THANK YOU *for* HOLDING

(On Hold Series Book #2)

JULIA KENT
and ELISA REED

Having it all is a fantasy, right?

Carrie Shelton thought her boyfriend was too good to be true. Her best friend's brother? A guy who loved antiquing? Who cuddled on the couch while watching foodie YouTube clips and talking about artisanal spices? Who helped her accessorize her outfits?

Right.

Fantasy.

So when he ran off with Kevin, the owner of an antique shop, right before his sister's wedding, Carrie's life went from fantasy to nightmare.

As maid of honor, she can't back out of the wedding. And her ex is the best man—but now he has his own best man.

She needs a date. Stat.

Enter Ryan. Sure, he's a hot male stripper at the O Spa where she works as junior designer, but he's a few years younger and just, you know—a friend.

Perfect. She needs a friend more than she needs a boyfriend.

A weekend of playing her boyfriend so she can save face is a lot to ask, but for some reason Carrie doesn't understand, Ryan's all in. Enthusiastic, even.

Especially when it comes to physical displays of affection.

Public kisses turn to private confessions, and pretty soon, Carrie can't tell the difference between fantasy and reality.

Because if Ryan's just pretending he's in love with her, then why does the chemistry between them—and between the sheets—feel so real?

Carrie can't settle for almost, though. She's already done that. She's not putting her life on hold anymore.

Turns out Ryan won't, either.

He's holding out for more.

♥ ♥ ♥

Thank You For Holding is a STANDALONE in the On Hold series. You do not need to have read book 1 in the series, but after reading about Carrie and Ryan's friends-to-lovers adventure, you'll want to. ;)

ACKNOWLEDGEMENTS

To Elisa, who has made writing this series so much fun.

To Clark, who continues to be my own personal Superman with a lovely geek streak.

—JK

For the beloved friends who spend so many hours on the phone with me . . . definitely including Julia!

—ER

CHAPTER ONE

Carrie

I SWEAR TO you, when I get married, I am NOT going to make my bridesmaids pay $250 for a dress. A hideous dress that makes them look like a) a grandmother; b) an elephant; or, in extreme cases, c) a grandmother elephant.

I'm not.

Just because it comes from J. Crew Weddings does not mean you can actually wear it again in real life. Trust me on this.

Also, I'm not making them fly to Las Vegas or Cancun and pay thousands of dollars to stay at a resort for three days just so I can post pictures on Facebook and Instagram of them toasting me by the pool. With fourteen-dollar cocktails. And a stupid caption, like, "What would I do without my besties?"

I am not doing this.

And yes, I know, they all said that, too. Before.

Perfectly reasonable women get engaged and apparently their memory banks are instantly wiped clean. Common sense, too.

They forget their college roommate's wedding, when—due to an unfortunate YouTube sensation—they were required to dance (*dance!*) down the aisle in a $300 sequin minidress (with coordinating sheer organza coat for modesty in church, $95).

They suddenly do not recall their cousin's sweet country theme, with the daisies and the barbeque and the IPA beer, and the $175 lavender flowered cotton maxidress with *puff sleeves* that went with it. Just try wearing that one to a future cocktail party. I dare you.

In my darker moments, I suspect there may be a kind of payback factor at work here.

Anyway, there's a reason it's called the wedding-industrial complex. And that's not the end! Then there are the *baby* showers.

Don't get me wrong. I love my friends dearly. I really *don't* know what I would do without them. I want their special day to be a treasured memory of perfect happiness, rare and well-deserved, documented in photographs. Their joy is my joy.

But my pain is apparently not their pain.

Let's look at the plus side.

I'm going to be the maid of honor in my friend Jenny's wedding. You probably saw that coming. I met Jenny at work here at the O Spa, the women's private club chain where I am the Assistant Director for Design. O Spas are the "fourth space" for women. Home, work, and other public venues are the first three.

We are meant to be the ultimate space. From highly-trained, well-oiled, hot massage therapists who wear g-strings that are outlawed in 111 countries, to a sex toy boutique with weekly workshops, to a new coffee bar with lattes that are better than sex, the O Spa caters to what women want.

A break, a chance, and a friend.

Jenny loved working for O, but she moved on a year ago, a promotion she could only get by changing companies. We were never just work friends. We're true best friends, and besides that, we could be sisters-in-law someday. I'm dating her brother, Jamey.

Who is standing in front of my desk right now, telling me about the tickets he just scored to Straight No Chaser at the Wang Center in November. We love *a cappella.*

"Fifth row, Carrie! And it'll be near the holidays, so maybe they'll do songs from their Christmas album!" His dark, wavy hair falls over his forehead in a boyish little curl. His eyebrows are perfectly arched. He gets them threaded more often than I do. His narrow chinos are rolled at the cuff, exposing his bare ankles in brown loafers. And is that *my* cotton scarf knotted around his neck?

I smile at him. Jamey is a great boyfriend because he always wants to do fun and unusual things. Has ever since we began dating two years ago. Our friends rely on Jamey to keep them current. When Steve Martin curated the Lawren Harris show at the MFA, we were the first people in the door. When Juliet opened in Union Square, we were tasting the tasting menu before anyone else had tasted it.

You can see why a lavender flowered cotton dress—with *puffed sleeves*—is of no use to me.

"We can go back to my place after the concert and I'll make cocoa. Bet you'd enjoy something sweet and hot," I say with a flirtatious grin. I give him what I hope is a smoldering look. He's holding my hand and his eyes widen in mock excitement, then he looks away.

I love Jamey.

And he loves me. What kind of guy stops by his girlfriend's work with Grind It Fresh! cinnamon lattes after finishing his Crossfit routine?

Jamey would fit in so well here at O.

A little *too* well. Looks like he's thinking about moonlighting here, judging from the way he's tracking Zeke, one of the master masseurs.

"Hey," Zeke grunts, his English accent somehow coming out even in a single-syllable sound.

Jamey doesn't say a word. He just keeps staring at Zeke, whose face hardens. His eyes dart to me, as if he's asking *What the fuck?*

I shrug. "Like what you see?" I whisper in Jamey's ear.

He jumps so high he nearly knocks my latte out of my hand. I recover quickly. Can't waste a Grind It Fresh! latte. But a few drops spill down the edge of my skirt.

"Whoops!" he shouts, a little too brightly. "So sorry, angel." His hug is swift and sweaty, his scent clinging, skin clammy and hot at the same time. Jamey is so affectionate. Always ready with a snuggle or a hug, a hand to hold while we go shopping.

Who needs lots of sex when you have a boyfriend who is prac tically a professional cuddler?

Not that we don't have sex. I mean, you know. We do. I'll bet we have as much sex as any other couple. Or *most* couples.

I guess.

Just . . . I am so fortunate to have a man who appreciates affection.

I take a sip of my drink. Now we both track Zeke's ass as he turns to the left at the end of the hallway.

"You would look great in that uniform," I tease Jamey.

He flushes, eyelashes fluttering. "What?" He clears his throat. "Why would you say that?" The judgmental tone is harsh, different from anything I've heard from him before.

I flinch. "I just meant, um . . . the way you were looking at his uniform, I thought . . ."

"You thought *what*?" He looks wounded.

Oh, God. I've offended him. I have to fix this. "Oh, I just meant, you know, that if you're thinking about getting a part-time job like Zeke's, you'd be fabulous here."

His eyebrow quirks. "Fabulous? I'm an associate professor of rhetoric and composition at an R-1 institution. I don't need a part-time job." His eyes go a bit dull.

Just then, one of the other master masseurs, Ryan, walks by. He's coming in to start his shift so he's fully clothed in faded jeans, flip-flops, and a ragged, tight t-shirt that shows off muscles on top of muscles. Ryan is my best friend here at the O Spa. We started on the same day, two years ago, so we bonded. We've been buddies ever since.

Jamey gives him a nervous glance. I think he's jealous of Ryan. How sweet is that? Look at the way Jamey combs over Ryan's muscular body . . . or maybe he's thinking about getting a tattoo? Ryan's arms are sleeved with complex geometric shapes. Jamey's pupils dilate and it's *so* obvious.

He's thinking about working here.

"I'll see you tonight, beautiful. I'll bring Thai," Jamey says, breathless, a genuine smile in his eyes. "Don't want you slaving over a hot stove when you could be rubbing my feet on the sofa."

Ryan gives him a weird frown, eyes doing that wide and narrow combination where you're not sure what the person is thinking, but it isn't good. He disappears down the hall to the men's locker room for staff.

Jamey kisses me on both cheeks. *So* European. Then, without even looking at me, he disappears in the same direction as Zeke.

I love Jamey. Did I say that already?

Ryan

I FUCKING HATE Jamey.

I tolerate him because Carrie thinks he hung the moon. When your friend is too clueless to realize she's dating the wrong guy, there's only one way to handle it.

Shut your mouth.

I scramble out of my street clothes and into my thong, moving quickly. Can't have waistband lines marking my body. We show up a little early to get in uniform and adjust to the spa's atmosphere. Women pay us a lot of money to be their oasis.

No man is an island, but for an hour or two, we can be a peninsula of pleasure.

"You rocked the Captain America costume yesterday," Carrie says, her troubled look fading as she turns her attention away from the disappeared Jamey. She happens to stare down the hallway as I walk toward her. Now I've got her full attention.

Which is how I like it.

"Thanks, but we're back to the standard uniform. In keeping with our new goal of remaining culturally relevant, the next costume is Dr. Strange." Her eyes creep over me, my blood's pace picking up. When Jamey gave me the once-over, it made my stomach clench.

When Carrie does it, other parts tighten.

"I wear more than that when I get a Pap smear, Ryan," she says with a smirk. A vision of Carrie naked, honey-colored hair fanned out behind her and over the edge of an exam table in a doctor's office with her shapely legs in stirrups flashes through my mind and *oh, shit*.

"How's Jamey doing?" I ask. I don't give a rat's ass about him. Talking about anything that will deflate my ever-growing boner is my goal. Think about Donald Trump. Hillary Clinton. Betty White. Jamey.

Perfect. Deflation sequence activated.

"Jamey is so sweet!" Carrie gets that weird look again. Her eyes fill with a mild form of panic, which fades quickly, leaving her chewing on a pen cap. "He got us tickets for a holiday concert and just stopped by with my favorite coffee."

"Nice. But every guy should do that for the person they're dating."

"Really?" She looks so surprised. I hate that she looks so surprised.

"It's pretty basic Dating 101 stuff, Carrie."

"Like you know anything about dating," she lobs back at me. "You haven't had a girlfriend since I met you." She walks into her cubicle and nods for me to follow.

My heart just got decimated by a SCUD missile. I can't look at her. I follow, then pick up one of the metal balls on her Newton's Cradle and let it clack against the others. The force shoves the ball on the other end to strike out in an arc.

"Well, you know . . ."

She snorts. "Yeah, I know. Why settle for one woman when you can have a taste of so many?"

I'm not sure when she got the idea that I'm some kind of playboy Casanova manwhore. That's Zeke. But no matter what I tell her, she doesn't believe me.

"Right." Our eyes meet and I can't breathe. You spend years pretending and hiding your feelings and when those little slivers, fractions of time that don't show up on a clock, protrude through your facade, you take them as they are.

Real, raw, and so hard.

But so good.

Her expression is serious. The world telescopes. Maybe now is the time. I swallow, my throat dry, and open my mouth as she keeps the gaze.

And then—*smack!*

A loud crack of a palm against ass cheek ruins the moment.

"You been upping the protein and dropping the carbs?" Zeke asks, butting in. He appraises me like I'm running for Mr. Universe, running his hand up and down my torso, counting my eight-pack. He mouths the numbers.

"You're more cut than usual," he adds. A smirk tickles his cocky English face as he widens his eyes, then gives Carrie a meaningful look. "What do you think, Carrie? Ryan's looking damn good." He turns me like I'm a piece of meat being inspected.

I fucking hate Zeke, too.

But Carrie, in that moment, does what people pleasers do. She follows his order, her inventory of my body starting with my feet. I can feel her attention, like a lingering touch, a visual caress that makes the hair on my body start to rally. Not quite gooseflesh, but damn close.

She passes up over my calves, across the knees, hesitating on my thighs, which are tight as I remind myself to unlock my knees. I have to control my breathing. Zeke crosses his arms over his chest and leans against the doorjamb. He's wearing the same damn shoestring costume I'm wearing as we start our shift, so it's not like I'm special here at the O Spa.

Carrie, though, makes me feel damn special as her look moves on to my package. I'm frantically trying to think about anything but how erotic this is.

Aside from Zeke, of course.

And then Carrie walks toward me.

Think about dead bodies. Rotting carcasses. Dead possum by the side of the road. Jabba the Hut having sex. Jamey having sex—wait, no, because then I have to think about Carrie having sex with that asshole, and I'll get an angry boner.

Which is worse than a regular boner.

"ZEKE!" Henry Holliday, our master massage therapist and unofficial leader of all the male attendants here at O, calls for him. Peeling off, Zeke leaves me alone with Carrie, whose eyes have narrowed, head tilted, that long hair brushing her shoulder right in that spot I've fantasized about kissing a thousand times before.

"You look good, Ryan," she says to my abs as Zeke walks away.

"Thank you. It's that all-coconut-oil diet," I joke.

She won't make eye contact, but her chest rises and falls a little faster, a light pink dotting the creamy flesh her open shirt displays. Her eyes dart around the hallway, trying desperately to look at anything but me.

Any other woman and I'd go in for the kill. I'd assume she's aroused and this is the perfect time to make a move. But if I'm wrong . . .

I freeze, my body ninety-five percent naked and my heart one hundred percent on the line.

She finally gives me a fuzzy smile, like she's trying to pack a thousand emotions underneath the one casual, bland grin that covers everything.

"You'll make a great Dr. Strange." And then she turns away and hurries off with a hand wave.

I slump against the wall and slowly bang the back of my head against it, like a heartbeat.

CHAPTER TWO

Carrie

"OH. MY. GOD. Oh my God!" Jamey is beside himself with ecstasy. "Carrie, look at this!"

He is holding up a disembodied hand made of white china.

"What is it?" I ask, laughing.

"A vintage glove form," he answers. "This is perfect for your bedroom, to hold your jewelry. So graphic and cool. I'm buying it for you."

We are in an antiques shop in a town filled with them, Essex, north of Boston. The perfect Saturday outing on a crisp September day. I'm flipping through a bin of hundred-year-old post cards, hoping to find a familiar scene. One of our hometowns, maybe, or someplace we've been together. I love to look at the messages written on the back in spidery script:

Dear Maudie the baby is much better. Amos went to Bangor. Your Sister Edith

And the impossibly brief addresses:

M Chapin Rural Delivery Bucksport Maine

"Very cool," I say, half distracted. "It *is* perfect for my bedroom."

I like to imagine life without email or messages or even phones, when important news arrived by postcard and the postman already knew where you lived.

Now the people answering the phone aren't even people. My new project at work is helping design the automated phone tree. You know, *press 1 for hours, press 2 for directions, to book an appointment press 3 or stay on the line . . .*

I'm going to suggest another option: *to describe your wildest sexual fantasy, press 4. Begin speaking at the tone; when you have finished, press O.*

My wildest fantasy? I make eye contact with Jamey, who grins at me.

And then an image of Ryan at work in that g-string invades my brain, unbidden and unwelcome. Where did *that* come from? I shake my head like a wet dog and move on, stroking a tea tray covered in hand-painted roses, ignoring the flushed tingles that climb up the back of my body from Achilles heel to neck.

How my name came up for this phone tree assignment at work is a mystery to me, unless someone noticed how often I have my cell phone glued to my ear and figured I was the world's expert. But I don't have to think about that until Monday.

Jamey buys the porcelain hand and a silver cocktail shaker. I buy a German glass Christmas ornament in the shape of a clementine, the glass so thin, I can't imagine how it has survived for one hundred and twenty years or so. I can't wait to hang it on my tree. Someday—maybe soon—*our* tree.

My girlfriends would *kill* to have a boyfriend who loves spending the day poking through dusty antique shops.

I am *so* lucky.

"We scored!" Jamey crows as I reach for his hand. He holds it with his fingers together, like a parent and child or brother and sister. We're *that* close.

Leaving the shop, we wander down the street toward the next one. Jamey has brought a wicker shopping cart on wheels to carry our purchases, and he pulls it along behind him. A few hundred yards down, he stops and pulls out his phone. From the wicker cart he extracts a selfie stick.

I'm used to this routine. I touch up my lipstick quickly, then press my cheek to his, flashing my widest smile. Jamey likes to document our fun; our Facebook friends don't miss a single thing. They call us the Happy Couple.

Sometimes I think I detect a certain sarcasm in their comments, but that's probably just me. Who could blame them if they were jealous?

The next shop specializes in old maps, not really our thing. We keep walking, but suddenly Jamey stops short.

"Remember we went in there once and the owner was a really nice guy? Really interesting? I wonder if he's working today." He peers through the display window. "Let's go in and see." When he looks at me, I get his eyes for a split second before he looks back at the shop. Excitement dilates his pupils.

"It's just maps," I answer, reluctant. Why do guys love maps? They all look basically the same to me. "Tell you what, you go see and come meet me at the next place."

He's already running up the steps to the door. Huh. The place must sell some really amazing antiquities.

I can get really absorbed in browsing through bins and shelves, hunting for some unexpected uber-cool object, but after forty-five minutes I realize that Jamey hasn't appeared. Odd. I head back to the map shop, and there he is, just coming down the walk.

"Hey, where've you been? It's no fun without you." I slip my hand through his arm, but he pulls away quickly and grabs his cart handle instead. He glances back at the store window.

"Old maps are actually fascinating," Jamey tells me. "I think I might start collecting them. Kevin says he'll take me on his next buying trip!"

"Who?"

"Kevin. The map shop owner." He lets out a little sigh, and then his face goes blank.

Really?" I say doubtfully. "That's nice. While we're here, we should look for a wedding present for Jenny and Aiden. The wedding's in a month."

Silence.

"I am so excited their wedding is at the Chatham Beach Inn," I continue. "Our room has a king-sized bed and an incredible view—it's going to be so romantic! And you are going to look *so* hot as best man. A whole long weekend together, oceanside," I sigh, imagining our nude bodies twisted in the sheets, so much sex we can't remember our own names.

More silence.

"Jamey?" He's studying a business card, which appears to be from the map shop. It has writing all over it. "Jamey?"

"Yeah," he says quietly. "Romantic."

He is uncharacteristically quiet for the rest of the day, actually. We have an early dinner at a restaurant on the water and head back to Boston. The top is down on his BMW convertible and the stars overhead are beautiful. We talk a little bit, comfortably, about my college roommate's job problems and Jamey's new department chair.

"Want to stay over at my place tonight?" I ask him in the car. "Seems like a really long time since we've . . . you know . . . we've both been so busy." I rub his neck and give him a hopeful smile. It's been thirty-two days since we did more than kiss and cuddle, but who's counting?

"I don't think tonight's a good time." He doesn't take his eyes from the road. "But thanks."

"Okay. Maybe tomorrow." A piece of concrete the size of my libido sinks into the bottom of my stomach.

"I'm going to Chicago on Monday morning for that conference, so I think I need to spend tomorrow preparing. But thanks."

I have to ask. I have to. "Jamey, is everything okay? With us, I mean?" My fingers worry a thread on the edge of the upholstered seat.

"Of course it is," he snaps. "Why would you ask that? You are so needy sometimes. I told you I have to get ready for a meeting!" The growl in his voice fills me with shame. I'm not sure why.

I am taken aback. "I'm sorry," I stammer. "You're right. I apologize."

But he continues to stare straight ahead all the way home. When we get to my apartment in Southie, he helps me carry my purchases, plus the ceramic hand, up to the porch.

"Sorry I wasn't very good company," he says, giving me a quick peck on the lips. "I guess I'm just stressed. I have a lot going on right now. I'll call you tomorrow."

But he doesn't.

Ryan

AFTER WORK MOST nights, Zeke and I head to this dive down the street from O, Tooney's Bar. It reeks of old cigarette smoke and unwashed men, the soured beers of decades past all absorbed into the cheap paneling. Dart boards are everywhere, and the two stained pool tables in the bar are constantly busy.

An antidote to a shift at O. No environment could be more different.

Carrie normally works regular hours, so she's not typically around for the night shift, which is what I pull four days a week. We pass each other mid-afternoon, like today, and then she leaves at 5:30 p.m. like all the other office drones, while the clients come pouring in.

Zeke and I spend the post-corporate hours massaging women, listening to them talk about their worries, flattering them, and trying to bring a little spark of fun and light into the lives of overstressed, overshamed, overwhelmed women.

Is our work frivolous? Should I go back to electrical engineering like my sisters all say I should? Robots don't sigh with relief when you unwind a nasty knot in their shoulder. They don't tear up when you tell them they're beautiful without the tummy tuck their new rich boyfriend insists they get.

Then again, robots don't pinch your ass, either.

"Made a move on Carrie yet?" Zeke asks as we grab a couple of bar stools and lean. My first shot of tequila goes down like that moment you get home and kick off your shoes.

"Shut up."

"Just asking. She was combing over you with those sweet brown eyes."

"Don't talk about her eyes."

His nose twitches. "Got it. Eyes are off limits. I'll talk about her tits instead."

I didn't know I could growl. Was pretty realistic, too.

"She's not yours, Ryan. She's Ja-mey's." His voice goes sickly sweet as he says Carrie's boyfriend's name.

"It won't last."

"No shit." He barks out a laugh that is half belch, half snicker. "Does she realize he's gay?"

I bristle. We're getting into dangerous territory. "You see it, too?"

"You'd have to be daft not to."

"Carrie isn't stupid."

"Then she's in denial, or they have some sort of an arrangement."

"Arrangement?"

"You read Dan Savage's column? Maybe he fucks whoever he wants on the side, and she. . . . I don't know. Who cares?"

"I don't think Carrie's the kind of woman to have an arrangement."

"You have no idea what kind of woman Carrie is in bed, Ryan. You're too chickenshit to find out."

"I know more than you think."

His eyebrows shoot up. "You made a move?"

"No." Fuck. I just walked right into a trap.

"She talks with you about her sex life? Jesus, Ryan, why don't you just braid her hair and paint each other's nails?" For whatever reason, this sounds way worse in an English accent as Zeke sucks down half of his pint of beer. He orders it straight from the tap in those big Pilsner glasses, wide at the top and more narrow at the bottom.

I tense.

"Oh, man . . . you *do* braid her hair, don't you? When you watch those stupid survivalist shows with her? Might as well cut off your cock and hand it to her." He holds an imaginary knife and cuts off his dick in Pretendland.

"It's not like that." I give the pool tables a look. Long line to grab one. I groan inside. That means Zeke'll want to play darts. I suck at darts. He's a king. I am convinced they start teaching kids darts in England before they're out of diapers.

Zeke continues pretending, cackling maniacally as he chops off his own dick. I'm damn close to moving him into Realityland.

"You friend-zoned yourself," he says, then finishes his beer, slamming it on the scarred wooden bar. The bartender starts pouring him another, the dark lager contrasting with the white foam that forms up on top, like a beer toupée.

"Shut *up*."

"Just tattoo 'Friend Zone' on your cock, man."

"Who tattoos their own junk?"

Zeke just cocks—no pun intended—one eyebrow.

I hold up my palm. "I don't wanna know. And besides, I hate that term. Friend Zone."

"Because you're it, dude. You turned yourself into The Nice Guy."

"I *am* a nice guy!"

"Nice guys don't get pussy."

"I don't want Carrie's—" Okay. Even I can't finish that sentence, because it's not true.

His eyebrow goes up, carrying the piercing along with it, like a ball of mercury in a thermometer, measuring something.

Measuring my stupidity.

"You want her bad, Ryan. Everyone in the spa can tell. We have a betting pool on you. There's a grid and everything."

"You—you *bet* on my feelings for Carrie? Like the Final Four?"

"Odds are 78 to 1 you'll never man up and tell her how you feel."

"78 to 1!" That's less than 1.3 percent. Damn.

"Once I tell everyone you braid her hair while you're watching *Naked and Afraid*, those odds will plummet even further."

"You'd seriously use what I tell you in private as leverage for a work betting pool?"

"Do you even know me?" He laughs. "If it ups the size of my payout, shit yeah."

"You bet against me?"

He shrugs. "Turns out I'm right."

"No, you're not."

"Prove me wrong, then."

CHAPTER THREE

Carrie

RADIO SILENCE FROM Jamey is like the air being turned off. He said he'd text me "tomorrow," and here it is. Tomorrow. No Jamey.

On a normal workday, he texts me like fifty times. He can do this because he's an associate professor, so unless he's giving a lecture or in a meeting, his time is pretty much his own.

Then there are his Snapchat photos. He spends his days in Harvard Square, so there's no lack of visual interest. Tats, burkinis, seven tour buses of Japanese families all taking pictures, virtuoso street musicians, fringe political protests, the limo of a visiting head of state. And that's on a quiet day.

If no head of state that day, I get photos of his manicure (no polish, of course), a shirt he might buy, a shirt he might buy for me, his sushi lunch, his cat Ina Garten.

It's a constant stream. And that's not even counting his Facebook posts or his tweets. I wait all morning for something to come in.

I am *not* going to call him. He said he would call. He *will* call.

"Carrie?" Chloe walks into the office, the very image of polished perfection. She's so smooth. I mean literally smooth. You know how everyone has stray hairs that glow in backlighting? Not Chloe. You know how everyone has that weird skin tag, or a mole in the wrong place, or a slightly asymmetrical smile?

Not Chloe.

She's dressed in this skin-tight gray crepe top paired with a prairie skirt and beaded shoes.

"Nice look. Retro," I muse, looking her over. "Retro with a disco flair and a western feel."

"Too much?" Her eyebrows go up slowly, face neutral. Chloe only gets nervous for two reasons: her boyfriend, Nick and her toddler daughter, Holly. Otherwise, Chloe is the epitome of cool.

She's my mentor. If I can cultivate one tenth of her sophisticated polish, I'll be lucky.

"There's a touch of MOMA in here, too," she adds, pointing to the beaded shoes.

I squint. "Is that de Kooning? In beads? On shoes?" I'm breathless now.

Her right eyebrow goes up even higher, which means I've impressed her. "Good call."

I shrug. "Twentieth century art history classes." But I'm secretly pleased. When you're a relentless people pleaser, praise is like crack.

She beams. "I know you just graduated last year. All that work paid off." She plops a folder on my desk. "We have some local bead-makers working with artisanal cobblers to come up with unique shoes we can market to clientele. All profits from these go to charity. This is a prototype. We need to work on rights acquisitions before we proceed." As she lifts her knee to show off the glittering shoes, Ryan appears in the threshold.

"Hey," he grunts, suddenly shy, clearly flummoxed by Chloe's presence. His eyes skitter to her leg, which is high enough in the air to show off substantial skin. Meanwhile, he's showing even *more* skin, dressed in skin-tight black leather shorts, wearing a policeman's hat and holding a riding crop. The hallway lighting highlights all the oil on his bare pecs.

Just another day at work.

"Hi, Ryan," she says calmly, then turns to me with an expectant look. I still can't read her, even after working here for two years.

She's either pissed we've been interrupted, inviting Ryan to join our conversation, or . . .

But my reaction is the same. I get nervous. When I can't read people, I assume the worst. I give Ryan a long, slow look to distract myself, but all that does is make heat pool in parts of my body that need to remain cold and dry for my professional life to function properly. The oil makes all the hard lines of his muscles stand out.

So does the tight leather. He, um, dresses left. *Far* left.

So far left, I think parts of his body might cross the international date line.

"I can come back later," Ryan says quickly, his eyes on Chloe's foot. "Nice shoes. They look like earrings for your feet." He gives me a strange look, then retreats like he's on fire.

"Does Ryan have a problem with me?" Chloe asks, puzzled. Then her face morphs into marvel. "Earrings for your feet! Love it! I'm stealing that phrase." She pulls a phone out of thin air and begins tapping the screen.

My own phone buzzes with a notification. I let out a long breath, not realizing I've been holding it. That has to be Jamey. *Has* to.

"What? Ryan? A problem with you?" I'm split in three, thinking about Jamey, Ryan, and Chloe at the same time. A tiny headache, a pinch really, forms at the bridge of my nose. I'm also caffeine deprived. That's the easiest issue to fix.

"Yes, Ryan." She straightens herself—as if she needed to be even more smooth—and gives me a serious look. "He runs away every time I appear."

I actually know why Ryan does that, but I can't tell her. Meanwhile, I need a cool drink to quench this strange burning feeling pulsing through me after looking at Ryan. I really need sex with Jamey. I am just a walking ball of libido lately.

"He's busy. Ryan, I mean. Trying to do a good job. You know." I am a terrible liar.

Chloe knows I'm a terrible liar.

We stare at each other in perfect harmony, both silently agreeing that I am really, really bad at lying. There's a reason why I changed my college major from public relations to design.

"Okay," she says in a clipped voice, smiling and frowning at the same time. "I came in here to ask about the phone tree again. Everything's on track?"

"Yes, including the new sex toy help desk."

She just blinks. "Help desk?"

I nod.

"We're adding a hotline for sex toy . . . *malfunctions?*"

I nod. "Marketing thinks it'll add more of a 'wraparound' feel to O. All your needs taken care of in one place. It'll be a protection plan you buy when you purchase a toy. We're hiring customer service reps as we speak."

She groans, but manages to look elegant as she laughs her way to a feminine little snort. If I did that, I'd sound like a donkey choking on an apple core.

"And financials?"

I give her a thumbs-up.

"This job," she whispers under her breath as she leaves my cubicle.

I scramble for my phone. The notification was from Jenny, posting a picture of a cat in a wedding dress.

No Jamey.

Around noon, I check Facebook. At the top of my news feed is a montage of four photos he just posted.

Okay, he's alive. *Whew.*

The first photo shows a shot glass full of clear liquid. Next is the doorway of a Cambridge body art studio called On the BrInk, then a selfie of Jamey smiling hard, and finally an obviously fresh tattoo of the words "Born This Way." The shot is too close-up to be able to tell what part of the body bears the tat. No caption.

"I knew it!" I hiss aloud. "He was totally checking out Ryan's tattoos. That explains so much." But why didn't he tell me?

Hey, I text him nervously, *All good?*

Nothing. No reply.

The day drags on. The evening drags on.

Until finally, around ten p.m., I glance at my phone and there's a message. I've been reading in bed, or trying to, but now I sit up so fast, my copy of *Me Before You* drops to the floor.

We need to talk

The four most dreaded words ever texted. My stomach drops through the floor, and my hands and feet go numb.

This makes no sense. What could we need to talk about? Nothing's wrong! Jamey and I get along perfectly! We're so happy! He probably means we need to talk about Jenny's wedding present, or which new restaurant to try Saturday night, that's all.

The phone I am holding rings, and I jump a mile. It's Jamey. I have to swipe three times before it connects.

"Hello?"

"Hey." His voice is quiet and flat.

"Jamey, what's going on? What's wrong? Are you sick? I've been so worried! Did you get a *tattoo*?"

"I need to tell you something. I'm so sorry, Carrie. I just—I can't do this anymore."

"What are you talking about? I can barely hear you! Can't do what? I don't understand!"

There's a pause. "I've met someone else. It's not you, you're wonderful. You're my best friend. It's me."

"Someone *else*? You've met *someone else*? *Who*? Who is she?"

"It's Kevin."

"Devin? Who is Devin? What's all that noise? Where are you?"

"It's *Kevin*, Carrie." He speaks very clearly and a little bit louder. "Kevin. From the map store."

"That's ridiculous, Kevin's a *guy*. This isn't funny, Jamey."

I think I hear a man's voice in the background.

"Carrie, listen. I'm gay. I'm gay! Kevin has taught me that I can't hide it anymore. It's been an incredible two days. For the first time in my life, I feel free. But I can't stand to hurt you. I'm sorry."

"You can't be gay! You're my boyfriend!" I think I might be

shouting. It's hard for me to tell, because there is a loud buzzing in my head. It's the sound of my entire world imploding. "You're my boyfriend, and we love each other, and we might get married, and everything is perfect! You don't become gay in two days!"

"I do love you, Carrie, just . . . not that way. It didn't happen in two days. I've always been gay. I've been pretending my whole life to be something I'm not." I hear a man's muffled voice again. "I have to go now," Jamey says. "They're calling our flight. I'll call you when we get back. Try to be happy for me. I am so sorry."

"Flight? Your flight? What? Where are you going? Back from where?" I yell, but the call is ended. He's gone. I sit on the edge of the bed, staring at my silent phone.

Gay. He's gay. Jamey can't be gay! If he were gay, we wouldn't have sex.

If he were gay, we—oh, God.

I don't know what to do. The world is spinning fast and mercilessly frozen at the same time.

When I don't know what to do, I always call Jamey. We're best friends. Okay, so Jenny is my best friend, too. And Ryan is my best work friend. I have a lot of best friends.

Or maybe not so much. Jamey no longer qualifies as a "best friend." Pretty sure dumping me by phone to run off with Kevin the Map Dude takes him out of the running.

And yet I instinctively want to call him and tell him about this, have him comfort me and make me laugh. Make me feel not alone. But he's not there now.

Desperate, I open my contacts list and scroll down. Ryan! I press his name.

"C-Shel!" He answers, thank God. There's music in the background. My name is Carrie Shelton, and Ryan came up with the nickname shortly after we met. It's adorable, even if I am not. "What's up, beautiful? Did you see *Empire* tonight?"

I open my mouth, but I can't speak.

"Carrie?"

If I speak, if I say it, it will be true. I can't.

"Carrie?" He's worried now, his voice deepening. "Carrie, are you there? What's wrong?"

"*Gay!*" I wail. "Jamey is gay!"

The phone goes silent, followed by a masculine sound I can't quite describe.

"I know," Ryan says, nonplussed. "You didn't know?"

"No, I didn't *know*! What do you mean you *knew*?" I'm shrieking. I know I shouldn't shriek at Ryan, but Jamey isn't here and Ryan has a penis. I need to yell at a penis.

Logic is long gone.

It got on a plane with a guy named Kevin and flew off, along with my dignity.

"He's your boyfriend. How can you *not* know?"

Right. Exactly. How could I not know?

"He *was* my boyfriend. Now he *has* a boyfriend. My boyfriend has a boyfriend! And we didn't have sex for a month and now we never will again because he's having sex with Kevin the Map Dude and oh my God, Ryan, what am I going to do? I'm *that* girl. I'm the girl who was too stupid to realize she was dating a gay man. There are entire *seasons* of Dr. Phil devoted to people like me!" I start to hyperventilate, replaying the short phone call with Jamey over and over, etching it into my brain.

This is real.

I've been dumped.

Jamey left me. Broke up with me *by phone* for . . . a man. Everything below my waist goes numb. I feel like I've malfunctioned.

Where is the hotline for vaginas that malfunction so badly your boyfriend turns gay? I start to laugh-cry, because my next project at work will probably be to develop *that* hotline, and why not?

I'm a fucking expert now.

He sighs. "Aw, C-Shel. This isn't good. Come over. Or do you want me to come to your place? I can bring Thai and we can watch *The Colony.*"

It's 10:30 p.m. I pull on jeans and throw a jacket over my nightie. It's only six blocks to Ryan's. "I'm coming to you. I can buy ice cream on the way. And your apartment isn't filled with antique finds from my weekends with Jamey," I sob as I grab my keys and purse and slam my front door.

Fury. Sorrow. Horror. Brokenness. Disbelief. All of it floods me as I storm my way into the convenience store, grabbing ice cream and peanut butter cups like it's the zombie apocalypse.

It is.

It's the sexpocalypse for me.

By the time I get to Ryan's place, I am a live wire. He opens the front door, dressed in a Cal Tech t-shirt and lounge pants.

I fling myself into his arms, drop the bag filled with comfort carbs, and kiss him.

Hard.

Ryan

SHE TASTES LIKE salt and sweetness, like all the soft warmth in the world is concentrated in her lips. We're clumsy, her lips hard against mine, wet from tears. Her hands grab my biceps, the kind of grip you have on someone you're pissed at and hold onto because you want them to bend.

At first, I'm stunned, the ice cream pint rolling out of the plastic bag, settling on my bare foot, the cold a tingling shock that contrasts with the warmth of her mouth. God, Carrie's mouth. My hands go up, like she has a gun pointed at me, then they land on her shoulders, one sinking into her hair, her messy bun coming loose as her lips soften and she starts to really kiss me.

I *really* kiss her, my mouth screaming *yes, finally, holy shit,* so many words my lips and tongue need to say. A kiss requires economy of language. You don't have the luxury of words, so everything I want to say has to come from a suck, a nip, a lick, the parting of her lips as my tongue blindly seeks answers in a new language.

Those hard hands on my biceps loosen, sliding up to the back of my neck, and as Carrie moves up my body, standing on tiptoe to rise up to the kiss, my heart tries to burst in my chest, like a water balloon tossed oh, so gently.

She shivers violently, suddenly, an electric jolt between us like I've stuck my tongue in a light socket.

Then she pulls back, eyes wide with alarm, hot with desire that fades so fast I almost don't even see it.

Panic floods her, followed by her chin jutting up as she says in an overconfident, fake voice, "There. See? I am *not* a broken vagina."

And she bursts into tears.

I don't know what the hell a broken vagina is, but I have a very unbroken cock tenting my pants right now. Desperate, I bend down for the ice cream and hold it right over my crotch.

"I'm sorry," she babbles as she walks past me into my apartment, flinging herself onto the couch, burying her face in a cushion. "I shouldn't have done that."

Oh, holy fuck, do it again.

"Done what?"

"Used you to prove that I'm not broken."

Use me. Use me all you want, baby.

Why does that inner voice suddenly have an English accent?

"You're not broken, Carrie," I choke out. As Ben & Jerry's becomes an ice pack for my dick, I stand in my kitchen, paralyzed.

What just happened?

And how can I get it to happen more?

"Jamey is gay. Gay!" she moans. Like a wounded animal, she's curled in a ball, panting hard, her face pressed into my sofa, little sobs making her ass shake. Her hair is everywhere, spilling over her shoulders and back.

This is one of those Nice Guy moments.

You know the kind.

Carrie is vulnerable. She feels broken. Jamey dumped her in the worst possible way—and now I *really* hate Jamey.

But he's given me an in.

A guy like Zeke would scoop Carrie in his arms and within half an hour be buried balls deep in her, taking advantage of her misery and heartbreak, using it to get into her pants, have her moaning under him, bare breasts shaking as he comforted her until Reverse Cowgirl became a form of revenge.

I am not that guy.

Why can't I be that guy?

I push my palm against my lips. She's still on the tip of my tongue, a salty, fresh taste I wish I could eat forever. I wonder what she tastes like in bed.

Damn it.

Not enough ice cream in the world to stop this hard-on, especially if I keep envisioning Carrie naked, spread out on the sheets, hair like the sun, radiating out to warm the world.

"Carrie." I put the ice cream on the counter and scoop out a big bowlful. Then I get out a bottle of wine. I pour her a full glass and take it over to her along with the bowl, sitting on the couch next to her. "You didn't do anything wrong."

"I did it *again!*" she wails.

"Again?"

"I picked a gay guy again! What is wrong with me? Why do I do this to myself?"

"You've dated gay guys before?"

Her glare melts the ice cream. "Not on purpose!"

I retreat to the kitchen, shove the ice cream in the freezer, and press my hips against the fridge for a second, willing my erection to go away. "No. Of course not," I say, struggling to figure out what, exactly, I'm supposed to do here.

"You have a penis!" she shouts.

My back's still to her, one hand on the fridge, the other discreetly holding the object in question, rearranging. I pause.

"Uhhh," is my intelligent response.

"Penises are what got me into trouble!"

I spin around. "You're *pregnant*? That fucker got you pregnant and left you for a gay dude?"

"WHAT ARE YOU TALKING ABOUT?" she screams.

"You said his penis got you in trouble!"

"Not *that* kind of trouble."

"Oh." My cock is still paused, about ninety seconds behind my brain. Usually it's my brain that's slower. Down, boy.

"We didn't have sex often enough for me to get pregnant!" she says with a sneer, a nasty tone I've never heard from Carrie pouring out of her. I refrain from telling her it only takes once. I assume they had sex at least once in the two years they've been together.

"'Let's just cuddle, Carrie,'" she says in a mocking voice, doing a damn fine imitation of Jamey. "'I just love waking up next to you and watching you sleep,'" she continues, face twisted with fury. She takes a big sip of wine.

Her cheeks are pink with rage, eyes red-rimmed and nose sniffling, and God help me, she's turning me on.

"He said that shit to you to hold off on sex?" I'm blown away. What guy has a hot woman like Carrie, ready and in his bed, and prefers to cuddle?

Oh. Right.

"He did! And he never mentioned anything like, 'Oh, by the way, I'm gay.'"

"Until today," I add.

And she bursts into tears, grabbing a Giants throw pillow and clutching it to her breasts.

I'm jealous of that pillow. Go Giants!

"No one will ever love me again!" she wails.

Now, a voice whispers in my ear. *Tell her now. Say something. Say anything.*

"And YOU!" She actually points at me.

"What about me?" Can she tell? Women can read minds, you know. I have four older sisters. Don't try to tell me they can't.

"You knew Jamey was gay and didn't tell me!"

I cross my arms over my chest, pretending my heart isn't trying to claw its way into the ceiling light fixture. "I didn't know."

"You suspected."

I can't argue with her. She's right.

I shrug.

"That's it? I get a shrug? Men. You're all the same." The Giants pillow hits me in the face. I catch a whiff of her perfume, a mix of her shampoo, some lotion she uses at work, and her unique scent.

"No," I say carefully, forcing myself to stop thinking about her scent. "We're not. For instance, Jamey is gay and I am not."

I'm *really* not.

"How do I know you're not gay?" she says in a vicious tone. "Apparently, I have no gaydar! Maybe you're gay. Maybe Zeke's gay. And what about Henry?"

"He's married to Jemma."

"All the good ones are taken!" Her hands go up in the air like she's at an evangelical revival.

I give her a look. She scrunches up her face, searching the room with her eyes, like a DEA agent on a drug bust.

"Where's the Thai?"

"On its way."

As if on cue, the doorbell rings. I pay the delivery dude and return. Carrie's already got the television on. She's halfway through an episode of a house flippers show, her wine glass empty, the pint of ice cream in her hand.

She's using an entire Reese's Cup as a spoon.

When you are the youngest brother in a family with four older sisters, you see a lot of break-ups. There's screaming and crying, cursing and condemnation. Lots of burning of things—letters, cards, Polaroids, diaphragms.

Pro tip: those don't burn. Trust me. And they smell really bad when you try.

But eventually, all that anger turns to one thought: *Why me?*

When guys get dumped, they drink heavily and recover by finding a piece of ass.

I wish Carrie were a guy.

Wait. That sounds wrong.

I hand her a carton of shrimp Pad Thai and grab the quart of Tom Yum soup. I take a sip.

"You're not going to slurp like usual, are you?"

I pause. "I don't slurp."

She points to the television screen with her chopsticks. "I can't hear the show over your mouth noises."

My eyes cut to the screen. It's a commercial for some plantar fasciitis foot wrap.

"God forbid you miss that important message because I am eating my dinner."

"*Slurping.* You sound like a walrus at a water fountain when we get Tom Yum soup, Ryan."

"No, I don't." But I slurp loudly on purpose, then look at her, eyebrows up.

"I'm sorry." She puts the carton of food down and covers her face with her palms, scrubbing her face, her fingers sliding into her messy hair, rubbing her scalp. "I don't know why you put up with me."

NOW, that damn voice screams. *NOW!*

I reach for her, my hand shaking. The wall between us is voluntarily broken on a regular basis. I've hugged Carrie. I've touched her hand, slung an arm around her shoulders, worked with her on fixing a leaky faucet or helped her move something heavy, our bodies brushing against each other in safe spots.

She's fallen asleep against me on my couch, and I've leaned against her while we watch shows.

It's not impenetrable. That wall, I mean.

It's just, you spend years not crossing that line and the moment it's time, the breach takes on gravitas. Meaning.

Intensity.

Just as I'm about to touch her jaw, a half second before I cradle her sweet face in my hands and pull her to me for a kiss I start, a kiss I want, a kiss I plan to turn into more, she pulls away, my fingertips brushing her back instead.

She comes in for a hug, all platonic, chin tucked down and into my shoulder before I can make a move to kiss her.

"You're different. I'm sorry."

"Different?"

"You're one of the nice guys." Her shoulders relax, her voice muffled against my shoulder. As she breathes, the heat from her mouth warms the cloth of my t-shirt.

Inches. I'm inches away from kissing her, from telling her how I really feel.

Fuck Jamey.

Fuck being nice.

It's time to be real.

Slowly, achingly, I shore myself up inside, knowing this is it. Do or die moment. I'm about to show her how I really feel and two minutes from now, we'll either be closer than ever, or—

I can't think about *or*.

"I'm so glad I have a real friend like you, Ryan," she says, sighing into my neck. "You're so sweet. Maybe I should take you to Jenny's wedding as my date." She laughs, then her breath evens out, body language clear. This hug is firmly in the Friend Zone.

Friend. All the bad words start with F.

My eyes fly open. I tense, all the muscles I've just willed into action going cold at her suggestion.

"Urg?" I say. No, it's not a word. I'm beyond words.

"I know, right? No one would believe it." Her laugh feels like fingernails raking my balls.

I'm speechless.

She pulls away and hits my chest pretty hard. "But next time I'm dating a gay guy, say something!" Her eyes are nervous as she moves away from me, grabbing her chopsticks like they're a shield, digging through her carton for a shrimp. "None of my friends in high school told me my boyfriend my senior year was gay, either."

"Uh." I'm down to single-syllable grunts. That's all I've got. My body is in flames, like a jetliner shot down by a rogue state.

A rogue state called Friendlandia.

"I mean, when I later realized he put more thought into his outfit than I did into mine for prom . . ." Her eyes go unfocused. "And he had much better hair."

"Maybe you have a thing for gay guys," I say.

I instantly regret the words.

"What?"

"Um, maybe it's just . . . there's some reason they appeal to you. They're your type."

"I don't have a type. I don't fall in love with a type. I fall in love with *people*. Not types." She snorts and chews, then swallows. "And from what Zeke's told me about you, you have a type, and it's not gay guys. We might both love watching stupid survivalist shows, but we don't both love the same people."

"What's Zeke said about me?" I'm going to kill him.

"You know. You two go on the prowl most weekends."

"On the prowl? I haven't heard that phrase since my grandma was alive." Zeke's lying. Sure, I go out with him to the bars a couple times a month, and some nights he finds someone to go home with. Not me.

I mean, I date, but . . .

"It's okay, Ryan," she says sincerely. "I get it. Guys like you, you know . . . you have different standards."

"Different standards?"

"For women. When you're a 10, you can pursue 10s."

"You think I'm a 10?" I sit up nice and proud, batting my eyelashes, buying time to control the crazy surge of need that makes me nearly lunge across the couch.

She sputters, then starts laughing, a hyena sound that ends with giggles. It's adorable. It makes me want her more. "You wouldn't be at O in your job if you weren't a 10. You're a 10. Zeke's a 10." She thinks for a minute. "And Henry's an 11."

"Hey!" I'm mildly offended, but happy to talk about anything that distracts me from the fatal mistake I almost made just moments ago. "I'm not an 11?"

"Henry is nearly seven feet tall, built like Superman, a gorgeous ginger like Prince Harry, and is married to the sweetest woman on the planet who is a whip-smart health journalist." She gives me a look that says, *Beat that.*

"But can he braid hair like me?"

Her lips puff out like she's considering the evidence. I want to kiss her again.

I shove a throw pillow over my crotch and stuff my face with Tom Yum soup, slurping be damned.

"Okay, you do get points for braiding. You're a 10.5."

"As long as I beat Zeke, I can handle that." I give her a serious look. "What would it take for me to become an 11?"

"Find someone as awesome as Jemma?"

I stare at her, the words caught in my throat.

The episode begins, and the first words out of the announcer's mouth are, "Kill two birds with one stone."

Yeah.

Right.

CHAPTER FOUR

Carrie

P EOPLE TALK ABOUT muscle memory all the time. It means when you do something over and over, you get really good at it. It becomes automatic. I was good at loving Jamey.

The heart's a muscle, right?

And now loving him is such a habit, I can't seem to stop.

I reach for my phone before I'm really awake in the morning, checking for his messages. It's not till I'm squinting at the tiny screen that I remember.

I stagger into the kitchen and pour my coffee into one of the beautiful French mugs Jamey gave me when I moved into this tiny apartment of my own. He bought them at Anthropologie, our favorite store. My kitchen is so small, he only bought two. One for each of us.

I want to go back to bed. If I can just stay asleep, I won't have to remember that I'll be drinking my coffee alone from now on. When other women get dumped, they can tell themselves, "He'll be back. He'll realize what we have, how great it is."

I don't have that comfort.

No matter what happens, Jamey is never coming back to me. I'm not his type. I never was. My heart isn't just breaking. It's slamming into a massive concrete wall of reality every time I remember.

Jenny hasn't texted me. Not even an *R U OK*. Maybe Jamey hasn't told her yet. I'm sure as hell not rushing to let my friend know that her brother dumped me for a guy. I'm not going to out him to his family before he's ready. I'm not that angry—and I'm not that person, either.

And what about the wedding? How can I show my face there? I joked about Ryan being my date because I need a date. Not Ryan, though. No way. He would do it if I forced him to, but I don't just need a date.

I need a *boyfriend*. A lust and passion-filled whirlwind romance that will shock Jamey to his core and make everyone not think of me as *Poor Carrie*.

The only thing worse than being dumped by a gay guy you didn't know was gay is being treated like Poor Carrie. Like it's not even two separate words. *Poorcarrie. Poorcarrie.* The whispers and gossip and sad puppy-dog eyes will kill me.

I have to back out of the wedding. I have to. Where am I going to magically find some guy who's madly in love with me, who can't keep his hands off me, who is sweet and kind and generous and broad-shouldered and muscled and so hot even Jamey lusts after him, thus making me the Queen of All Comebacks? In only three weeks?

Right. Never going to happen.

It's too late for a shower. I can barely drag myself to the closet to get dressed. Who cares what I look like? It's just work. It's not like I have a date tonight. Or *ever*.

The black knit skirt I wore yesterday is lying on the floor by the foot of my bed. I pick it up and give it a shake. No one will notice if I wear it again today. Most of my clothes are in the laundry basket now, but I pull an old white shirt off a hanger. I add black boots, simple flats that scream Soviet era utilitarianism.

Good enough.

It's not till I'm trudging down the stairs to the T station that I remember: I have a meeting today. A big one. The Anterdec team is coming to talk about our new phone tree customer interface, and Chloe asked me to sit in because of my involvement in the project. I freeze on the stairs, forcing the hordes of hurrying workers to dodge around me.

Right now, I am less well-dressed than the woman standing by the subway entrance holding a sign and collecting cash in a cup. I'll bet her last boyfriend didn't dump her for an antique maps dealer.

"Or what if he *did*?" I gasp, muttering to myself. A bearded hipster carrying a folded bike with a hemp strap around the handlebars looks at me like I'm losing it.

Because I *am*.

My hair is dirty. I have no makeup on and there are dark grey circles under my eyes. There is no time to go home and start all over again.

Amanda Warrick is going to be in that meeting. Crap. She's always perfect.

I make a U-turn and run back up the stairs. There's a CVS on the corner of this block. It's not Sephora, but it will have to do. Eight minutes and $57.45 later, I am back out on the sidewalk, carrying a plastic bag with foundation, mascara, lipstick, blush, a brush, and a hairclip. Also a can of dry shampoo and a pair of black tights.

I toss some change in that poor woman's cup. She gives me a conspirator's smile.

According to the drug store register receipt, I saved eight bucks with my customer card. It's my lucky day.

Customer card . . . interface . . . an idea attempts to form in my thick and foggy brain. Could we give our O clients a membership card that confers benefits? Not just "buy nine massages, get the tenth for free," but something really fun and unexpected? I need to talk to Ryan. He can tell me what the clients would love, *and* he'll understand the programming issues. That was his minor in college.

I take off my jacket in the O Spa lobby and stuff it into the CVS bag, hoping to look like I've been at work for hours. Given the dirty hair, tired under-eye circles, and yesterday's skirt, I really do look like I never went home last night. Great.

I duck into the ladies' room and wash my face with the Tropical Paradise hand soap from the dispenser, drying it with paper towels. My skin instantly feels like it's going to crack and fall off, and I am not going to escape the scent of chemical pina colada today. I unpack my purchases and get to work with them.

Makeup is really just hope in a jar, or a tube, or a pencil. Doesn't matter if it's CoverGirl or the priciest brand at the Neiman Marcus counter, I defy you to open the package without believing on some level that you are about to be transformed into Gigi Hadid.

No matter how many times I have bought a new lipstick, since I was thirteen years old, I still pull off the cap with the expectation that my life is about to change forever.

It's worth eight dollars just for that moment.

When I emerge from the bathroom, no one mistakes me for Gigi's older sister, but they don't reach for their tissue boxes, either. Hayley, the receptionist, looks up when I pass her desk. She brightens.

"Carrie! You look like you got some sleep." She jumps up and hugs me. "See, I told you it would get easier!"

I got sleep because I went to bed at 7:15 last night with two Tylenol PM. But she doesn't need to know that.

"I know just what you're going through. When Carlos broke up with me last spring, I thought my life was over," Hayley confides. "I stayed home three nights in a row, crying and eating Oreos. My mother was so worried." Hayley is twenty-one. "But then my girlfriends made me go out dancing with them, and what do you think? I met Javier that very night! And we've been together ever since! It was fate."

"That's great," I say weakly, hating her on the inside.

She smiles a satisfied smile. "Our song is 'Single Ladies.'"

This is clearly supposed to make me feel better. It doesn't. Tears prickle behind my eyes. No. No crying. Not until I'm at my desk.

"Thanks, Hayley," I manage. "What time is the Anterdec meeting this morning?"

She checks the schedule. "Ten o'clock."

"Thanks again."

I head back to my computer and open up my phone tree script. Somehow I've got to focus my brain on this. I've got all the basic options and responses down, but some of the more specific questions still need to be considered. I've spent hours interviewing Hayley and the spa receptionists downstairs to identify the most common requests.

And the most unusual.

It's O. We get quite a large number of unusual requests:

What wine pairing do you recommend with strawberry massage oil? (I'll connect you to our catering manager.)

The key to my handcuffs is lost, how do I get them unlocked? (Bring them back and we will give you another key. Unless someone is wearing them, in which case, use bolt cutters.)

Can I book a vaginal massage party for my book club meeting? (Yes. What book are you reading?)

I need to determine how deep the technology can go before the call has to be handled by a live person. For cost savings and improved efficiency, the more the process can be automated, the better. But O is decidedly not your average call center. Hours and directions are easy. Retail clients looking for standard appointments are referred to our website to see our menu of services and book online. Club members, of course, have their own special service team.

But O is all about customized, personal service at every level.

My computer makes a sound and I jump. Chloe, my boss, has sent me a message.

Carrie, can you come in for a minute?

I pause in the open door to her office. She looks up. As always, the surface of her glass waterfall desk is clear and pristine. A single white rose stands in a polished steel vase. The gauzy Roman shades on the windows filter the light into a soft haze. No matter what crazy stress is going on at O, Chloe's office is a peaceful retreat. It's like a spa within a spa.

"Hey," she says calmly. "Ready for the meeting?"

"I think so. I made a chart of the phone tree that shows all the options and where they lead. And I have sample recordings of three different voices, two men and a woman. After I get today's feedback, I'll arrange a focus group. That will help us understand how clients will respond."

"Great," she says, studying me. "You look pretty good for someone having a pretty bad week."

"You heard?" Chloe is a little older than me, but not much. She's so together—she has this great job and an adorable baby girl and her boyfriend Nick is *amazing*. She has everything. Her life is moving forward perfectly.

I have nothing. My life is now actually sliding backward. My broken vagina changes the laws of thermodynamics and makes Einstein rethink his theory. I can reverse human progress.

Or, at least, forget to shower on an important career day.

"I heard. You've been crying for four days and you've worn that skirt for three. So I asked Henry what happened." She shrugs, a delicate gesture that looks so elegant on her. When I do it, I look like Shrek's cousin.

I sink down into a chair across from her and bury my face in my hands. Great. If Henry knows, then the entire staff knows. And if the entire staff knows, then I'm already part of the rumor mill. Poor Carrie, they're all thinking.

Poorcarrie.

"Carrie, I know how you feel. It's awful. You feel so alone, and you're sure you'll never meet anyone else, and you miss him like crazy. You want to call him. You think you are never going to have fun again in your life. It's a physical pain, and you don't know how to make it stop hurting."

Exactly. I nod my head, my face still hidden.

"And you are embarrassed."

I look up. "You heard that part, too?"

"It wasn't hard to figure out."

I hide my face again and groan.

"The reason I know how you feel is that I was in the same place last year. Carrie, if you have forgotten my breakup with Joe, you're the only person at O who has. Or ever will. You think *you're* embarrassed? Joe showed up here, drunk, and had to be removed by security! He hit people! He threw up in the reception area!"

She smiles ruefully. "And it was the best thing that ever happened to me."

"I don't understand . . . ?"

"Somewhere in the back of my mind, I knew everything with Joe was all wrong. But it was *something*, and I didn't have the courage to let it go. What if I'd stayed in the relationship? It scares me to even think about it." Chloe reaches up to her neckline and plays with a beautiful necklace, one that her boyfriend Nick gave her. It looks like a delicate, gold gyroscope.

"But I didn't know anything was wrong between Jamey and me, Chloe. How could I *not know*? Everyone else knew! I feel so stupid. I can't even figure out when a guy is with me because he wants companionship or passion!"

"Maybe you just wanted it to be right so much that you ignored what felt wrong? And you have so much love inside you, and that kind of took over your rational brain. Jamey's a really nice guy. That wasn't the problem, right?" Her words are nonjudgmental. Comforting. Friendly and wise. Chloe is everything I could ask for in a boss. Her chocolate brown eyes are filled with sympathy and understanding.

"Right." I'm going to cry again, I can feel it coming, and then I'm going to have to start all over again with the Maybelline Instant Age Rewind Concealer. They should make Instant Boyfriend Rewind. That would be a big seller. I'd buy a case.

"I know you don't believe it, but this is going to be the best thing that's ever happened to you. How can you meet the right guy if you're busy with someone who's wrong for you?"

"That must be what Jamey was asking himself," I say bitterly.

Chloe smiles sadly. "Now go get ready for the meeting. They'll be here in half an hour." She hesitates. "You want to borrow a hair clip?"

A subtle hint. I touch the unpolished straggly mess that's spilling down my back. The dry shampoo could only do so much.

"No, thanks though. I have one at my desk." I suddenly feel an impulse to get away from her, even though she's so nice. Appearances are everything at O, and I'm definitely under-performing right now.

I need to triage my situation. I wish there was time to run to the spa bathrooms and grab a shower. I wave and bolt out of her office like a scared little rabbit.

Turning the corner into my cubicle, I run smack into Ryan. He's holding a bag, or he was until I knocked it out of his hands. Our bodies meet, his hard, mine anxious. He's so warm, my hands brushing against the ironed cotton of his soft denim shirt.

One of his hands reaches out, landing on my hip, while I grab his shoulders to avoid falling over. His breath smells like sugar and coffee. It's warm against my cheek and my heart flutters in my chest.

He holds onto my hip a second longer than he should, then pulls away. I let out a long sigh and wonder what the hell my body thinks it's doing. This is Ryan. *Ryan.* I am just confused after Jamey. It's been proven my wires are crossed inside, a jumble of circuits that make no sense.

"What are you doing here so early?" I pick up the bag to have something to do, to evacuate the burning sensation of his hard chest against my palms. I look inside. "Glazed cake! My favorite!"

"We're having a planning session in Entertainment. Something about a new phone tree system. I was walking by City Donuts on my way and I thought of you. The line was pretty short today, I only had to wait twenty minutes," he says, looking down at me. He's so tall.

Too tall.

I look at my boots. Flats. I forgot.

"Thank you so much!" As our eyes meet, something sparks between us. A flash of memory of that rushed kiss from the other night won't leave my mind. It invades, resting there like a movie, flickering between us. My rational mind knows he can't see it, but my arousal system decides to send blood rushing to places that begin to pulse, as if a ten-alarm fire were called for my libido.

What is wrong with me? The guy brought me donuts. It's not like he's in love with me. I'm so desperate for any male attention— straight male attention—that I'm inventing things.

Although he did wait in line twenty minutes to buy me two donuts.

And he remembered which kind I like. I've never been a chocolate girl. I know, right? You can't imagine this. No one can. But these deep-fried, sugar-glazed rings of vanilla cake are my weakness. They actually do make me feel better. Just holding one in my hand is comforting. I may not have a date for Saturday night, but I can have this little round piece of pleasure. No one can take it away from me.

It's no accident that it's shaped like an O.

Ryan leans against the wall and inspects me as I commune with my donut.

"You have a big meeting today too?" he asks.

"Yeth." My mouth is full. I swallow. "Phone tree meeting. Same one. I guess we're in for a couple of hours together."

"Are you ready?" His tone makes it clear that he's skeptical.

"Why is everyone asking me that? Of course I'm ready!" I pull open my desk drawer, looking for the hairclip I bought. "I just need to fix my hair."

He mumbles something I can't hear.

"What?" I ask, still hunting for the clip.

"I said, I'll braid it for you. If you want." I look at him and blink exactly once, as if my mind is taking a picture. His hair is curling slightly, a little longer than usual, and it's tousled like a little boy in the wind. Those golden brown eyes smile at me, but with a hint of nervousness, something that's increased lately. He's wearing a faded blue denim shirt that is unbuttoned, a tight black t-shirt underneath that shows his washboard abs. His forearms are tanned, covered in sandy-colored hair, with colorful geometric tats showing as he uncrosses his arms and walks toward me, the smile fading.

"Seriously? Here? I would love it!" I chirp, sounding too eager, too spritely. He's rescuing me, for sure.

"Um, how about in the conference room?" he suggests.

We look in and it's empty. His eyes dart over to the hallway and he closes the door, even though the room is nothing but windows and glass walls.

I settle into a chair and let my shoulders drop. Having my hair brushed is better than sex any day. Jamey used to brush my hair while we binge-watched *Scandal*, and I swear I would get to such a sensual place, I'd almost come.

Almost. And then we'd fall asleep. It was lovely.

This isn't like that, of course.

Ryan has told me all these stories about his four older sisters. When he was five, they noticed that he liked to build intricate and creative systems with his tiny LEGO blocks. The Donovan girls quickly found a more useful activity for his dexterous fingers: French braids. The man creates body art. Could this have inspired his love of tats?

Ryan's hands in my hair put me into a trance. Brushing, quickly dividing, gently tugging and sliding, his fingers woo my head as it leans into the movement of his hands.

"Almost done," he says, and I half-open my eyes.

At that moment, someone walks past the glass wall of the conference room, stops short, and peers in.

"Fuck," Ryan says under his breath.

The door opens. "Hello, kids," Zeke calls, grinning. Like Ryan, he's dressed in actual clothes, so it takes me a minute to recognize him. "See you in the planning session, RD," he says to Ryan. "I see we're meeting in the Friend Zone." He smirks and moves off down the hall.

"What does he mean?" I ask Ryan. "Where is the Friend Zone?"

"Nowhere, C-Shel. Absolutely nowhere," he says with a sigh as he moves back. "Done."

I reach up and touch the braid, grabbing my purse for a compact with a mirror. As I study the artwork he's done with my hair, I see hope again.

"This is amazing!" I squeal, dropping the compact and throwing myself into his arms for a hug. His arms circle around me and he smells so good.

Our hug deepens. His breath gets shaky and I should let go. Need to let go. This is the part where the hug is supposed to end, right? A simple *thank you* hug is a quickie, a brief embrace that communicates gratitude, a social nicety.

I'm grateful. He just saved my ass.

Speaking of my ass, his hands go to the base of my spine, and then—

"Ready?" Chloe asks through the glass as I pull out of Ryan's arms, shocked by the intimacy, those damn signals crossing again. He looks down at the ground and turns to the door, opening it like a gentleman. I hurry out and we join Chloe, who is talking about metrics for customer service, and how Amanda Warrick from headquarters is already down the hall, waiting for the team.

Half of me listens to her.

The other half is back in that conference room, in Ryan's arms. I imagined that, right? Ryan wasn't being—you know—that wasn't sexual or anything.

Of course not.

Now I'm misreading cues from *straight* guys. I need to google convents. Stat.

"Nice hair!" Chloe says, really looking at me. We stop at the coffee station and fill up before the meeting.

"Thanks," I say as Ryan pours milk into his coffee cup. "Ryan did it."

"Ryan?" Chloe turns to him, touching his hand. "Who knew you had these fine motor skills? I've always seen you as more of a gross motor guy. You have some magic hands."

Right. Magic.

Ryan

CHLOE TURNS ME into a tongue-tied little boy caught with his hand in the cookie jar. Normally, that's bad enough.

But *Carrie* is the cookie jar right now.

I want her cookie, and I want it bad.

Chloe reminds me of my oldest sister, Ellen. She's fifteen years older than me and a second mother. Ellen's eyes have two expressions: 1) wide with incredulity and 2) narrow with speculation.

No one has ever told Chloe she reminds me of my oldest sister. And no one ever will.

Chloe is touching me, her manicured fingers examining my palm.

The same palm I've been dating ferociously since Carrie kissed me the other day.

"We could add braiding to the service menu," Chloe says under her breath. "We have the hair salon, and our stylists are top of the line when it comes to hair care."

"But this isn't about style," Carrie interrupts, her voice gathering excitement. "It's about the rush of having a man's hands on you, fingers tugging at your hair, touching you in this half-intimate, half-compassionate way that just makes you feel so *cared for*."

Chloe's eyebrows go up.

And there it is.

Wide-eyed incredulity.

A rush of pleasure and impulse pounds through me as Carrie looks at Chloe with a flushed face, her eagerness still there for a split second before it drains out, embarrassment replacing it.

Then she punches me. It's playful and it kills the mood.

Her laugh is tinny and thin, weird and awkward. "You know," she backpedals. "For the paid customers. They'll eat it up. Not only can he dance and massage you, he'll braid your hair. Plus, evolutionary biology says that, you know, primate behavior makes us feel more like part of a social group when others touch our hair. Pick out nits. Eat the bugs. Groom. You know."

Now Carrie's just babbling. I want to save her, but Chloe's holding my hand and I'm enjoying listening to Carrie ramble about how having me braid her hair turned her on. That's my translation, and I'm sticking to it.

Chloe's eyes turn to Carrie and narrow. "Eat the bugs?"

"Chloe!" calls out a familiar man's voice.

Carrie looks relieved. Saved by her boss's boyfriend. Nick Grafton walks down the hall, confident in that way older men have when they've been successful in the business world long enough to know they've earned it. His suit is tailored and he's wearing cufflinks like the ones I inherited from my grandfather. Tall like me, but with more of a marathoner's build, Nick has a touch of silver in his hair and that casual assumption that when he speaks, he's in charge.

I like him. Unlike the men who work at O, he's not jockeying for the role of alpha male. Most of the guys here have a thing about their looks—Zeke especially. Henry's the unofficial pack leader here, and he's welcome to that role. I wouldn't want to deal with all the petty shit people dish out. Work is a place where I earn a paycheck and have some fun.

And, lately, find reasons to run into Carrie.

"Ryan," Nick says, giving me an obligatory handshake where we mutually crush each other's knuckles as testosterone takes over. "How's it going?"

"You know. The uniforms get smaller and the tips get bigger," I reply with a smile.

Chloe lets out a soft laugh at Nick's surprised response, his bewilderment rippling through the confident expression he normally has. Then he laughs as he wraps a possessive arm around her shoulders and plants a kiss on her cheek.

"Half an hour ago, I was in a design meeting for a chain of funeral homes. Or 'transition centers,' as they're calling themselves. O is a refreshing change of pace," Nick observes.

"From coffins to sex toy hotlines," Chloe muses, smiling up at him with that flawless grin. "You're quite the Renaissance Man."

My throat tightens. I want someone to look at me like that.

Carrie catches my eye.

I want *Carrie* to look at me like that.

Instead, she's giving me the stink eye.

"I thought I was the Focus Man," Nick teases Chloe as Carrie motions for me to come closer to her.

"Do I really look okay?" Carrie whisper-hisses, her nervousness calming me. I become the comforter, the confident one, the leader. "I need a handler, Ryan. Did I really go on about monkeys eating bugs as a form of foreplay?"

I choke on my coffee. "I wouldn't put it that way, but . . ."

"I'm not fit for public interactions," Carrie hisses. "This is all Jamey's fault!"

I'm not even going to try to understand how Jamey made her talk about primates eating hair bugs. Anything that makes him the bad guy works for me, though.

I reach for her shoulder and press gently, as if pinning her in place so she doesn't shoot off to the moon, fueled by adrenaline. "You're fine. You'll be great in this meeting."

"There's Amanda Warrick!" Carrie gasps, reaching up to touch her hair. "I look okay?"

"You look fabulous. Calm down."

"I am calm!" she hisses just as Amanda appears. Amanda Warrick is the assistant director for marketing for our parent company, Anterdec. She's engaged to the CEO, Andrew McCormick, and all the guys here at O know a dirty little secret about her.

Last year, Amanda came to O with a very enthusiastic older woman who sipped shots out of Henry's navel like it was a baby bottle. They were mystery shoppers—*the* mystery shoppers who wrote up the report that set Chloe's hair on fire.

Zeke remembered Amanda but no one believed him. Then Andrew McCormick's brother got married and when Declan McCormick escaped from his own wedding with his bride, the crazy older blonde lady was all over the news. We happened to be in the employee lounge when some cable news channel interviewed her going on about how the president stole her daughter from the wedding.

Henry told us never to say a word to anyone. Not sure why, but when Henry tells us to do something, we do it.

Every time I see Amanda, though, I can't help but smirk. Like right now, as I shake her hand and say, "Hello." She has beautiful auburn hair, a shade redder than Henry's, and big brown eyes that are perfectly round.

Eyes that narrow as I smile at her. It's like she can read what I'm thinking.

Nick, Chloe, Carrie, Amanda, and I all exchange handshakes and pleasantries, the kind of corporate shit I hate. Chloe insisted Zeke and I sit in on this meeting. Normally, Henry would handle it, but he has some class he can't get out of at Harvard, where he's working on his master's degree in public health.

Overachiever.

Once we're settled in at the big conference table, I realize this meeting is bigger than I thought. Diane from accounting has joined us, and some guy I don't recognize is sitting next to Chloe. Nick's on her other side. I angle for a spot next to Carrie, but end up sandwiched between Zeke and Diane. There are two other men in the room, dressed in t-shirts and jeans. I look down at my denim shirt and frown.

I didn't have to dress up after all.

The two men are arguing about something on a laptop. I didn't catch their names so I think of them as Geek and Geeker.

"But it looks all wrong," says Geek. "We have to make it look exactly like the O Spa's branding."

Geeker snatches the mouse and hisses to his partner, "But look, it does everything we need. Emails, text messaging, and each rep can customize their own messages. It's already all paid for."

Now I'm getting interested. "That's perfect. All you have to do is customize the branding to make it look like the O Spa, and all the hard work is already done for you."

Geek and Geeker stare back at me like I've just farted in an elevator.

"What is your job, exactly?" Geek asks with a sneer, eyes on my tatted arms.

Chloe stands. "Thank you, everyone, for coming to this very interesting meeting." She clears her throat gently, suggestively, and everyone grins. Geek turns away from me.

"Instead of making everyone go through introductions, allow me. I'm Chloe Browne. This is Amanda Warrick, assistant marketing director from Anterdec, our parent company. Nick Grafton, branding director from Anterdec. Ryan Donovan and Zeke Kelsroy are master staff members here at O, and will be manning the phones as beta testers."

"Nothing beta about me," Zeke whispers under his breath.

"Diane Delman from O's accounting team is with us, as is Jack Simonds from our New York office. Assuming all goes well, New York will be the phone line's next target market. Carrie Shelton is my assistant designer here at O, and has managed the details of development and content for the phone line." Chloe pauses, the silence ticking, taking on meaning.

We all look at Geek and Geeker, who are currently looking at their phones, ignoring the rest of us. Some subterranean part of their minds kicks in, like a second grader who realizes the classroom is a little too quiet, and they both look up, ostriches emerging from a hole in the ground.

"Advanteque Systems sent two of their primary developers here to help with specific coding and tech questions. Welcome Justin Rantz and Sanjay Mehta," she adds.

Both grunt out something close to "Hello" and raise their hand as Chloe says their respective names. Sanjay looks at Carrie with more interest than he has any right to.

"Let's get down to business. Carrie, it's your floor."

At the mention of Carrie's name, Sanjay's eyes widen and he does the once-over. I know exactly what he's doing. Carrie is being graded.

"If you look at the outlines in front of you," Carrie says confidently, pointing to our papers, "you'll find the basic phone system that an O member will experience when they call the number:

Press 1 to schedule a massage appointment

Press 2 to request a master masseur

Press 3 to speak with a coordinator about bachelorette or divorce parties

Press 4 to purchase merchandise

Press 5 for device troubleshooting

Press 6 for an intimate chat with a master masseur

"Device troubleshooting?" Diane asks, her brow down with confusion. "What sort of device?"

"Sex toys," Chloe answers cheerfully.

"Oh," Diane says, her face turning a furious red, matching the bright lipstick she wears.

"That's right!" Carrie says, a little too cheerfully. "O!"

I groan. Nick raises an eyebrow. Geek and Geeker don't react.

"But," Chloe adds, brow knitting, "if that term is too confusing, maybe we should simplify."

"How about 'battery-operated boyfriend'?" Zeke helps out.

"Marketing can handle name generation," Nick adds smoothly, not taking the bait.

"We have the system set up in advance. All of the options except number six are free, and included in O club membership. Intimate conversations with master masseurs are a separate charge, and require a permission-based system," Carrie continues.

"Opt-in," Sanjay mutters.

"Right," Carrie replies. "On multiple levels."

"The operative word being 'multiple,'" Zeke jokes.

Chloe shoots him a look that says, *Really?*

He just grins back.

Until Nick gives him a staredown.

"Clients are charged one-eighty per half hour for these conversations."

Justin the developer lets out a choking cough and gives Carrie an incredulous look. "That's more than Sanjay and I make!" He gives Zeke and me a glare of outrage. "To talk to a bunch of horny women?"

"You can only aspire to have my skill set one day," Zeke declares, flexing a bicep.

Nick's jaw tightens. Chloe just rolls her eyes. Carrie starts to panic. No one else in the room can tell, but I see it.

"Master coders don't pull in $360 an hour," Sanjay protests.

"Do you argue with all your clients like this?" Nick asks in a low, neutral voice that manages to sound more threatening than a shout.

Sanjay shuts up.

"Customers will have credit cards on file, and master masseurs can access a smartphone app to pull up the customer's file for background information when they call. The point is to be a good listener. This is not phone sex," Carrie clarifies.

"Wait. It's not?" Justin looks up, long brown hair flopping over his face. He tucks it behind his ears, over the stems of his glasses.

"No. That is a hard *no*, too," Carrie elaborates, staring at Zeke. "We could get shut down if we tried it."

"Then what the hell are women paying $360 an hour *for*?" Sanjay asks in a voice that makes it clear the guy doesn't get it.

"Companionship. A listener. The feeling that she gets a little piece of me to herself," Zeke replies.

Justin and Sanjay just gawk.

"That's so . . . stupid," Justin finally blurts out.

"Welcome to reality, gentleman," Zeke crows.

"Tuck the peacock feathers back in, Zeke," Chloe whispers across the table.

"I'm just having fun with them," he whispers back with a grin.

"I am going back to the office and asking for a raise," Sanjay says, swiping on his phone.

"Can we get back to discussing the specifics of this project? You know, the one Anterdec is funding?" Amanda Warrick finally joins the conversation, her words cutting through. One eyebrow goes up, an expression like Chloe's, and all eyes are on her.

Money always gets the eyes.

Except while everyone else is looking at Amanda, I'm looking at Carrie.

"The guidelines for intimate conversations have already been banged out," she adds.

Zeke snickers. I kick him under the table. Sanjay yelps. Wrong foot.

I don't care. Sanjay breaks his evaluation of Carrie. Two birds, one stone, all that.

"What we really need to concern ourselves with is the financial system and permissions-based aspect here. We don't want regret to drive credit card chargebacks and disputes," Carrie explains.

Justin gapes at her. "Huh?"

"We don't want customers to claim they didn't understand the expense of the call. So the tech side of this is clear."

"Phone sex hotlines have a warning at the beginning. A pre-recorded message that informs the user of the exact charges, and they have to press one to accept, or two to decline," Zeke says matter-of-factly.

We all just watch him.

"What? Everyone knows that," he says defensively.

"We don't want to be so . . . vulgar," Chloe weighs in, her voice deliberative.

"O's branding isn't about sex," Carrie adds.

Zeke starts laughing.

"Don't make that mistake," she emphasizes. "It's about freedom. About owning who you are." Chloe is watching Carrie with the look of a pleased mother. "We don't want to cheapen the brand by making people equate this new phone system with 1–800-HAND-JOB."

She spells out the last seven digits.

Zeke is in the middle of drinking his coffee and sprays it all over Geek and Geeker, who jump up and howl in protest.

Nick, Chloe, and Amanda all begin speaking at once, ignoring the coffeefest.

"What about bundling the fee—"

"How about a gratitude-based message rather than—"

"If we added a video component, maybe we—"

"If you turn to page three, you'll see I've addressed all of this," Carrie interrupts calmly.

My phone buzzes. So does Carrie's. We simultaneously ignore our phones.

"If we make this about how the woman *feels*, we'll nail it from a branding perspective," Carrie begins.

"Nail it," Zeke says, snickering again.

I really kick him. "What are you? Twelve?" I hiss.

Carrie gives me a look that says, *You too?*

No. Not me, too.

My phone buzzes again, though. I grab it and look.

It's a text from my oldest sister Ellen. *Did you finish the grad school application?*

I ignore it.

"Go on, Carrie," I say loudly, trying to clear some of the static from the room so poor Carrie can finish. I don't sit in on meetings other than staff gatherings managed by Henry or Chloe. This is a snoozefest.

"We focus on how she feels. Thank her for her call. Talk about how privileged O is to provide this support to her in a time when she is working on personal growth. Have the masseurs emphasize their gratitude to her."

Sanjay makes a mock gagging motion.

"What does that have to do with the tech angle, though?" Amanda muses. "How do we design a tight system that gives us permission to charge their credit cards and keep chargebacks at a low rate?"

"What about a follow-up?" Carrie mentions, pointing to page four of her handout. "We have an automated check-in later in the day. Opt-in. We could text her—even have the master masseurs write a personal text and the system could schedule it. We would have strong return business, too. Build a relationship between the masseur and the client."

"This is so fake," Justin says with a sour look.

"Can you do it from a tech standpoint?" Amanda asks, giving Justin and Sanjay a challenging look.

"Of course," Sanjay says. "Not hard at all. We'd need to connect customer records with phone and texting systems. Do you want email integration, too?"

"Absolutely. VR as well," Chloe adds.

"VR? Virtual reality?" Sanjay's eyebrows go up.

"We're experimenting with it. If we could have synergy between all the systems, that would be optimal."

"Great idea, Sanjay!" Zeke says, pretending to clap. "I like it."

Everyone nods. Carrie's face falls. Sanjay beams while Justin pats him on the shoulder.

"It was Carrie's idea," I say, clearing my throat. Carrie looks at her phone as I talk and frowns. The skin at the corner of her eye starts to twitch, then tighten.

Oh, no.

I know that look.

She's about to cry.

"Well, she had the general idea, but—"

I put Sanjay's protests to an end. "She had the entire idea fleshed out."

Zeke snickers.

"And you need to leave if you can't stop acting like a teen boy in his first sex ed class," I tell Zeke in a calm, cold voice that makes it clear I'm not fucking around.

Carrie won't stop looking at her phone. What was in that text?

Nick Grafton speaks, splaying his hands on the table, leaning in and looking at Geek and Geeker with the eyes of a closer.

"Can you accomplish the autoresponder sequence with texts and emails that are customized by the master masseur to the customer? Yes or no?"

"Yes," Justin stammers. "But it's complex, and all the new requirements are going to take longer and cost more. "

"No, it's not," I bark, reluctant to jump in, but they've given me no choice. "All you have to do is customize the branding to feel and sound like the O Spa. You already paid for a phone service product that does the heavy lifting for you," I add, giving Chloe and Nick a pointed look. "The rest isn't that hard."

Nick looks back at me, grabs a pen, and jots something down on his notepad.

Sanjay shrugs. Justin scowls.

The room goes silent. Carrie's looking at me, lips parted, teeth separated, her face filled with surprise.

I shrug. "I have coding experience."

"The man braids hair, dances beautifully, keeps the customers happy with his hands, and can code. Is there anything you can't do, Ryan?" Chloe jokes.

I look at Carrie.

Yeah, I think. *There is.*

CHAPTER FIVE

Carrie

W E KNEW SATURDAY was going to come, right? A gorgeous Saturday in late September, the month when New England in general—and Boston in particular—comes alive with events and energy and impossible natural beauty. In a city full of universities, the new year really begins on Labor Day.

We—the old 'we,' Jamey and me—were going to drive out to the country today and pick apples. Then we were going to come home and bake a pie. A beautiful pie, with a perfect fluted crust sprinkled with cinnamon and sugar, and a little slice of cheddar cheese on the side. Or homemade ice cream. Whichever we felt in the mood for.

I feel more in the mood for applesauce. You know, where you peel off the skin and cut up the fruit with knives and then boil it until you end up with mush. So it matches your heart.

For our apple-picking date, I was going to wear a cute little corduroy miniskirt and a bright quilted vest. Instead I am wearing plaid flannel pajama bottoms that say Northville Polar Bears across the seat (Christmas gift from Mom and Dad), and slippers with polar bear faces on the toes (Christmas gift from Teddy). The slippers scuff and slap as I trudge up and down from the basement laundry, four flights down. For those of you with elevators, that's sixty steps each way, times four (wash and dry), for two loads. Two hundred forty steps, half of them carrying a basket of clothes. Who needs a gym membership?

BUT if you are five minutes late for your cycle? (No, not *that* cycle!) Someone will have removed your wet laundry and left it on top of the machine. Either add one hundred and twenty more steps or wait forty minutes in the windowless, humid laundry room, so you don't miss your chance.

Anyway, the muggy laundry room with its peeling green paint feels about right today. There are no chairs, but if I sit on the machine, the steady vibration and rocking motion might just distract me for a few minutes.

My new boyfriend, Kenmore. I can set the dial to Large Load. Ha.

I pull out my other boyfriend, Smartphone. The one who is such good company, always willing to entertain or inform me, any time of day or night. You're never alone when you have an iPhone.

I press SHD in my contacts list.

"Hi Daddy, it's me." During the meeting at work, Dad texted me. I couldn't deal with him then. Laundry time is down time, perfect for calling home.

"Carrie Baby! Hold on!" He holds the receiver away from his mouth. "Yes, thank you, Mrs. Patterson, and don't forget you can store wet brushes in the freezer overnight! Saves on cleanup! Come in again soon!" My dad's sentences always seem to end in exclamation points.

"Sorry, baby," he says. "Busy day—fall is fix-up-your-house time!"

"I know, Daddy," I smile. "I can almost smell the paint."

"Remember when we used that slogan in our ads? 'Wake up and smell the fresh paint!' But then it turned out that some people hate that smell." He chuckles.

My parents own Shelton's Home Decorating in Northville, Michigan. They sell paint and basic wallpaper, plus all the tools and accessories to do it yourself. And they hold classes. I have taught literally hundreds of people to use a utility knife.

Making things look better is in my blood. I'm a total sucker for before-and-after magazine spreads, doesn't matter if it's houses or hairdos, cosmetics or closets. In the checkout line, when I see a People Magazine cover that says "I Lost 100 Pounds!" or "Veteran With Six Foster Children Gets New Home Surprise!" I cannot get $4.99 out of my purse fast enough.

"What's Teddy doing?" My brother still works at Shelton's. He and his girlfriend, Andrea, fixed up an apartment over our parents' barn. The paint and wallpaper were free. It's cute.

"He's around here someplace. In the stockroom, I think. Did you want to speak to him?"

"No. I just wanted to hear your voice." I sniffle. Damn.

"What's up, sweetie?" His voice is immediately full of concern. "Everything okay at work?"

"Oh, yes, everything's fine. I just miss you, and Mom, and . . . home."

"Carrie, you can come home anytime! You know that. Your room is waiting for you, and Mom and I would love to have you back. And so would all your high school friends, the ones that stayed around. Mom hates cooking for just the two of us, and she has no one to go to the mall with anymore. Why don't you come for a weekend and think about staying?"

"Thank you, Daddy. I'll be home at Thanksgiving. I'm fine. I love you."

I don't point out that they have never visited me in Boston. "Too loud and busy," they say. Mom and Dad never planned for Teddy or me when it came to college. They assumed we'd stay put and take over the business. And I did—stay put, that is. Just long enough to realize I was literally spending much of my life watching paint dry.

I left home when I was twenty-five. Moved to Boston nine years ago. Took the long route to getting my degree. I've built a fine life.

I *am* fine, right? I mean, I have a great job, even if it doesn't pay very much yet. I'm in debt up to my eyeballs, too, but who isn't? Changing careers means some sacrifice, but I knew I wanted to be in design, not public relations. Now I have my degree, and I'm back on track.

Career on track. Love life off the rails. I just can't explain this situation to my father.

Saved by the *beep*.

"I have to go, Daddy, my friend Jenny's trying to call. She's the one who's getting married in a few weeks. I'll call Mom later. I love you."

"Sure, baby, I'll tell her. Love you back."

I click over to Jenny as my machine boyfriend clicks over from 'wash' to 'rinse.'

"Hi Jen."

"Hey, what's going on?"

"Going on? What do you mean?" *How much does she know? What is she really asking?*

"I mean, like, what's going on? What do you mean, what do I mean?"

"I'm in the laundry room standing guard over my load of darks."

"Never try to get the machines on a Saturday, you have to fight all the people who have nothing better to do." I *am* the people who have nothing better to do, but apparently she doesn't know that yet. "I thought you'd be on your way to the apple orchard by now. You're running late—or are you staying in the country tonight? Jamey always finds those adorable inns where they roast the venison over an open fire or whatever." She chuckles, proud of her creative brother.

"Um, no. That was the plan but . . . Jamey had to go out of town. At the last minute."

"Really? That's weird, he always lets Mom know where he's going to be."

"I think he had a lot on his mind." Can you die from lying by omission? I'm about to find out.

"Oh. Well, since you're not doing anything, why don't you come meet us? I'm taking Savannah to pick out her flower girl basket, and then we're going to Cheesecake Factory for an early supper. It'll be so much fun!"

You see? You *see*? This is what my life is going to be from now on. Dragging someone's whiny four-year-old niece around on the T, followed by gluey fettucine Alfredo at 5:00 on Saturday night. Home in bed by 8:45. Alone.

"That definitely sounds like fun, Jen, but I think I'm going to use the time to work on a special project Chloe gave me. It's a little different for me and I want to do a good job."

"Okay, sweetie," she says, her mind already moving on to the next wedding-checklist item. "When Jamey comes back, let's get dinner, the four of us."

"That would be great."

It would be great, all right. Just four friends, two happy couples, grabbing dinner. But Jamey's not coming back—not to that life, anyway.

We say our goodbyes and I'm alone with my spin cycle again.

Jenny hasn't heard the news. That's obvious. I don't think it's up to me to tell her. You don't out people. That's not how this works. Even if I hate Jamey—and part of me does—I'm not cruel. There's a reason he hasn't told Jenny the truth yet. While he's been horrible to me, I don't have to stoop to his level and be horrible back. When he's ready, he'll tell Jenny.

I'm pretty sure showing up to the wedding with a boyfriend will tip his hand.

This is like living in some alternate reality: in one version, Jamey and I are living out a cozy and predictable romantic comedy, happily ever after, except in my parallel universe, the comedy is *Will & Grace*.

Being the keeper of Jamey's secret is harder than it should be. Frankly, it's unfair. I feel a sudden and desperate need to talk to someone who knows the true story.

That would be Ryan.

Hi! I type, and delete.

Hey! delete.

What's going on? Delete.

What is the matter with me? It's just Ryan—it's not like it has to be the cleverest line ever written.

Do you like apple pie? I hit send.

When everything is finally dry, I pile both loads into my laundry basket and start the final ascent to the third floor. I'm developing thighs of steel. Although I've never been sure if that's really a good look.

Still no answer to my text.

In my bedroom, I dig through the clean clothes until I find a pair of jeans and a long-sleeve tee. I pull my hair back with an elastic, grab my wallet and that quilted vest.

"Your plan was to bake an apple pie today and, with or without a boyfriend, that is what you are going to do," I tell myself. Or applesauce. Not sure yet.

No answer.

At the Tedeschi store down the street, I buy a bag of McIntosh apples, some brown sugar, and a little block of cheddar cheese sealed in plastic. Jamey would never tolerate ingredients from the convenience store. If it wasn't from Whole Foods, you'd think it was rat poison.

No answer from Ryan.

Back in my kitchen, I get out a bowl and start peeling. Okay, this is where it's more fun if you're doing it with a partner. It's a lot of apples. Jamey would have researched all the different types of apples and he'd explain which was best for what use. He would get the stream of "Wait, Wait, Don't Tell Me" on NPR, and we'd laugh at the jokes. We'd drink hard cider.

We had so much *fun*. So much damn fun.

"If you stretched these peels out end to end, they'd reach to Worcester." It's been so long since I spent an entire day alone, I am starting to talk to myself, just to see if my voice works. "Springfield maybe."

No answer, either to my comment or my text. Maybe I should get a pet to talk to. A Betta fish. They have to live alone, too.

I make the pastry for the crust and roll it out. You didn't know I had these culinary skills, did you? The granddaughter of Emmeline Shelton was not raised to buy frozen piecrust at the supermarket, no sir. It cracks a little in the center but I pinch it together. No one will know.

By 5:00, the scent of hot apples, cinnamon, and sugar fills my apartment and probably the apartment across the hall as well.

By 7:00, a golden brown and beautiful pie is sitting on my counter, cool and ready to cut. I briefly consider an Instagram shot, but truth be told, the lattice crust is patched in two places; Jamey would not approve.

At 9:00, I take a fork from the drawer and dig in, eating from the center of the apple pie out to the crust. Why bother with a plate? There's no one here but me. I lick the syrupy juice from my finger.

Still no answer.

Ryan

WE HAVE FIVE kids in my family: Ellen, Michelle, Dina, Tessa . . . and me.

Notice something different about that last kid?

Yeah. Mom and Dad heard it once I was born. "Kept trying till you had that boy, huh?" Wink wink. Nudge nudge.

Pretty sure it got old pretty fast.

Being the baby boy in a family full of older sisters means there are loads of picture albums with me wearing makeup, dressed in heels and dresses, and being paraded around like a pet. That's pretty much what I was—a pet.

Because Mom and Dad didn't expect to have a bumper baby at 43.

Tessa is the next in line, seven years my senior, and she lives on the South Shore outside of Boston. Everyone else is back home, in Concord, California, outside San Francisco. I came here first, a few years ago, and Tessa's husband happened to get transferred here a year later.

I'm thinking about Tessa because I'm staring at a text from her right now. It's Saturday. She has twin four-year-old boys. Which means this text is about:

We need you to babysit so we can go to a hotel and have wild monkey sex for a few hours, the text reads.

Tessa has no filter.

Carlos has blue balls. The buildup of semen is so bad, his irises are losing color. If this continues, his accelerated hair growth will be a function of the semen pressing on the hair roots.

STOP! I text back. *None of that is biologically possible, but I get the picture. When do you want me to babysit?*

How about four days ago? she replies.

I don't have a time travel machine, I tell her.

Can't you invent one, Mr. Cal Tech Engineering Grad? Slacker.

Oh, brother.

Er . . . sister.

Tonight? I'll get pizza and watch Mythbusters with the twins.

Sounds good. Just don't teach them how to build a toilet bomb. Be here at 3.

Toilet bomb? What kind of uncle does she think I am?

That's for second grade. They're still in preschool. Molotov Cocktails first, then we're going to hack musical birthday cards to play burping sounds. A man has to pace himself, I reply.

Once a nerd, always a nerd, she answers. *I have pictures of you when you were a kid. Get too cocky with my twins and I'll embarrass you,* she shoots back.

Show pictures of me when I was younger to anyone I care about and Carlos will drown in his own semen.

I get a smiley face in return and run through my day.

It's Saturday. A rare weekend night off for me.

Carrie just got dumped and turned me into Friend Central. Call me Mr. Huggy.

Zeke's grinding me mercilessly about being a wimp.

And he's right.

Tessa's dig about my former nerdiness makes me decide my next move. Lifting. When you lift, your world becomes nothing but metal and gravity. People pay thousands of dollars a year for testosterone supplements. I just need my apartment set of adjustable weights and some music to pump by.

Lifting is the answer to everything.

Bzzzz. It's my apartment door. I press the call button.

"Yeah?"

"It's me." I only know one person with that accent.

"What do you want, fuckface?"

"That's what my hens call me, Ryan. Unless you plan to actually fuck my face, you get to call me Zeke."

"Why would I want to do that?"

"Because I've got a damn fine face. Let me in."

"Why?"

"Because I can outlift you and you need someone to push your testosterone levels back into man range. I swear you have a tampon string hanging where your dick should be. I caught you braiding Carrie's hair yesterday. You need an intervention."

"Fine." I buzz him in just as I get a new text on my phone.

It's my oldest sister Ellen again. *You sure you finished the grad school application?*

I type back, *What grad school application?* because I love imagining her head exploding.

RYAN! she screams via text. Don't think it can't be done. My sisters are masters at it.

Mission accomplished.

You have asked me twenty times. Every time I tell you yes. Stop asking, I respond.

Just making sure, she replies.

I'm not twelve years old, I answer.

In my mind, you are. Plus, it's important to Mom and Dad. Having you move back home is really critical.

I've applied to grad school in California. Berkeley, Stanford, and Cal Tech. Made the mistake of telling my sisters. Ellen hasn't stopped asking about it for two months.

No one here knows about my application. Not even Carrie.

Zeke bangs on the door before I can even try to shove that thought away, saving me from my own denial. Dad's slow slide into early dementia has meant increased pressure from my sisters to go back home and help.

"I'm thinking about a change in hairstyle," Zeke announces, walking in with a giant gym bag and two smoothies from a juice bar down the street. "Can you give me some highlights and lowlights?"

"Lowlights for a lowlife?"

"Do you braid pubic hair? Chloe would love to add that to the spa menu."

"How would I do that when every woman who comes to O gets a full Brazilian? There hasn't been any pubic hair on women since 2005."

"Leave it to Chloe to figure out a way. Maybe you'll single-handedly create a bush fashion trend. If anyone can do it, you can, mate. You were epic today."

"Thank you."

"Epic fail." He studies me. "I don't get it, man. Really. Just make a move. You haven't even kissed her."

From pubic hair braiding to Carrie in two seconds.

"Yes, I have," arguing automatically, cringing as I say the words.

"That mistletoe at the office Christmas party two years ago doesn't count."

"Not that."

Eyebrows up, Zeke grabs my weight set and starts doing curls. "Spill."

"The other night. She came here, upset because she was dumped. And she kissed me."

"*She* kissed *you?*"

"Yeah. But I kissed her back."

"And?"

"And what?"

"Did you sleep with her?"

"No."

He recoils like I poked him with a hot iron. "Why not?"

How the hell do I answer this? While my logical brain tries to figure that out, my stupid brain spits out, "Because she was worried she has a broken vagina."

Stupid brain has impulse control issues.

He squints. "There are tests for that. Easy. Go to the health department, get some antibiotics, you're good to go. Not that I would know," he adds quickly.

"Not that. She felt . . . vulnerable. Worried about what it meant to be dumped by a gay guy again. I couldn't just make a move on her in that state, so—"

"Again? This wasn't her first gay boyfriend?"

"Damn it."

"What the hell are you doing here, Ryan?" He hands me a 55-lb dumbbell and I work my triceps. "Either act or move on. Sounds like she's a hot mess."

"Carrie is great. Better than great. You're the pot calling the kettle black."

"I'm a pot who gets laid. Unlike you. I don't get it. You have some weird, crazy hang-up about her. She's not a unicorn. There are plenty of other women out there if she rejects you."

When, the voice inside my head says, crackling like a handbrake on a train being pumped. *When she rejects me.*

I shrug. "Why are you so obsessed about this? It's my life."

"Because it's too painful to watch, man. You're pining away for her and she likes you, and you don't see it."

"We're friends. She doesn't like me."

"You said she kissed you."

"To prove she's still attractive to men. Or something."

"She picked you to kiss. Not me." Shrug. Lift.

I grab the second dumbbell from him and work on toe lunges while he starts doing burpees. "So?"

"Women don't just pick random guys to kiss when they're trying to prove a point. Guys are random. Women aren't."

"You're suddenly an expert in human psychology?"

"Aren't we both? You have to be to do our jobs at O." He powers through more burpees, panting hard. "Think of Carrie like she's a client at O."

I groan at the thought. "What?"

"Seriously. Apply work standards to her. You know when a client has the hots for you, right?"

"Yeah."

"What tips you off?"

"The crotch grabs." I make it through another set of lunges and drop the dumbbells. "Carrie hasn't gone in for the kill."

"Yet."

I don't even dignify that with an answer.

"She spends all her free time with you. You curl up on the couch and watch prepper shows. You share pints of ice cream. I'll bet you even share the same spoon."

No comment.

"We're *friends*."

"She lets you braid her hair."

"Friends."

"She came to you in a moment of weakness and kissed you to prove a point."

"Friends."

"Does she do that with her female friends?"

I'm losing this argument.

"If—and I'm only hypothetically entertaining this to prove you wrong—if Carrie's into me, she has a terrible way of showing it. After that kiss, she pulled back and went on and on about what a good friend I am, how she's so glad we're friends, friends, friends, friends."

"That's your fault."

"I know."

I give up.

"You need to fix this. Go for it. Kiss her. Be the aggressor. Kiss her like you mean it, then screw her silly."

"I don't want to screw her silly. I want more than that."

"A silly screw would be a start. You need to start somewhere."

I hold the 55s over my head and turn, doing pivot lunges, calves screaming.

"You're right," I grunt out.

"Excuse me?"

"You're right."

"About time you admitted it." His face is beet red as he grabs a water bottle and chugs. Then he sets his jaw in a funny way, rubbing his chin as he watches me with cat-like eyes. "What about the wedding?"

"What wedding?"

"Jenny's wedding."

"You going?"

He gives a half grin. "Hell, yeah. I love it when my exes get married."

"You slept with Jenny?"

"Years ago. Way back. She was fine."

"Jenny and Carrie are best friends."

"And Carrie needs a date." Zeke's words fill my living room. So does a strangely compelling odor. Some guys get sweaty and just smell like effort. Other guys get sweaty and smell like—

"Jesus, Zeke, did you have *sex* before you came over here?" I sniff the air.

"Yeah. Uber driver." He grins.

"You had sex with an *Uber driver*?"

"UberX, man. Eight-passenger SUV. Nice, flat backseat. She had bottled water and snacks and everything." He shakes his head. "Never knew how convenient those little travel packs of baby wipes could be."

"You met a complete stranger through Uber and had sex with her in her car?"

"Trust me. Better than PlentyOfFish or Match.com."

"Uber isn't an online dating app!"

"It is now."

"You reek of pussy."

"Glad to know you remember what it smells like."

"I know what it smells like."

"I meant other than sniffing your own armpits."

"Remind me why I am friends with you."

"Because I give you all the good ideas. Ask Carrie to be your date for the wedding. We're all going."

"Why would I be her date?" He's onto something, though.

"Because you like her. Because chicks love weddings. Weddings are like stirrups at the gynecologist's office, mate."

I don't want to know.

He doesn't wait for me to ask what he means. "They make women's knees fall wide open."

"You're sick."

"I'm not the one walking around with blue balls."

"Speaking of blue balls," I say, looking at the clock, "I need to go help my brother-in-law."

Alarm fills Zeke's face. "Man, have I been wrong about you and Carrie? You're into guys now?"

"What? No!"

"Then how the hell are you helping him with a blue balls problem?"

"Babysitting. Remember the twins?"

"You mean the demon spawn."

"They're not that bad."

"Those two little Tasmanian devils gave themselves a powder bath in my five gallon bucket of protein shake mix. Burned through a couple hundred bucks of whey. I'm still finding powder in crevices in my apartment after that time you brought them over. Why would you willingly babysit on a Saturday night?"

"To help my sister."

"You gonna braid her hair too, mate, or is that just for women you're afraid to hit on?"

"Shut up."

"Ask Carrie to the wedding. Tell her something. Hell, tell her you'll be her fake boyfriend. Anything to get an in."

"An *in?*"

"Think about it. Spend a weekend on Cape Cod making her look good in front of her friends. She's already been humiliated by being dumped by a guy who likes hot dogs more than vertical tacos."

"Vertical . . ." My mind forms an image. "Jesus, Zeke. You're disgusting. Seriously."

"What? Tacos are delicious." He winks at me. "Going as her date is genius. Tell her it's all pretend. You're doing her a favor. Be affectionate in public. Be the hot guy she landed on the rebound. Then make your move."

I can't believe I'm considering this, but he might be onto something.

"Offer to rescue her," I say slowly.

"Right. Be the nice guy who's going already. Give her a way to save face while you figure out how to get her to sit on yours."

I throw a towel at him. "Stop it."

"Stop what? Telling you the truth?"

"Talking about Carrie like that."

"Jealous?"

"No. Just . . . don't."

"You realize she's hot, right? Hot enough for some other guy to make a move before you do."

My balls turn into ice cubes at the thought.

"You need a date, anyhow. Something other than babysitting rugrats."

I snatch the towel up and walk away. "Speaking of which, gotta shower."

"That's it? I thought we were lifting."

I look at the clock. "Fine. Let's run stairs."

Zeke hates stairs. He groans.

I grin.

♥ ♥ ♥

WALKING INTO CARLOS and Tessa's house is like going to a daycare center run by hummingbirds who moonlight at Starbucks.

Before I can shout "hello," I step on a pile of LEGO blocks, lose my balance, catch myself on the edge of the couch, and feel warm breath on my calves.

"UNCLE RYAN!" two little boys scream, lunging at me.

"Did you bring soda?" Elias asks, his little butt firmly on the top of my foot. His brother, Darien, is settling into the same position on my other foot. I carefully lift each foot, wondering if I could do toe lunges with one kid in each hand.

"Good thing your mom didn't have triplets," I announce, looking down at them. I feel like the Jolly Green Giant.

"Why?"

"Because then I'd need to grow a third foot."

"But you can't. You only has two foots," Darien explains seriously. He looks like Carlos, with deep chocolate eyes and dark, wavy hair.

"Two feet," Elias corrects him. With features like Tessa's, only translated into XY versions, Elias looks more like the men in our family.

Which means when I take my nephews out in public, everyone assumes he's my son.

Surprisingly, I don't mind.

"MOOOOOOOMMMMMMMMMMMMMYYYYY!" Darien screams. "Can people have three feet?" He gives me a fearful look, pressing his palms against my calf. "Where would it grow out of?"

"What are you telling them now? People can't grow extra feet." Tessa comes around the corner from the hallway, her fingers working an earring.

"I said if you'd had triplets, I'd need a third foot." I start shuffling around the room, using the little boys' backs as brooms to push toys aside. They don't seem to mind.

"If I'd had triplets, I'd trade your third foot for a third breast. Way more useful." Tessa looks me up and down. "You look good."

"Um, thanks? You suddenly become a client at O? Why are you commenting on my appearance?"

She studies my face. I study her right back. Her hair's been cut and styled, and she's wearing makeup. A dress. Her feet are in high heels and a light, floral scent fills the room.

Tessa generally lives in yoga pants and whatever shirt she threw on after her nightly bath, so. . . .

"Something's changed," she says, pursing her lips in contemplation. Her eyes narrow. "You're dating again?"

"What?"

"You're—I don't know what to call it. If you were a woman I'd say you're glowing. What do you say when a man is glowing?"

"Is Uncle Ryan radiactic?" Elias asks, unraveling from my foot. "Cause that's what happens on *Fantastic Four*. The men glow because they got radiactic."

"What does radioactive mean?" I quiz him.

He shrugs. "I think it's when you fart and get superpowers."

"Nice," Tessa says, giving me the hairy eyeball. "Carlos must be letting them watch Cartoon Network again."

"Only *South Park*," Carlos calls out from the kitchen. "Nothing too risqué."

"That's not funny!" Tessa calls back as I laugh.

"You're all dressed up. Where are you going?"

"To a hotel," she says. "I told you."

"Yeah, but why get dressed up if you're just going to a hotel to get undressed?" The words are out of my mouth before I realize I have zero desire to hear my sister answer that.

She frowns. "Wait. Where's Carrie?"

"Nice topic change, sis," I tease, secretly relieved not to have to suffer through her answer, but on edge about Carrie.

"She always comes with you when you babysit."

"That's because you have the best selection of ice cream in town."

"We do," Tessa agrees. "We really do."

The twins start chanting, "ICE CREAM! ICE CREAM!" Tessa's eyes widen as Elias, fingernails coal black, runs his hands up and down her leg.

"Mommy!" he says as Darien continues the chant, "what happened to the caterpillar?"

"Caterpillar?"

"The one who lives on your legs. The one that's so hairy all over from your knees to your toes."

"I shaved, honey."

"You shaved a caterpillar?" The corners of his mouth turn down. "Why?"

"CARLOS!" Tessa screams. "WE NEED TO GO NOW!"

He ignores her. She shrugs. "So . . . Carrie?"

I shrug. We're a shrugging family.

"When are you finally going to make a move?"

"Did you change your name to Zeke today?"

"You make no sense sometimes, Ryan. Make that most of the time. And you're stalling. Didn't work when we were kids, won't work now."

"I'm going to a wedding with Carrie." It's a lie. A big one. Zeke's suggestion apparently took over my subconscious.

"As her date?"

"Yes."

"So you two are dating?"

"Kind of. We're going on a date."

"Which is the very definition of 'dating.'"

"If you say so."

"You two are practically married, anyhow. She's perfect for you. Anyone who willingly watches those stupid prepper and naked-in-the-jungle shows is a saint."

"Is that a compliment to Carrie, or an insult to me?"

"I have twin preschoolers, Ryan. I'm the ultimate multitasker. It's both." My phone makes a powering-down sound.

"You let your phone battery die again?" Tessa groans. "Mr. Electrical Engineer lets his phone get to four percent charge."

"I never claimed to be Dad," I shoot back, searching the room for her charger.

"I don't have one that works with your phone, Smartass," she says, clearly figuring out my need. "And you'll become Dad when you start filling the gas tank whenever it drops below three-quarters full."

Like magic, or—more likely—driven by his own need, my brother-in-law appears with two plastic bowls of ice cream for the kids.

Disengagement occurs immediately, my legs freed as sugar saves the day.

"Hey, Ry." Carlos gives me a fist bump. "Leave while we can," Carlos whispers to Tessa. The two kiss the twins' heads and tiptoe to the door while the boys sound like pigs at a trough during feeding time.

"You know the drill," Carlos says to me, giving me a quick bro hug.

"Right. Sugar 'em up, let 'em drop where they pass out, and more sugar for breakfast."

Tessa's about to throw a clot.

He shrugs. "Works for me. I get eighteen hours of sex in exchange."

Tessa stops at the doorway and peers at me. "We're not done talking about Carrie."

"You're losing precious blue ball evacuation time worrying about my love life."

"You told him about . . . that?" Carlos's eyes bug out behind his glasses, sharp rectangles with a silver edge that make him look like the accountant he is.

"It got him here, right?" Tessa shrugs.

"Bro Code," I say somberly, giving Carlos another fist bump. "Never let a bro suffer."

"Hey, man, let me tell you, it's been so long that I'm backed up and I swear I can taste my own—"

I hold up a palm. "Bro Code has limits. She's my sister." I put my fingers in my ears. "Lalalala."

The twins imitate me.

And that's the soundtrack as my sister and brother-in-law peel out of the driveway and take off for the business district in town, where the hotels cluster together.

Leaving me with mini Carlos, mini me, fourteen half-full pints of ice cream in the freezer, and Cartoon Network.

"It's mantown!" I shout, the twins jumping up and grabbing my arms. I march around the room with boy meat hanging off me like beef jerky drying on a clothesline.

"ARRRRRRRR!" Darien shouts.

Elias drops to the ground like a ripe apple releasing and scurries back to his ice cream, scraping the bottom of the bowl then looking at me, hopeful.

"Uncle Ryan? More?" The look on his face says he knows his mom and dad would never let him.

"SURE!" I call out, reaching into the freezer to line up all the pints like little kids getting ready for recess. "Pick your poison." I spot Carrie's favorite flavor in there. I grab my phone to text her, wondering if she's free.

Of course she is. She just got dumped. I should have called her sooner.

And—damn it. Dead phone. Shit.

"It's not poison! Mom says ice cream is a kind of love potion."

"She does?"

"She tells Daddy it gives her organisms when she eats it. I heard her the other night when I got up to pee."

"Okay, buddy." I rush through scooping a big pile of ice cream into his bowl so he'll stuff his face and we can end this topic.

And move on to the real fun.

Bingewatching *South Park.*

Haha. Kidding.

CHAPTER SIX

Carrie

J ENNY'S WEDDING IS now ten days away. As far as I know, Jamey still has not come out to his family, and I think I would have been the first to hear about it if he had. Is there any etiquette for this, a standard procedure to be followed when your serious boyfriend switches teams a few weeks before a major family event in which you are both involved, yet doesn't breathe a word to his closest relatives?

Do I at least give them a heads-up that something's different? I mean, at the very least there's going to have to be an extra place setting for Jamey's new date at the reception, right? What about hotel rooms? If there aren't any extra rooms, I guess I'll have to share with another single bridesmaid.

Great. Not exactly what I had in mind.

What I had in mind went more like this: *Jamey and I arrive at the Chatham Beach Inn a day before everyone else. We walk the dunes holding hands. We browse the galleries and he buys a lovely seascape, a small oil in soft blues and aquas: a memento. We drink sophisticated cocktails. My hair is perfect. Back in the room, Jamey is suddenly overcome with lust and passion for me, and we make love for hours while gazing out at the ocean view.*

The big day arrives. We are paired in the wedding party, and everyone says what a perfect couple we make. What with the beach-walking and the cocktails and all the acrobatic sex, I have lost two pounds. After witnessing Jenny and Aiden's romantic vows, Jamey is inspired to drop to one knee and propose to me on the dance floor. I accept, weeping tears of pure joy (but my eyes do not puff and my nose does not turn red). The reception explodes with applause, and when Jenny tosses her bouquet, I catch it. Happily. Ever. After.

That is what I had in mind.

Now, apparently, it's going to play out a little more like this: *I leave work at noon on a Friday and head to the Cape, just like everyone else in Boston. If my car doesn't break down and leave me stranded on Route 3, I eventually check into a room shared with Angela, who arrived early and took three quarters of the closet, most of the counter space in the bathroom, and the bed with the ocean view. I missed cocktail hour. Angela snores.*

The big day arrives. Jamey and I are paired in the wedding party, but he barely notices me and spends most of the ceremony looking at his Apple watch, surreptitiously texting someone. Which is just as well, because I have gained six pounds since the last time he saw me. At the reception, Jamey and his date steal the show with a choreographed swing dance routine that clears the floor and ends in an explosion of applause. It later becomes a viral YouTube sensation. When Jenny tosses her bouquet, I don't catch it because I am in the ladies' room weeping and eating a little gift bag of Jordan almonds. I think I read online that almonds contain trace amounts of cyanide. Maybe if I chew enough of them . . . ?

Sighing, I sip my coffee and try to focus on my computer screen, where I have the virtual reality phone script open. I know how to design beautiful and sustainable rooms, but creating an imaginary space with words and sounds is different. What do women want to hear while they are on hold? Brazilian samba? Waves on the beach? Male moans?

I channel Yoda: Do. Or do not. There is no try.

To be honest? I'm having a hard time caring about the deeply personal satisfaction and radiant inner glow of every potential O client (translation: every female on the planet). My own inner glow feels more like a nuclear meltdown, evil green radioactive slime. And how does a virtual reality phone script even *work*?

So when my phone pings with a text, it's actually a welcome distraction.

It's Jenny: *Is this some kind of practical wedding JOKE? Like short-sheeting our bed??*

Looks like Jamey finally got around to sharing.

Not a joke I type. I consider adding a sad-face emoji, but that seems a little inadequate. And maybe inappropriate. This feels like when friends announce they're pregnant, or getting a divorce. Best to stay neutral and follow their emotional cues before committing to a feeling.

WTF? Does he think these seating plans are easy to rearrange? He can't just do this at the last second!

Jenny is obviously well beyond the bridezilla stage where her close friend's heartbreak has any impact at all. Not to mention her brother's life transformation.

I don't think it was really a last-second thing, Jen, I type, hating Miss Manners right now. Where's the style guide on this? Maybe Dear Prudence has some advice.

Did you know about this? Jenny shoots back. Oh, God. I'm going to have to answer this question for the rest of my life, aren't I? Only most people will really be asking, "How could you sleep with a gay guy and not know the difference?"

I doubt Jenny's asking about her brother like that, but the rest of those nosy assholes sure are when they ask.

Not really, I type back. It's the only true response I can think of. I'm too emotionally spent to lie at this point.

There's a pause. Then: *OMG Carrie*

That's my Jenny. She got it. She's not so far gone in caterers and cake toppers that she's lost her heart. She remembered that I'm collateral damage here, that my life just came to a gigantic traffic sign: Road Closed Seek Alternate Routes. She's trying to figure out how to comfort me.

Three bouncing dots, then: *OMG Carrie, you're still going to be my maid of honor, right? Because you're the perfect height for Jamey.*

Okay, maybe she *is* too far gone.

Are you sure you still want me? I mean, this is going to be awkward for Jenny and her family, too.

OF COURSE I DO!! And sweetie, I'm so sorry. My brother is an ass. We're all in shock. I don't know what to say. Boss just walked in for big meeting. Call you later xoxo

I'm still not exactly sure whether she has more concern for me or for her careful plans, but at least the whole fiasco's not a secret anymore.

"'Did you know'?" I mutter, my fingers worrying my braids. "'Did you know'? How am I supposed to answer that?" I take out my frustration on the cold cup of coffee in front of me, ignoring the thick layer of milkfat that sticks to the top. One swig and I cringe. House coffee is better than this. Barely, but it is. I get up and head to the employee lounge.

"Oh, you already have one." Ryan's voice sounds disappointed as I startle, midway into the small kitchen. .

I turn to see him standing behind me with a Grind It Fresh! go-cup the size of a small fire extinguisher. I love that their cup-size names make sense: small, medium, large, and life-support. No silly fake-Italian words for them.

"It's left over from this morning," I tell him. "It's cold, and not in a good way. Is that really for me?"

Ryan's getting to be like a canteen truck lately. You can be pretty sure he'll show up with coffee, donuts, maybe a yogurt parfait or a soft pretzel—you just don't know exactly when he'll arrive or what he'll be offering.

What *is* he offering, exactly?

"I thought you could use the energy."

"Is caffeine the same as energy? I think there's a nutritional difference. But that's okay, I need them both." I reach for the enormous cup he's holding. It's really too big to call it a cup. Vat? "Thank you."

"How's it going with virtual reality?" He sips from his own normal-size cup, but it smells more like spiced chai.

"Not great, but better than real reality."

"That's the whole point, right?"

"I guess so." I hold up my phone. "Jenny texted. Jamey finally came out to them and she was worried that I wouldn't want to be in the wedding anymore."

"Did you tell her I'm coming as your date?"

I pause and study his face. We talked about this once, just as a joke. He might still be joking. I can't quite tell. But . . . oh my God . . . it could actually work. I wouldn't have to show up alone, sit alone at the reception, leave alone, while Jamey and my replacement reenact a scene from *Dancing with the Stars* and his grandmother asks me when we're getting married.

"I can't ask that of you! It would be three whole days, and we'd have to share a room," I point out. Might as well be clear about the downsides. "And you couldn't hit on any other women. No matter what."

"Seriously? A weekend at a beach resort on the Cape, with an open bar and a beautiful date? I would *pay* to do that!" He grins and looks a little too much like Zeke for my comfort.

This could actually work.

Hmm. Maybe there's a third scenario after all: *Ryan and I arrive at the Inn a few hours early. We walk the dunes, telling O stories and laughing. We browse the local shops and he buys me an aqua baseball cap embroidered with a scallop shell: a memento. We stop at a pub for fried clams and beer. My hair is pulled into a ponytail that sticks out the back of my new cap. Back in the room, Ryan feels tired, so we lie down and he naps. I'm not sleepy; I watch his face and wonder what he's dreaming.*

The big day arrives. I do my maid of honor thing, Ryan plays the role of attentive boyfriend whenever anyone is looking. And sometimes when they're not. He really is a great dancer, which is fun, and as a surprise he and the other O guys do a show to Brunos Mars' Marry You that clears the floor and ends in an explosion of applause. When Jenny tosses her bouquet, I catch it, and I do not cry.

"Carrie? What do you say?"

Ryan

THIS IS YOUR chance! My mind screams at me, like a football coach on the sidelines in sudden death. My blood is pumping in my ears, and I'm on the verge of making a huge mistake.

So I don't.

I don't fuck this one up. For once.

"Carrie," I say slowly, as if the idea were just coming to me slowly, like I hadn't been stewing in it. "I'm not kidding."

"Really?" She's so cute when she scrunches up her face like that.

"You know," I say with studied casualness, adding a shoulder shrug for emphasis. "We go as friends. But we'd pretend to be boyfriend and girlfriend."

Our eyes lock when I say *girlfriend*.

"Why?" she gasps.

Oh, shit.

"I—I mean, oh. Oh. Um. . . ."

This is worse than that time I jumped a chainlink fence when I was nine and got my underwear caught on a wire, gave myself a wedgie, and old Mr. Agliotti had to come out and cut me down with pinking shears.

"But," she says, her cheeks turning pink, her gaze still on me as I force myself to smile. "No one would ever believe we're together. You're *way* out of my league." She waves her hands at me, palms flat, like she's washing a glass shower door.

Or rubbing my oiled pecs.

I like that second image better.

I give her a half smile. "No, I'm not. That's crazy." If I've gone this far, I might as well push it. Without worrying she'll notice, I take in her body, enjoying the openness. She's wearing black on black, with flat shoes and her braided hair. I know *she* thinks she's plain and boring, but she's wrong.

Carrie is gorgeous. Not just on the inside, but in every possible way.

She gives me an epic eye roll. "Please, Ryan. Don't even bother. I'm not being modest. I'm stating a fact. You're a master masseur at the O Spa. You're a 10."

"A 10.5," I correct her. "You said so the other night."

She blushes even harder at the mention. "Right. So, I mean, it's a nice offer and all, but I can't accept. And asking you to waste your weekend wouldn't be fair."

And then she mutters under her breath, something I can't hear. "What was that?"

She turns red. "Nothing."

I reach for her arm and pull her closer. "What did you say, Carrie?" My voice goes low, an emotional rumble, and suddenly all my worry about this is gone. Heat flashes through me, the space between us changing as she slowly tips her head up, catching my eye.

Without flinching, she says, "Because I'm a 4 at best."

Before I can answer—and my response would have been a kiss, goddammit—we're rudely interrupted by a talking cockroach.

"WHAT?" A distinctly unwelcome British accent fills the air. "Did Ryan just call you a fucking FOUR, Carrie?" Zeke swaggers into the lounge and gives me a mock look of anger. He grabs Carrie out of my arms and spins her down into a dip, like they're dancing.

Rage makes me damn near blind. My arms are empty.

And Zeke's are full.

"You are a 7 on your *worst* day, Carrie. An 8.5 if you work on it," he says, examining her face from their half-bent position.

"Uh, uh, thanks?" Carrie gasps. "But I don't think you're very good with math. Maybe you're using the metric system?"

Zeke's eyes narrow. His nose runs along her collarbone and I'm an inch away from breaking his dick off and stuffing it up one nostril.

"Nah. I know the difference." He shoots me a look.

"Thanks," she says, a nervous laugh coming out of her. "Let me go, though."

"A beautiful woman in my arms wants me to set her free?" He kisses her on the cheek, but puts her upright. "Don't let this bag of deflated ball sacs tell you you're a four."

"I didn't," I say through gritted teeth. "Carrie gave herself that number." I look at her pointedly. "And she's wrong."

"You two are good for my ego," she says with a giggle, pink returning to her cheeks.

"Heard your ego needs a boost since you got dumped by the guy who used to come to O and treat it like a feast for his eyes. Man, the way he ogled Ryan," Zeke says as he shakes his head and makes himself a cup of tea.

"What?" She gives me an accusatory look. "Jamey didn't, he wouldn't . . ." Her eyes drift over my body, light and airy, like a butterfly landing on blades of grass.

"Oh, he did. We should have charged him for visiting you here at work."

"Shut up, Zeke," I warn him.

"Why were you giving each other numbers?" He looks me up and down. "Ryan here's a 7 at best."

"Hey!"

"No, he's not," Carrie protests. She squints one eye, like I'm a diamond she's evaluating for flaws.

"Carrie told me I'm a 10.5," I shoot back at him.

Zeke's snort sounds unimpressed.

"What are *you*, then?" I challenge. "On Carrie's scale, I'm a 10.5 and Henry's an 11."

In a rare display of modesty, Zeke nods. "Yeah. That fucking redwood tree is an 11. I'll give you that. But you ain't close to a 10.5, mate. If anyone's a 10.5, it's me." He preens, showing off his guns, giving Carrie a come-hither grin that makes me homicidal.

How did we get from Carrie in my arms to eye-candying Zeke's arms?

Carrie starts to walk toward the door. I know her deal.

Not letting her get away with it.

"You need a date," I start, tapping her shoulder. She halts.

"A date?" Zeke puts his arms down and grabs his tea. As he sips, his eyes tip up, the lashes long. Those eyes miss nothing. He's the biggest gossip at O—although he's told everyone I am—and whatever I say to Carrie now will be repeated all over.

"I—you know Jenny's getting married. I'm the maid of honor. Jamey's the best man."

"Right. Gotcha. So you need a crackerjack stud to take as a date." Zeke purses his lips and thinks for a minute.

"Exactly," she says, breathless, her eyes darting to me then away.

"Two birds, one stone," Zeke adds cryptically.

"Huh?" Carrie asks.

"Impress the women who'll think you're a pathetic loser who just got dumped—"

"Hey!" I protest.

"—and make the gay ex a little jealous."

"Hey," I protest a little softer, my response a Gordian knot of confusion.

"Too bad you have to settle for Ryan. He's a 7, you're an 8 . . . I'd take you myself but I've made other promises." Zeke winks at me. "Brilliant idea, though, mate." He pulls Carrie close and fake whispers, "Think about how it'll play. Your best friend at work. You've carried a torch for him for years."

My skin starts to buzz.

"But I—" Carrie looks anywhere but at me.

"For show, Carrie," Zeke stresses. "You've spent all this time dreaming about him, wondering what it would be like to kiss him, to make love with him, to fuck him in the backseat of the car, how his hands would feel on your hips while he bends you over a wood fence at a Montana ranch—"

"We get the picture," I growl.

"Go on," Carrie says, mesmerized. Her tongue peeks out between her lips and she licks before swallowing, hard.

"And all this time, it turns out the flame he carries for you—get it? *Carries?*—is even bigger than your little torch. The cute surprise love story practically writes itself," he adds with a flourish and a smirk, chucking her chin.

"Nice fiction," I say in a low, tight voice.

"This could work?" Carrie's voice goes up, high and thready the way women can get when they're unsure.

I take the lead.

"Yes. Absolutely. Zeke's story is a great fairy tale."

"Yeah, mate, well . . . some fairy tales can come true."

Carrie's phone buzzes. She looks at it. "Jenny. Begging me not to back out of the wedding." Uncertain, she gives me a look I can't decipher. My bones feel bigger. The air feels thinner. Her eyes beckon, asking me to save her.

"Tell her you met someone," I reply back, confident and strong. "He was right under your nose all along."

"But you're half a foot taller than me," she points out.

Zeke throws up his hands. "You two are hopeless." He punches me in the gut. I tighten, catching the blow, pretending it doesn't hurt. "We're two minutes late for that divorce party." He flashes Carrie a thousand watt smile. "Think about it. And if you don't want Ryan, I can always change my plans."

I grab his arm and drag him down the hall. I can drown him in one of the 55-gallon drums of massage oil, right? Justifiable homicide.

CHAPTER SEVEN

Carrie

L EFT TURN INTO the drive, between stone pillars with a carved sign: Chatham Beach Inn. Underneath the logo, the words "An Anterdec Property" are painted in small, discreet letters. My prehistoric Hyundai seems to take a deep breath before climbing the hill. The air conditioning died about an hour into the trip. Normally that wouldn't be a crisis at this time of year, but this has turned out to be that strange fall weekend when it's eighty degrees.

It's a spectacular Cape Cod October day, but Jenny can't be happy; her gown is heavy white satin.

Angela, a bridesmaid, sits beside me. She's been navigating since we turned off Route 6.

"I cannot wait to get to my room and take a bath," she says with a sigh of relief. "We have two hours until Jenny wants to meet with us. When does your boyfriend get here?"

"He's already here," I answer.

She looks at me, puzzled. "I thought he was coming later?"

"Oh, right, Ryan!" I say quickly. "Right. He'll be here later. He couldn't leave work early."

"You were so lucky to find a new boyfriend so quickly," she comments. "Last time I had a breakup, I didn't have a date for six *months*. By Month Five, I was rubbing up against doorknobs."

"Right," I repeat, quieter this time. "Lucky. I sure am. I'm lucky."

We pull up to the main entrance. I hand my keys to the valet and open the back of the car to unload our suitcases and the garment bags with our dresses.

The maid of honor outfit isn't as bad as I feared. In fact, as these things go, it's pretty great. I could have spent that $350 on other things, like, say, my cellphone bill, but still.

The dress is strapless, knee length, navy blue silk faille. It's fitted, and the top dips between my breasts. Best of all, it came in Tall sizes, so the waistline is actually in the general vicinity of my waistline. Navy suede strappy heels—four inches—thank God Ryan is tall. Jenny gave us dangly pearl earrings and necklaces as gifts, and she also gave us navy flip flops with silver seashells on them for dancing at the reception.

My suitcase is packed with my own outfit for the rehearsal, and everything else I might need for the weekend. A sweater, jeans, shorts, some tops. The sleepwear choice was harder, considering my roommate. I settled on a silk slip, not too long, not too short.

It's not like Ryan and I are really together, but you know, I can't wear pajama bottoms and a baggy t-shirt. Someone might see, and get the wrong idea.

Or the right idea. Whatever.

Angela and I haul our bags out of the car and head into the lobby to the registration desk. We get our keys—our rooms are on the same floor—and turn to look for the elevator. I'm scanning the lobby when I see two very tanned and handsome men coming through the entrance door, wearing white shorts and polo shirts and carrying tennis racquets. They are laughing.

My heart lands in my stomach.

It's Jamey. And . . . Devin? No.

Kevin.

I spin around and face the elevator, praying that the doors will open *now* and swallow me up. Before the new and improved Happy Couple gets over here.

"So, Angela," I start, "Want to meet up before we meet up with Jenny?" I don't even know what I'm saying. I am babbling.

Open, please, please *open.*

The light that shows where the elevator is has not moved. Apparently an entire family is moving in on the third floor.

"Carrie?" I hear behind me, in Jamey's familiar voice.

It's showtime.

"Jamey!" My voice reflects nothing but surprise and pleasure. "Oh my gosh, how have you *been?*" I lean forward and kiss him on both cheeks.

He looks at me a little oddly, but air-kisses me back.

"Um . . . you remember Kevin?" Jamey asks, eyeing me nervously.

"Of *course* I remember Kevin! From the map store, right? It is *so* nice to see you!"

Kevin is having a deer-in-the-headlights moment. Angela is smiling politely, waiting to be introduced.

The elevator door finally opens. The passengers file out and we crowd in.

"This is Angela. She's a bridesmaid. Angela, this is Jamey and, um, Kevin. Jamey is Jenny's brother. Kevin is, um, Jamey's friend." That all sounds perfectly normal and reasonable. "We're on the fourth floor," I add.

"Boyfriend," Kevin corrects. "I'm Jamey's boyfriend. We're on the fourth floor, too."

"*My* boyfriend will be here in a few hours," I announce. "He had to work today. I'm so excited for everyone to meet him. Jamey, you might remember him from O? His name is Ryan. He's really tall and handsome and has an engineering degree from Cal Tech and we love all the same movies and I can't wait to see our room, I think it has an ocean view and a huge bed and we'll probably be late for everything because we just won't want to leave the room, Ryan just never wants to get out of bed, you know how it is when you're in love—"

Everyone is staring at me.

Shut *up*, Carrie.

Mercifully, the elevator stops and the doors slide open.

Jamey clears his throat. "Well, okay then. What number are we, again, Kevin?"

"412."

I look at my room key. 410.

Great. Just . . . great.

"Looks like we're neighbors," I say.

"I'm 431. Guess I'm in the other direction," Angela says, with what sounds like relief. "See you all later." She sets off to the right, trotting.

The rest of us turn left, trooping down a long, hushed hallway hung with prints of sailing ships.

I stop at number 410. "So we'll see you at the rehearsal tomorrow," I offer, my hand on the door handle.

Kevin keeps walking to their door. "I really need a shower. You coming, Jamey?" He disappears inside.

"Just a sec." Jamey hesitates, shifting uncomfortably from foot to foot. "It's really good to see you, Carrie. I think about you all the time. I . . . I miss you. Are things really going well?"

"What do you mean? Of course! I've never been happier." I push the door open and drag my bags inside. Jamey moves to help but I turn, blocking his way. I do not want him inside this room . . . *our* room. Where we were supposed to stay, together. Like always. "Thanks. I have to get ready for Ryan now. He'll be here soon. Any minute. So . . ." I'm closing the door now, not looking at him.

"Maybe we can talk later," he says.

"Maybe."

The door clicks shut and I lean my back against it, eyes shut tight. I will not cry. I *will not* cry.

My phone pings with a text, and I pull it out of my bag.

It's Ryan: *Hey beautiful almost there what's our room number?*

Ryan

I SWING INTO the semi-circular driveway at the resort and end up third in line. Valet parking. Of course. My 1992 Mazda Miata is an oldie but goodie, the original red shine a little duller, but she made the trip from California to Massachusetts just fine when I moved here a few years ago. Weekly car washes in the winter keep her rust-free.

My sisters call her my first love. Pretty sure they're right. Dad helped me buy her and we rebuilt the engine together the summer between high school and college. 119,000 miles and going strong. I love going for rides during leaf-peeper season in Maine and Vermont, the only time of year I run up the miles on my baby. Fun day trips.

Now that I've seen more of the Cape, I'm thinking we need some summer excursions, too.

We. Me and Carrie.

I move up to second in line and run my hands on my thighs, hoping I don't leave sweat marks. It's all pretend, this boyfriend-for-the-wedding act, but it's also real. Too real. It's almost more real by being fake.

I get to touch her. Kiss her. Be an animal in public who can't get enough of her, all to show everyone that she's moved on.

But this is also my chance. Fake it 'til you make it, right?

A valet takes my information, asking for the room number. I text Carrie. I give him the number.

A hotel room. One bed. Ocean view. Alone with Carrie at a romantic seaside inn, at a wedding. Weddings are like tiramisu for women. The aphrodisiac that just keeps on coming.

Or something like that.

I check in and take the stairs up, hanging bag in hand. By the time I use my cardkey, I'm a little sweaty, a lot excited, and as I enter the room I freeze.

Carrie's luscious ass faces me, on the bed. Her head is down and she's crying.

Not the greeting I expected.

But that view. That ass. Her skirt is pulled up, exposing her knees and thighs, the soft undercurve of her sweet, round ass just peeking out from the hem. Her entire body is shaking and she's sobbing, her fists punching the pillow she's buried her face in.

Without taking my eyes off her, I hang my suit bag on the closet door and stop, taking a deep breath. She doesn't realize I'm here. I have an unadulterated, unfettered view of pretty much every man's fantasy (minus the clothing), until she sits up and turns around, still on her knees, ass up, her hair swinging over the back of her shoulder, her face submissive and pleading.

Oh, kitten.

I know, I know. Her emotional state should trigger empathy in me, right? I'll get there. I will. Give me a minute. Maybe even two.

"Ryan!" Carrie starts sobbing, again, her face crumpling. I take one big step toward her and halt, struggling not to show that I need to adjust my, uh. . . . stride before I can reach her.

I sit on the edge of the bed and reach for her shoulder. "You saw Jamey, didn't you?"

"How did you know?"

"Wild guess."

She lets out an adorable little huff of sad laughter. I look at her, stroking the wet hair off her face, tears ravaging her makeup. With wide, red-rimmed eyes and flushed cheeks, she looks so helpless.

So beautiful.

"I got here too late, huh? Sorry, traffic on Route 6 was terrible."

"You're actually early. It's okay."

"No, C-Shel. It isn't. No guy is worth being like this over." *Except me*, I think, *and I'd never do this to you.*

"Thanks. It's just . . . Jamey was with Kevin, and—"

"So he did bring him after all?"

"YES!" she wails. "And he's cuter than me!"

I look at the stamped-tin ceiling and scratch my chin, trying not to laugh. "I seriously doubt that."

"He's tan. And fit. Fit like *you!* And he has great pores! It's like God's mindfucking me. I mean, who finds a guy with great pores? My pores are like the Grand Canyon cloned a million times! I've been replaced by a Ralph Lauren ad. Kevin runs an antique map store and he has better skin. And better clothing taste. And—"

"And he's gay," I say softly. "Like Jamey. Your pores had nothing to do with it. You did nothing wrong, kitten."

She frowns. "Did you just call me 'kitten'?"

Oh, shit.

"Um, yeah. Just, you know—practicing. I came up with some great names for you. You know. For when we're being boyfriend and girlfriend."

The frown disappears.

I leave out the words *in public* on purpose.

"Oh." *Sniff*. "That makes sense." *Sniff*. "I like it." My hand migrates to her back, between her shoulder blades, and I rub the spot, feeling her melt beneath my touch.

"You do? Okay, Kitten."

She smiles. "Like a sex kitten." *Sniff*.

"Right." I put my free arm across my lap because this conversation is having a very obvious physical effect on me.

"You're really good at this sex stuff."

Oh, come on. I look up at the ceiling, as I can see God up there, pointing and laughing at me.

Funny how he looks like Zeke.

I lean in to Carrie, moving my hand from her back to her shoulder, and plant a kiss on her cheek. "If we're going to convince everyone out there, we might need a little practice."

Her breath comes out of her nose in these short little rasps, sniffs here and there slowing down. Our faces are inches apart. I'm still in scramble mode from the road trip here, half starved, mind going a mile a minute, so my rational brain isn't exactly at full attention.

Unlike my other brain. The one in my pants.

Leaning in, I kiss her on the lips, soft and slow. No tongue. Don't want to push it.

Carrie kisses me back, hands going to my shoulders, sliding up to the back of my neck. I kiss her again with more urgency, our mouths slanting, her lips capturing my top lip, nipping. My hands cradle her face and I go for it as her lips part, my tongue exploring her. God, she tastes like spun sugar, fired by the heat of my blood, and soon one of my hands has a fistful of her hair, years of hunger coming out in this kiss.

Tap tap tap.

"Carrie?" a woman says from the other side of the hotel room door. "You there? It's Angela. Jenny's downstairs having a meltdown and I could use your help. The florist is bailing on the wedding and Jenny and her mother are acting like a meteor hit Boston."

"Just a minute!" Carrie calls, staring at the back of the door, her fingertips against her lips as her eyes lock with mine.

I stand up. Damn. I resist the urge to rearrange.

"Uhhhh," Carrie says.

"That was great. Good practice, C-Shel." I give her my best flirty half-grin while I dig my cardkey into my thigh like I'm pulling a bone marrow biopsy. "Let's show 'em how it's done." I walk to the door and open it just as Angela has her fist in the air, ready to knock again.

"Oh!" she says, then looks me up and down. "Ooooooohhhhhh," she says, drawing this one out. "You must be Ryan. I didn't interrupt anything, did I?"

"No," Carrie says. I die a little inside but don't show it. "You didn't. Sounds like I need to go downstairs," she says, giving me a pleading look that either means *Pretend to be my horny boyfriend* or *Get out of the room so I can get ready.*

I go with the former, grab her around the waist, and plant a huge, over-the-top kiss on her neck.

"Sorry," I say to Angela, clearly not sorry. "Four hours away from her and I just need to recharge my Carrie battery, if you know what I mean." I flash Angela a grin. "How about I get you two some lemon water while Carrie freshens up. Not that she needs to." I kiss her cheek. "I'm just inventing reasons to leave you alone to figure out how to help the bride."

"Actually, we need to go *now*," Angela says, giving me a wild look. The whites of her eyes get big. That's what weddings do to women—turn their eyes into the color of the wedding dresses.

"Then I'll just meet you downstairs," I say, pleasant and smooth.
With that I leave her and Carrie speechless, eyebrows up.
And get the hell out of there so I can breathe.

CHAPTER EIGHT

Carrie

T HE BIG DINING room for the wedding reception is full of round wooden tables, not yet covered with their linen tablecloths. In a storage room off the main dining room, one table is littered with shells, boxes of pillar candles, and bags of smooth stones. On another, clear glass containers are stacked in a pyramid. Huge buckets of beach sand rest on the floor.

A dozen or so women in cocktail dresses and perfect hair are standing around in small clusters, talking nervously. Jenny, who is weeping, is being comforted by her mother and sisters.

"What's happening?" I ask, confused. This is the problem with always running ten minutes late. I'm forever trying to figure out what everyone else already knows.

"These centerpieces were supposed to have been assembled by the florist!" Jenny moans. "We paid Petal Pushers fifty dollars *each* for twenty-five 'Beachscapes'—that's over a thousand dollars! And she's gone and we have nothing for the tables!" Her mother is frantically dabbing Jenny's cheeks with a handkerchief where the tears are streaking her makeup.

"Oh no . . . who would do that? She probably just ran out for more coffee or something," I soothe. "I'm sure she'll be back."

Jenny just hands me her phone.

The text on the screen reads: *My band just signed with UMG leaving on tour tonight so sorry have a great marriage! Nova*

"Okay, not coming back," I concede. Jenny gives a ragged sob.

I look over the raw materials spread out on the tables. "Jen," I say slowly, "listen. I can do this. I'm a designer. No problem."

I lift a glass container from the stack and set a fat white pillar candle in the center. Using an empty cardboard coffee cup, I scoop in enough sand to hold the candle in place. So far, so good. I drop in a few shells and arrange them evenly.

Angela comes up beside me and watches for a moment. "I'll help you," she offers.

Jenny looks torn between hope and guilt. "Oh Carrie . . . could you really do this? But, oh, the rehearsal dinner tomorrow and then the bachelorette party—your new boyfriend is here—it's too much to ask . . ."

"Ryan will be fine. He can talk to some of the other O people. You go to the dinner. Angela's going to help me."

"I will, too," Diane volunteers. "If you can show me what to do?"

"Thanks," I smile at her gratefully. "With three of us, it won't take long at all. Go on now, Jen, everyone will be looking for the bride."

"I'll check back in a little while," she says. "You guys are the best friends ever! I don't know how to thank you!"

"A bottle of wine would be a good start." I wink at her. "And three glasses."

"Coming right up." She heads for the door, followed by her posse of female relatives.

I turn to my two assistants, who are already taking off their heels, getting into craft-project mode. "If you two can set the candles and fill in the sand, I'll do the stones and shells. I think this raffia is to tie around the outside."

Diane is unwrapping candles. "So, Carrie," she asks curiously, "I didn't know you were dating Ryan. Is that new?"

Could there actually be someone at O who hasn't heard the whole gruesome story? Must be because Diane's in accounting; they're on a different floor of the building, separated from daily spa operations.

"Pretty new," I answer cautiously. I have to make this story be-lievable. "You know, when Jamey broke up with me, I was a wreck. Ryan was totally there for me. He held my hand, and he listened no matter how long I went on, and he let me cry on his shoulder. He did all these really nice things to try to cheer me up."

So far, all true.

I look at Diane's face. This woman, a strong and successful execu-tive, is listening with rapt attention, like a little girl hearing a fairy tale.

Because it *is* a fairy tale.

"We were already friends, but then one day I just looked at him and realized that he's the perfect guy for me." Zeke's script flashes in my brain. "I mean, I used to wonder sometimes what it would be like to, you know, *be* with him. But we were just good friends. I was dating Jamey. But then I wasn't. Dating Jamey. Obviously."

"Ryan is *so* handsome," she sighs.

"He is," I nod. "And he's really smart, and funny. He makes me laugh, even when I'm in a bad mood." This is also true. "He even braids my hair."

"Wow," Diane whispers. "It's like it was meant to be. I wish something like this would happen to me."

Ha. I wish something like this would happen to me, too.

"I always thought it would be incredible to date one of the O guys," Angela comments. "You'd get professional massages for free, anytime! They know everything about a woman's body. And just watching them dance, you can tell by the way they move that they'd be amazing in bed."

She looks at me for confirmation.

"Right!" I agree, not quite meeting her eye. "Ryan is amaz-ing . . . in bed . . . he, um, does this thing with his tongue . . ." Here I stop short. I'm on shaky ground. I have no idea what he might do with his tongue, besides talk, eat ice cream, and slurp Tom Yum soup.

Jamey didn't even like to French kiss, never mind French-kissing anything below my waist.

Angela and Diane both sigh. So do I, but for a different reason.

And as if on cue for an O dance routine, Ryan appears in the door, with two bottles of wine tucked under one arm, a bottle of sparkling lemon water under the other, and four glasses in his hands. He's wearing a navy jacket over a pale blue dress shirt, no tie. His light brown hair is brushed straight back and curls a little over his collar. Seeing him dressed like this, he looks different. He looks . . . *manly* is the only word for it.

What *would* he be like in bed? What lovely things *might* he do with his tongue?

We are all staring at him. He heads straight for me. "There's my girl," he says, setting the glasses down. I take the bottles from under his arm. "Working hard. Carrie makes every room more beautiful. Decorations not needed."

His hands now free, he takes my face and gently, lingeringly, kisses my lips. His breath is warm and delicious. I wobble a little bit on my heels. Who needs wine with kisses like that? Diane and Angela watch intently.

Don't overplay it! I think, opening my mouth to say precisely that, but then I just moan. Even syllables won't form.

He grins.

"I don't want to distract you ladies from your work," he says, pulling a corkscrew from his pocket. He twists it into the cork, which slides out with a little pop, and he pours the wine. As he hands me my glass, he runs his other hand slowly down my back. "I just wanted to be sure you have *every*thing you need." His voice drops low on the word 'everything.'

"Thanks," I answer faintly. "We're good. I'm good."

"You sure are. " He kisses me again, this time on my temple, his hand migrating down my waist, very publicly squeezing my ass. His palm is so warm. So big. Kinda rough.

Funny. I never knew how good a little *rough* could be.

And with that, smiling, he takes his glass and leaves.

Angela and Diane watch him go. Their mouths are open just a tiny bit.

So is mine.

As he heads out the door, Jenny is headed in. Ryan pauses and kisses her cheek, chats for a few seconds, then continues on his way.

"These look amazing!" she cries when she sees the assembled centerpieces. "*You* are amazing! Thank you *so* much!"

"It's really not a big deal, Jen. We're just assembling what's already here. But at least you don't have to worry about it now."

"There's a lot of worrying involved with a wedding," she says ruefully. "I've never worried this much in my life! Will it rain? What if I forget to pack my shoes? What if my cousins who don't speak get seated next to each other by accident?" She pauses. "What if my brother figures out he's gay and breaks up with my dear friend a few weeks before they're both in my wedding? Are you sure you're okay?" She gives my hand a squeeze and smiles at me with a knowing look.

"Oh, well," I laugh nervously, "that was kind of a surprise, but it turned out fine." I suddenly become intensely interested in tying the perfect raffia bows around the glass containers.

Bows have meaning, you know? Tying the knot?

"Seems like it," she says, watching me speculatively. "I just ran into Ryan on my way in. And Jamey and Kevin are around here somewhere. Maybe it did all work out for the best, but I have to say, it's a little hard to get used to."

"I guess it all happened pretty fast. For something that's been coming for years." I turn to her suddenly. "Jen, was it really a surprise to you? Did you know? About Jamey, I mean."

She thinks. "Yes and no. Jamey was never the kid playing ice hockey or blowing up mailboxes with cherry bombs, but that doesn't mean anything. And he always had a girlfriend around. And then you two were going out . . . didn't *you* know?"

"No. Maybe. No." I sigh. "I don't know."

"You and Jamey seemed like such a perfect match, but now I have to wonder if I just really wanted you to be part of the family forever. It was so convenient, my best friend and my brother." Her brow wrinkles a little as she considers. "Maybe you were a perfect match for the rest of us."

I put down the ribbon and the scissors I was holding. "You're not losing me, you know! You think I'm going to give up your mom's manicotti because of this?"

"Ryan's a big change," she observes. "The total opposite of Jamey."

I burst out laughing. "I know, right? I don't know what to expect next with Ryan!"

I don't know what to expect next with Ryan.

Exactly.

Ryan

IF THIS IS pretend, then Carrie deserves an Oscar for best performance. That kiss was anything but pretend. The kiss back in the hotel room, too. Leaving her alone with Jenny and all the wedding details like that isn't just me being a guy who doesn't want to get embroiled in all the crazy details. Who cares about raffia ribbon or the correct ratio of lilies to hydrangeas?

I got out of there because I'm damn close to losing it and telling Carrie how I really feel.

Too close.

Practically running, I get to the stairwell and pound my way to the outside door, walking fast on the long deckwalks before hitting the beach, dress shoes be damned. Deep breaths, I tell myself. Breathe in ocean air to replace the carnal need. Salt air is a balm, right? Calms the nerves. I'm nothing but short circuits and overloaded transformers right now.

A live wire with a need to connect.

"Ryan?" A bikini-clad woman on a towel next to a guy sits up, covering her topless half with a towel. "Is that you?"

Redhead. Wide green eyes. Mole above her eyebrow. Wide smile. Oh, shit. She's either a client at O or—

"You were at my bachelorette party two weeks ago!" She nudges the guy next to her, who turns over and glares at me. "Honey, this was the stripper!"

Master masseur. But I don't bother to correct her.

"Hey," the groom says with as much enthusiasm I would muster if my new wife were gawking at a stripper from her bachelorette party.

I mean *master masseur.*

"Hey," I throw back.

"What are you doing here?" she asks, blushing. "Working?" Her eyebrows go up, hopeful.

"I'm here with my girlfriend at a friend's wedding," I offer, her eyebrows dropping, husband's face splitting into a grin.

"Perfect place for a getaway, man" the guy says. "Beautiful weather, off-season rates, stellar food." He grabs his wife—whose name escapes me—and kisses her neck. "Lots of privacy."

His look tells me to fuck off.

The word *girlfriend* made my ex-client's eyes glaze over. "Well, good to see you Ryan. Have fun."

Fun. Right.

I wave and get the hell out of there. I don't really exist unless a woman's using me to get something. Being spotted by a client is unnerving, but I can handle it. It's not like it happens every day. Besides, this is an Anterdec resort property, so I shouldn't be surprised.

What does surprise me is Carrie. All the thick lines around our friendship have faded to wet streaks of grease pencil, smudged and smeared until the boundaries aren't clear.

Is this all still fake? Was *some* of the kissing real? I grabbed her ass back there for show, but also because I wanted to. It's a highly grabbable ass.

The line between real and fake isn't just blurred. It's a giant skidmark.

Back up. Not the image I'm going for.

Carrie's feeling it, right? These kisses and caresses go way beyond pretend. Have we reached a point where we're pretending to pretend?

My phone buzzes. An actual call. It's my Mom.

"Lenny's Bail Bonds," I say, resurrecting an old joke.

"I'm not sure if that's a worse job than the one you have, sweetie," she says with a laugh. It took me more than a year to admit to my family that I wasn't an engineer anymore, hiding massage therapy school from them. Mom still doesn't quite know how much my job at O involves walking around in various states of undress.

I plan to keep it that way. She's pretty cool, but still.

"Bail bondsmen deal with money all day, Mom. I come into contact with fewer germs even when I touch people all day for a living."

"Wires and circuits don't have germs, Ryan."

"Is this a lecture about going back to engineering?" She has no idea I've applied for grad school back home. Ellen and Tessa are keeping my secret, but for how long?

"No. I can do that anytime. This call is more specific. Dad really wants to see you."

"Is something wrong?" Alarm floods my extremities, cortisol suddenly flowing through my brain like a dam spilling over, about to burst.

"No, actually," she says softly. "He just keeps talking about you."

"Is he there?"

"Golfing with Fred and the other guys from the firm. I wanted to talk to you separately. Is this a good time?"

"I'm at a wedding on Cape Cod."

"A wedding? Whose?"

"An old co-worker's."

"Do you have a . . . date?"

"Mom," I say with a sigh.

"Well? Do you?"

"I'm here with Carrie."

"Carrie your friend?" Normally, the way she says *friend* makes my teeth ache. This time, though, it makes me smile.

"Yes. She needed a date, and I—"

"You're *dating*? Dating that nice, sweet woman Tessa's always telling me about?"

I'm going to kill my sister. Or let Carlos die from blue ball explosions by withholding babysitting services for the next six months. That's effective.

"We're just here as friends."

"How long are you there?"

"What?"

"This wedding—is it a day wedding?"

"We're here for the weekend."

Mom lets out a sound of jubilation. "You're at a hotel! You're sleeping with her!"

"Mom!" I sound like a choked fourteen year old. "I'm not talking about this with you!"

"Not talking about what?"

"Sex!"

"Ryan Gabriel Donovan, you are twenty-seven years old. If you can't tell me you're seeing someone and it's serious enough to sleep with her, then when can you?"

"I am convinced that you and dad had sex exactly five times and did it with your eyes closed via telepathy, Mom. I'm not talking about this with you." I'm forced to say that last sentence through her laughter.

"I'd like to meet my grandkids, you know," she finally says. "You're my baby. We'll never be spry with yours if you don't start having them soon."

I don't know what to say, so I say nothing.

"Is it serious? With this Carrie?"

"What? No. We're friends. Nothing more than friends, Mom. I'm just helping her out here by being her date for the wedding." As I finish explaining, I hear a shuffling sound behind me and turn to find Carrie standing there, holding a plate with donuts on it, wearing a grimace she quickly changes to a bright smile.

"Oh, I'm so sorry!" she gushes, bending down to place the plate next to me. "I didn't mean to interrupt."

"You didn't. It's okay. I'm just talking to—"

Too late. Carrie gives me a huge smile and waves me off. "It's fine! I have a million things to do to help out. Go back to whoever you're talking to." She disappears around a corner, out of sight.

I hear footsteps gain speed, then the unmistakable sound of running.

"Ryan? Dear? Who was that?"

"Oh," I say, watching the last spot where I saw Carrie's back. "No one. Just a friend."

CHAPTER NINE

Carrie

"I THINK JENNY'S mother is a little drunk," I whisper in Ryan's ear. The casual dinner for the wedding party and any early guests is over, dessert plates and coffee cups littering the tables. This is the last chance anyone has to relax. Starting tomorrow, we go into full-throttle wedding mode.

No one's listening to us, so we can talk the way we always do. Normal. Relaxed.

Like he said to that person on the phone earlier, we're nothing more than friends.

Right? *Right.*

"What was your first clue?" he whispers back. "Was it when she stood on her chair and sang "I Will Always Love You"?"

"Actually, I think it was when she sat on your lap and showed you Jenny's first grade picture." I'm giggling helplessly. "She is going to have a wicked headache tomorrow morning."

"Aiden's mom isn't too far behind. I just saw her leaving with an entire platter of chocolate tarts."

"We should follow her. This can't be good."

"It'll be fun to watch her try to press the elevator buttons, though."

I gather my bag and my wrap and we hurry to the lobby. Sure enough, there's Aiden's mom, Annette, standing in front of the elevator with a huge tray in both hands, looking helplessly at the button on the wall. Her cheeks are very pink and she has a zinnia from the centerpiece in her hair. She looks like a tipsy elf.

"Can I give you a hand with that, Annette?" Ryan takes the tray from her as I press the button. "It looks heavy."

"Oh, thank you so much!" She smiles up at him crookedly. "Sometimes I get hungry in the night. You should take a few, you never know when you're going to need a little snack at four a.m."

"That's so true. Take a few, Carrie," Ryan says, looking at me with an expression I can't interpret. "We might need a snack. At four a.m."

What could he mean? We'll be asleep at four a.m. But I take two plates from the tray.

When the doors slide open, Ryan winks at me and says, "I'll help Annette to her room. Meet you back at ours."

"Okay," I answer faintly. Off they go, Ryan bearing the tray, Annette chattering away beside him.

It's not easy to work the cardkey while juggling two dessert plates and my clutch, but I manage to get in the door without dropping anything. As I head to the desk to set everything down, my fingers start to shake. I lose my thumb-grip on one plate and—of course—it tips toward me. I should have seen this coming. Of course the tart hits my dress chocolate side first. Of course it slides all the way down before landing on the beige carpet. Of course.

For a long minute, I stare down at the mess on me and the floor. Then I get a towel from the bathroom and start scooping up chocolate filling and smashed pastry. The inn will probably charge me for new carpet.

Perfect.

At least my dress is dark brown silk—chocolate brown, as a matter of fact.

See? Things can always be worse. Almost always.

The door lock clicks and Ryan comes in. He registers me on my knees, scraping at the mess, mutters "Damn," and goes straight for another towel.

Kneeling down beside me gingerly, he studies the situation. Then, without saying a word, he reaches over and dips two fingers into the whipped cream on my skirt. He licks one finger experimentally and smiles. He holds the other to my lips.

Well, what would *you* do? Refuse? I open my mouth and take his finger in gently, sucking the delicious sweet cream from his skin.

And at that intense and unpredictable moment, a piece of heavy furniture falls over in the next room, shaking the floor. We both jump a mile.

"Oh my God, what was *that*? That's Jamey's room!"

"Jamey's room? He's next door to us?"

Just then, a man's deep moan comes through the wall.

"He's hurt! What should we do? I think you should go check." I imagine Jamey trapped under the armoire, bleeding to death internally, while I am wantonly licking cream from Ryan's body not twelve feet away. I can see the front page of the Boston Herald now: "Guy Kicks While Girl Licks" . . . "She Was Coming While Her Ex Was Going" . . .

Another moan follows, this one louder and longer. It goes up oddly at the end.

Ryan and I look at each other.

"Yes! Kevin! Give it to me! Harder!" The voice is muffled, but the words are clear. There's a smaller crash, like a lamp hitting the floor.

Ryan's mouth twitches on one side as he tries not to laugh. "Are you sure you want me to go knock on the door?"

"Maybe not." Despite myself, I feel a giggle bubbling up. "Or maybe yes!"

Ryan walks up close to the wall.

"Oh, Carrie, oh baby," he says loudly. "Oh, baby, you are the *best!*"

I stare at him, speechless—what is he *doing*?—but then I get it. I scurry over next to him and join in. "Ryan! Ryan! I want more of you, now! Oh, God, that spot—yes! Right there! Right now!"

He starts smacking the wall rhythmically with the heel of his hand, faster and faster. Tears of laughter are streaming down my face.

"Carrie! Oh God! You're so pink and wet and luscious!"

I clap my hand over my mouth at his words, holding back giggles.

"Ryan! Extend the spreader bar!" I pant and moan.

Ryan freezes and gives me an arched eyebrow, then slowly crosses his thick arms over his chest. His expression says, *How in the hell do you know what a spreader bar is?*

What? I've seen *Fifty Shades Darker*. Read it, too. It's a requirement when you work at O.

Suddenly BANGBANGBANG at the door.

"Hey!" Kevin's outraged voice shouts from the hall. "Keep it down in there! People are trying to sleep!"

For a moment, we are too amazed to make a sound. Then we fall onto the bed, laughing so hard we can't breathe. Every time one of us subsides, the other one snorts with a giggle and we're off again.

Finally I prop myself up on one elbow, and that's when I notice the pastry dotting the bedcover.

"Oh no!" I jump up from the bed. "My dress is getting the bed dirty!"

Ryan stands up too, and surveys the damage. "It's not too bad, mostly crumbs." He folds the bedcover down. "But you should probably get out of that dress."

Not meeting my eye, he adds, "Here, I'll unzip you."

Turning my back to him, I gather my hair and pull it forward. I wait. Nothing happens.

"Ryan?"

Then he's behind me, his hands finding the zipper tab. He pulls it slowly, achingly slowly, his fingers brushing the skin of my back as they travel down. He's standing so close, I can feel his body heat, his breath on my exposed neck making me shiver.

"Okay then, thanks!" I say a little too brightly, failing miserably at ignoring the flush of heat that just rushed across every inch of skin I possess. I grab my nightgown and robe from the closet and dash into the bathroom, closing the door behind me.

What was *that*? Just a little friendly help with a hard-to-reach zipper? Like you would do for a roommate, or a sister? It didn't feel very brotherly.

It felt wonderful.

This is ridiculous. Ryan's not interested in me, not that way. We're pretending, that's all. We're friends. He's doing me a favor, like he said to that person on the phone.

Anyway, Ryan's straight. Straight guys aren't attracted to me. It's a proven fact. I brush my teeth.

Finally, I tie the belt of my robe tightly, take a deep breath, and reach forb the door handle. Wait—just a little spray of perfume behind my neck. Just to be considerate. It's close quarters here.

Very close quarters, actually. One king-size bed. The bed that Jamey and I were supposed to be sharing.

When I emerge from the bathroom, all the lights are turned off except the soft glow of the desk lamp. Ryan's standing at the window, his back to the room, looking out at the moon shining on the ocean. He's wearing a t-shirt and soccer shorts, loose and comfortable.

I wonder if that's what he wears to bed every night.

Or does he sleep naked?

My mouth goes dry.

"So," I start. "Which side of the bed do you want?"

He doesn't move. "Either one. You choose."

His shoulders are so broad. One of his hands is on his hip, the other pressed flat against the window, like he's trying to touch the sea. I watch his steady breathing and find myself matching his rhythm. The air changes. We're in the dark. In a hotel room. I'm wearing just a light robe and a nightgown. It's not a very short nightgown, but it's sheer and lightweight. Every time it brushes against my smooth thighs I feel sexy. Sensual.

I look at Ryan's back.

And now I'm throbbing.

What is he thinking about?

Slipping off my robe, I slide under the covers on the right side. "Big day tomorrow," I offer. "It's late. We should get some sleep. Thanks for doing this, Ryan. I know it's not easy pretending. Thank you for everything." I turn off the nightstand light. I stare at the ceiling, willing my throbbing blood to stop crashing against the tidal wall of my body.

He's magnetic. How else can I be so drawn to him? It's Ryan. Good old Ryan. This is idiotic. I just need an orgasm or nineteen and I'll be fine.

With Ryan, a voice inside me whispers.

I roll on my side and punch my pillow. Impulse and need flood my skin and my heartbeat migrates south, between my legs. Suddenly, the sheets feel too well starched, brushing against my nipples through the nightgown, making me squirm. And when I change position, my calf brushes against my other calf just so, until I swallow hard, curling my hands into fists, grabbing the bedsheets.

So I don't stand up and walk over to Ryan.

So I don't offer myself to him and make a fool of myself.

He's being nice. We're friends. I can't ruin that just because I misread a few signals from him. I mean, how embarrassing would that be?

"Sure." He's still at the window, staring out. "No problem, C-Shel."

Ryan

I CAN'T TURN around or she'll see the tent.

You know the tent. Every guy gets the tent. Sometimes the tent is a Boy Scout pup tent. Sometimes it's circus-tent size.

And then once in awhile, you get full-blown state university graduation tent size.

Yep. If I lean an inch forward I'll poke my own eye out.

I can see her in the glass's reflection, her face turned just enough toward me to watch as she stares, wide-eyed, at the window. Watching her like this—when she doesn't know I'm doing it—is a guilty pleasure. The moon seems to treasure her as much as I do, stroking a line like an artist, the glow of the moon's edge marking a trail along her profile.

If I close my eyes, I can feel her behind me. I'm fifteen feet away, but damned if she isn't in the air we're both exchanging right now. Damned if her breath isn't touching the back of my hands like a soft caress from a lover's soothing palm.

Damned if she isn't in my arms, seeking a kiss, a stroke, a tight clasp, and so much more.

Damned if I'm not getting harder than ever.

It takes more control than you think to breathe evenly, to hold back emotion, to hide how you truly feel about someone you love.

Love.

There. I thought it.

Too bad I'm too much of a coward to say it.

I can be in a room with people I loathe and they'll never guess how I really feel. Managing expressions, respirations, tone of voice— that's child's play compared to this.

Because when you dislike someone, all you have to do is cover up the negative.

When you love someone, you have to cover up your heart. And unlike anger or disgust or irritation, the feelings the heart emits don't cover easily. They bleed through, pumped in an unremitting, steady stream that pushes through every defense and reveals itself in every action.

My throat won't stop tightening, as if my heart is crawling up my chest, seeking Carrie. I let go of the glass and let the words come into my mouth, feeling them there like her lips, her tongue, the soft sweetness of her neck against my cheek as we played earlier.

This isn't pretend, my tongue wants to say. *This is anything but pretend.*

"Ryan?" Her voice makes me jump, and now my heart is in my cheek, tucked there as it pounds mercilessly against my jaw. I do the best I can to make myself able to speak.

"Yeah?" I grunt out, the sound bizarre to my ears.

That was about as far from *This isn't pretend* as you can get.

That's it. I square my shoulders and taking in a long, deep breath.

I ignore the flurry of rejections past. I push away the images of bullies who told me I was lesser. Weak. Not worthy.

The man I am needs to connect with the woman she is. It's time. It's past time.

She yawns, rolling over onto her back just as a strand of moonlight makes her gown translucent, one breast hollowed out from the fabric, ripe and lush. It's a work of art. I can't help myself.

I stare. The words disappear in the distance between my eyes and her fine skin.

"Thanks for doing this, Ryan. I know it's not easy pretending. Thank you for everything."

And with that, she rolls over, her breathing slowing.

"I—" Choking out a sound that isn't connected to anything but my own desperation, I grab the window for support. What the hell is wrong with me? No other woman makes me feel like this. Not one. Why can't I just say this?

Because Carrie isn't just any other woman.

Slowly, with great purpose, I make my way to my side of the bed. Her back is to me now, the raised curve of her shoulder cutting through the view of the sea outside. As the waves start to match the rhythm of her breathing, I pull back the covers, sliding one leg in, then the other, until I'm on my back next to her, fingers threaded behind my head, staring straight at the ceiling.

Touch her. Touch her. Touch her. My heartbeat suddenly has a mantra, a voice.

It sounds like hers.

"Carrie?" I whisper, ready to try.

Silence.

I fall asleep to the sound of my coward's heart beating like a drum of warning, off in the distance, muted but carrying a message of the inevitable.

♥ ♥ ♥

I WAKE UP to the intoxicating aroma of faint perfume, silk, and sweat, with Carrie pushed up against me, spooning. She's curled into my arms and her ass presses against my front in a way that makes me suddenly hold my breath and tense, like I'm a wax statue.

With a sword between my legs.

I don't want to wake her up. Actually, I *do* want to wake her up. My arm is wrapped around her and the gentle weight of one of her breasts against the bones of my hand is killing me. Electricity shoots through me, from the root of my cock into the top of my head as I close my eyes and nuzzle her neck, breathing in the scent of the possible.

The scent of *now*.

And then I remember.

I know it's not easy pretending.

My gut curls in, away from her body. She moves backward instinctively, seeking me out, her hand finding my hand and pulling me in.

If I go by her words, we're just friends.

If I go by her body, she wants more.

Tap tap tap.

I startle, half flying off the bed as someone knocks on the door. Racing to answer, I open it a crack and find a big grin on the other side.

"Slacker. It's seven. Get your ass out here for a run and some lifting. Unless you already worked those arms with some pushups over Carrie last night?"

Zeke.

"Shut the hell up," I snap, closing the door in his face. But I grab my water bottle and socks and shoes, then slip my cardkey in my pocket. I know how this works.

He'll wake her up if I don't get him out of here.

I'm in the hall in seconds. Zeke's inspecting me like I'm a medieval bride and he's looking at the wedding-night sheets for proof of sex.

"Nice tent. I take it you struck out."

I suggest he have sex with himself while I get my socks and shoes on.

"I don't have to, mate. I can always find a filly happy to ride me."

"You're comparing yourself to a horse?"

"I'm hung like one." He shrugs and laughs. "You look like shit. You get any sleep?"

"Some. Not much," I admit, as he takes me down the stairs and out a door to a trail that runs just above the beach.

"Your bedhead could win awards. You spent all night in bed with a woman and didn't sleep *or* get laid?"

"You planning to flap your lips or run?" I challenge as I stretch.

"Seems like the only lips in your life that are flapping are mine."

And with that, I sprint, because it's either start running or start punching.

CHAPTER TEN

Carrie

WHEN I WAKE up, the room is quiet. The kind of quiet that lets you know you are completely alone. I squint at my phone and see it's 8:15 in the morning.

Ryan's gone.

Where *is* he? His side of the bed has been slept in, but I don't remember him next to me. Last I recall, he was standing at the window, back turned, mind elsewhere as I undressed just a few feet away.

"He slept next to me all night and never even touched me," I whisper slowly, trying to make sense of what's happening.

And what's happening is: nothing.

Of course. That's the deal. It's pretend. Right?

It's hard to focus my eyes, but I type out a text: *hey good morning all good?*

Please let him appear with a life-support-size coffee. *Please*. I close my eyes and visualize him standing by the bed in sweaty running clothes, holding out a giant steaming cup and smiling down at me. Like at O, only better.

Nothing happens. I visualize harder.

Still nothing.

Jamey used to bring me coffee in bed in the morning. I would smell it before I even opened my eyes. You know those articles that always come up online? "Ten Ways to Know Your Partner Truly Loves

You"? I always read every single one, and we always got a perfect score.

He brings you coffee in bed? *Check (although I was in bed and he wasn't)*

He always kisses you goodnight? *Check (although it was just a kiss)*

He gives you affectionate little touches? *Check (although only in public)*

Perfect score, 10 = Total Denial. Congratulations.

Next time I fall in love, if there *is* a next time, I am going to be completely aware of what's going on, right from the start. I swear I will never be fooled again. I will learn from experience. I will know the real thing when I see it, when I feel it.

What I feel right now, though, is a desperate need for caffeine. I pull on jeans and a t-shirt, and hang up my nightgown. Before I shut the closet door, I run my hand down the rose-colored silk, loving the sensual liquid softness. Ryan's definitely a better roommate than Angela would have been. I have almost the entire closet to myself, except his suit, a jacket, and two dress shirts. And I have the whole bathroom counter, other than his shaving kit. Jamey always took up more than half the closet real estate, but the bathroom wasn't so bad.

"Of course," I mutter to myself, "that's because we used the same skincare and hair products."

I step into the lobby and follow the delicious smell of dark roast (undertones of cinnamon and sugar) around the corner. It looks like a new coffee bar is going in. There's quite a long line of sleepy-looking people. Some are chatting, but most are staring silently down at their phones.

Carpenters are hanging shelves and signs behind the counter, and the baristas are dodging around ladders. A pretty woman with long, shiny brown hair is working calmly but quickly, grinding beans and steaming milk, not a movement wasted. She has a surprisingly good manicure for someone in food service. Her partner, who is taking customer orders, is a tall, handsome man in a very tight t-shirt that reveals muscles he did not acquire by filling cardboard containers and making change.

About a dozen people ahead of me in line, I spot a familiar and elegant head.

"Chloe?" She looks up and smiles when she recognizes me, then motions me to join her.

"Hey, good morning! I was just checking in with Jemma. She and Henry are taking care of Holly this weekend so Nick and I could come to the wedding. It feels so strange not to know what she's doing."

"What is all this?" I wave at the crowd and the construction chaos.

"Grind It Fresh! is opening in all the Anterdec properties. Looks like our lucky weekend."

"Pretty sure this is not my lucky weekend, but I'm happy about the coffee." I watch the counter to see how quickly the line is moving.

"What's going on? Aren't you here with Ryan? Where is he?"

I should *not* tell the truth here. This is not part of the approved script, but it's so hard to pretend every minute, and Chloe is always so comforting to talk to. She looks perfect on the surface, but she's very real underneath.

"No idea," I confess. "He was gone when I woke up this morning."

"Hm. He probably went for a run. Did you check to see if his running shoes were gone?"

"Oh no, I wouldn't look in his bag!" I am horrified at the idea.

"Really? I'm in Nick's bag all the time. Just last night my feet were cold, and I needed to borrow a pair of his socks. I'll bet he never goes in mine, though." She chuckles. "He wouldn't know if he'd find a garter belt or a binky."

"I don't think Ryan and I know each other well enough for that," I say doubtfully.

Just then a camera crew from the local TV station starts setting up directly in front of the coffee bar, forcing the line to snake around the equipment. The reporter touches up her makeup as if fifty strangers weren't watching her. Lacking a hurricane, a beached whale, or the filming of a Casey Affleck movie, this coffee shop opening is breaking news. Chloe and I shuffle forward as we talk.

"How long have you been together now?" she asks. Normal

question, right?

"Um . . . well . . ." I stutter, "we've been together since . . ."

Chloe looks at me oddly, and I almost crumble. I almost say: *I don't know! I mean, we're not together! I mean, we're here together, but we're just friends! But nobody is supposed to know that, it's a total secret! Because, you know, Jamey dumped me and he's here with his boyfriend!*

Instead, I feel a touch on my arm and turn. The TV reporter is standing next to me with her microphone angled toward my mouth. I see the camera just behind her.

"Tell us what brings you here to Chatham Beach Inn," she says in a professionally pleasant media voice. "Is it the new Grind It Fresh! bar?"

I look at her, and I look at the camera, and dear God, did I just almost tell the entire world that I'm a complete loser?

I open my mouth but not a word comes out.

Then there's an arm around my shoulders and Ryan is leaning forward to the microphone. He is shirtless, covered in a fine layer of sweat that darkens all the hair across his chest and torso. The same t-shirt he wore to bed last night is around his shoulders, soaked through.

His happy trail thickens and the hair seems to curl in formation, as if Ryan has some kind of general in charge of his army of sexy hair. His eight pack goes up, out, and in as his chest expands, his smile so broad and happy it's infectious.

Every woman nearby grins at him. I haven't seen this many teeth since a design conference I attended two years ago was in the same hotel as the Miss Teen Alabama pageant.

"My girlfriend and I are in town for the wedding of our good friends," he says in his deep warm voice as he plants a hot kiss on my cheek. The combination of his sheer athleticism and the affectionate gesture makes heat pool between my legs, my throat closing, my own abs contracting with pure, unadulterated desire. Corded muscle in the form of his arm crosses my ribcage and waist as he pulls me in. The scent of hard exertion, sand, salt and sheer animal magnetism makes me want to lick his shoulder.

Oh, God, Carrie! I scream in my head. *Do not lick him! Not on camera!*

A small crowd has formed around us. Instinct makes me put my arm around his waist, too, finding slick, marble-like muscle. I accidentally brush against his ass.

It is hot, tight, and some part of my mind just melts as I turn into a throbbing hormone. A 5'9" live-streaming podcast of want.

He's wearing lightweight soccer shorts, and when I look down, I see the inside of his thigh. Short socks and running shoes complete the look. As I look up, I realize every other woman is checking him out, too.

Of course they are.

I tighten my hold on him and stand on tiptoes. He plants a light kiss on my cheek, then turns to the camera and says, "But finding a Grind It Fresh! right here is a fantastic surprise. We'll probably come back to the Inn again just knowing we can have our favorite coffee. Home away from home."

He flashes a blindingly handsome smile, gives my shoulders a squeeze, and then kisses me on the lips, all in full view of the camera.

News Woman visibly melts a bit.

"I think I need to change my panties," some anonymous woman in the crowd whispers.

"I think I need to change my husband," says another.

Titters fill the air, but they're like static, a kind of white noise machine that I vaguely sense as Ryan's hot, sweaty skin connects with as much of my body as he possibly can touch, his one hand at my neck, the other on my ass.

On camera.

He's smiling as he kisses me, my tongue engaged in a light-hearted battle with his, the messy, primal maleness of his body after a long run making me turn into one big wordless, boneless woman who can only make little moans in the back of her throat. On live television.

With a stage presence that is so persuasive I almost think he really is attracted to me, he ends the kiss and gives me a convincing grope, making my hips shiver, abs tightening.

"And we here on the Cape certainly hope you do," the reporter says a little too warmly, ignoring me now, focused entirely on Ryan, who has me in a lover's hold. "Please come back very soon." She moves off, but Ryan's arm stays firmly around me.

All the O guys have incredible bodies. I've spent years in the enviable position of being able to look all I want, all day long. It's part of their job, and I admire them from a distance every day. But now my arm is pressed tightly against his abs, and I'm starting to sweat, too.

Look? Sure.

Touch? Never.

But never say never now . . .

"Well, hi, Ryan," Chloe says in an amused voice. "Excellent timing."

"What can we get you?" the barista asks. We have finally arrived at the head of the line. Not that I noticed. All I can see is Ryan's chest, going up and down like a hot pec buffet of rollercoaster.

I know that makes no sense, but I can't put two words together right now. Ryan's arm is still around me. He can stop now. The cameras aren't rolling.

"*Declan?*" Chloe's voice rises with incredulity, staring at the tight-shirted barista with her jaw open. Dark, wavy hair. Thick eyebrows with green eyes the color of emeralds in a cup of tea. A square jaw and a serious look that makes you stop breathing. Declan McCormick is famous in Boston for being a hot billionaire, but in the flesh, he's even more breathtaking than I'd ever imagined.

Now I understand the local news camera crew.

"Chloe!" he says with a dazzling smile, wiping his hands on a towel and reaching for her hand. "I'd kiss you, too, but the counter's too wide."

"I didn't recognize you without a jacket and tie," Chloe marvels. "I assumed you were born wearing a suit." She regains her composure and gives him the kind of smooth smile I can only deliver after three drinks.

"Apparently you don't take sculpting classes at the Westside Center for the Arts," the other barista says drily.

"Shannon!"

Things are moving a little too fast for me here. Shannon and Declan *McCormick*? The former vice president of Anterdec and his wife? The new owners of Grind It Fresh! are *here*?

"What are you doing making coffee?" Chloe asks. "You own the chain."

"Shannon's years working as a mystery shopper taught her that there's nothing like first-hand experience when it comes to customer satisfaction," Declan says with a rueful smile. "So here we are at 8:45 on a beautiful Saturday morning, grinding it fresh first-hand."

He holds up his right hand for emphasis, then places it squarely on Shannon's ass. She swats it away, but their eyes meet for a hot second.

Jealousy blinds me. I blame it on caffeine deprivation. I wish someone would grab me like that.

Wait a minute. Ryan just *did* grab me like that.

But I want the real thing.

"You'd be working anyway," Shannon chides him. "Might as well be here on the Cape as at home."

"Well, since I'm supposed to be working, what would you like, Chloe?" Declan asks.

"A medium latte for me, a macchiato for Nick, a life-support latte for Carrie, and Ryan . . . ?"

"Large black coffee, please." He puts down his Grind It Fresh! card. "My treat, though."

We move along to the pick-up counter to wait. "Thanks for coming, you guys," Shannon says as she delivers four steaming cups. "Call me, Chloe!" She waves and turns to the next order.

"What are you two planning till the wedding?" Chloe inquires. Ryan sips his coffee and uses his t-shirt to wipe sweat off his abs.

"*Wedding*?" I gasp. "We're not really thinking in those terms— we're just dating!"

They both look at me, nonplussed.

"I think she means Jenny's wedding. You know, tomorrow at four?" Ryan offers, mouth doing that sexy lip-biting thing where he's trying not to laugh.

I can feel my face turn scarlet. Red is an actual facial expression for me.

"Right, of course! Ha ha. Of course. Well, I have some time till I have to show up for the rehearsal and the bachelorette party. And then there's hair and makeup tomorrow after brunch." The wedding is at 4 p.m., so plenty of time for Jenny and her mother to have their hair catch fire over and over—metaphorically, of course.

"It's a great morning—want to take this coffee down to the beach?" Ryan asks.

"You two go ahead," Chloe says, adding milk to one of her cups. "I'm going to take this up to Nick. I'll bet he's still asleep."

Ryan and I head for the main door and the path to the ocean. No one's on the beach yet. It really is a beautiful morning, warm and bright, and without the humidity of summer the air is crisp. There's a gentle breeze. We settle on the sand, facing the ocean. It's a moment of peace before the craziness of the wedding formalities kicks in.

Just sitting together in the sun feels so comfortable. Jamey would have searched for twenty minutes for the exact perfect spot, dug a hole for his Provençal umbrella, set up the wood and canvas sling chairs, poured mimosas (with mint leaves and orange slices) in plastic champagne flutes, and started work on the sandcastle. A replica of Neuschwanstein. With turrets.

Ryan is so . . . low maintenance.

"How do you think it's going so far?" he asks. "Are your friends buying our act?"

"I think so. Angela and Diane were certainly convinced last night. That uh, show you put on for the news woman will certainly cement it." My eyes drift to his bare belly. I lick my lips. "Thank you again, Ryan. I know this is a lot to ask of anyone, maybe too much."

He's quiet for a minute, squinting out at the waves. A few people are starting to appear on the dunes, unfolding chairs or spreading towels. Some are walking along the edge of the surf, shorebirds scattering ahead of them.

"It's not too much," he says finally. "It's easy. I could do this every day." He touches the back of my hand lightly, tentatively, with one fingertip, and I shiver in spite of the warmth. "It's the opposite of too much. It's not enough. I was thinking about this all night . . ."

A seagull dive-bombs a group behind us, the sudden flurry of activity making us both turn and look. And then—

"Carrie! Is that you?" Someone in a floppy white hat and big sunglasses is calling and waving. I look up from Ryan's intent face and there's Jess, Jenny and Jamey's college-age little sister, barreling toward us. Yes, their parents did the cute same-initial thing. Their family dog? Junebug. You should have seen their Christmas cards.

"Hi, Jess," I say faintly.

Go *away*, Jess.

There is really not one thing she could say that I would be interested in hearing at this moment.

Is that rude of me? Because I don't know where Ryan was going with what he was saying, but something in me wants to find out.

Nope. Jess is on a mission.

"Carrie, come on, we're supposed to all have brunch together!" Jess reaches down and picks up my empty coffee container. "We barely have time to get dressed!"

She appears to notice Ryan for the first time. "Oh, hi, I'm Jessica, I'm Jenny's sister, nice to meet you!" She holds out a sandy hand.

Ryan shakes his head once and stands up.

"Jessie, this is Ryan Donovan, my . . ."

"I'm Carrie's date. Her boyfriend, actually."

"Really?" Jess looks from Ryan to me and back again, obviously astonished. "Wow."

It's unclear whether this means "wow, that was fast" or "wow, he is *so* out of your league."

I sigh. "Let's go to the brunch, then."

"I think I'll hang here for a while," Ryan says. "I'll see you back at the room later."

In perfect boyfriend mode, he puts one hand on the back of my neck and pulls me in for a kiss. As I balance myself, one of my hands lands on his hipbone, the other on his abs. I'm getting used to the taste of his mouth, the male scent of his skin. New but somehow familiar. I lean into it a little bit, breathe him in.

Just a little. Just for now.

Just pretending.

He pats my ass with a loving touch and a half grin that makes Jess gape.

Who knew Ryan could be such a good actor?

"Don't be gone too long," he says with a wink, then turns away from us, his attention on the horizon.

"Right," I say faintly, my butt tingling from that affectionate love pat.

As Jessie and I trudge up the dunes toward the hotel, something catches my eye a little way up the beach. It's an umbrella, in what looks like a Provençal print. A man sits beneath it in a canvas sling chair while another man kneels in the sand, building a sandcastle. Jamey and Kevin.

Huh. Nailed it.

And the funny thing is, I feel a sense of relief. If the orange juice isn't fresh-squeezed, if the greenheads are biting, if the iPod dies, it's not my problem. I'm not going to be in the Instagram shot of the perfect Cape Cod beach day. Kevin is.

I glance back at Ryan, sitting in the sun with his coffee, quiet and casual, completely unrehearsed.

I wish I were sitting next to him.

Ryan

THE LAST THING I need right now is a shot of excitement from caffeine, but I need to do something with my hands and mouth before I use them both on Carrie in extremely not-safe-for-public ways.

Gulping a Grind It Fresh! coffee so fast it burns my throat is a luxurious form of masochism. I'll take it.

She smells so good. Tastes like honey and sunshine. The wall inside me between real and pretend is being demolished.

And not just by my horny jackhammer.

I stand and move up the dunes to where the inn has lounge chairs lined up facing the water. Choosing one on the end, I stretch out, coffee in hand, October sun giving my body a nice, light toasting as my heart rate goes back to pre-kiss levels. The run was for cardio.

But there are other ways to get your heart rate nice and high, and they don't involve miles on the beach.

"Chill out, man," I mutter under my breath, curling up to take a sip of my coffee. Abs tight, I make myself stay in place, lats tensing, working my core to get some composure. Staying centered emotionally starts with being centered in the body.

Or something like that.

I open my eyes and catch Carrie as she disappears into the hotel with Jessie. As if she feels my gaze, Carrie looks over her shoulder at me, longing etched in her face.

Yeah. If I had to choose between a brunch with a bunch of crazy wedding women and hanging on the beach sipping a latte, I'd pick coffee, too.

I smile at her, but she doesn't smile back. Instead, Jessie pulls her arm impatiently, and Carrie trips slightly, righting herself quickly, moving with long strides that turn her ass into an animated upside down heart.

I make a sound that's half exasperation, half arousal.

"Coffee that good?" A woman pulls her chair over to me, a floppy sun hat hiding her face. She sits down, making no effort to be modest with legs that go up to her chin, in a short skirt that shows me she favors thong underwear. "Sounds positively orgasmic."

I'll give her credit—she knows when to make a sultry entrance. Long, blonde hair highlighted by a color artist, curled into a loose french knot that stays in place as she peels off her hat. Toned arms, perfectly tanned, shoulders kissed by freckles. Her bright red sleeveless sun dress shows off a pair of sculpted breasts, unnaturally big and perfectly symmetrical. The toothy smile greeting me as she cradles a coffee cup in her hands on top of knees that brush against my thigh is about as obvious as a crotch grab.

"Good coffee is good coffee," I say with a polite smile.

"And good orgasms are even better," she replies with a wink.

Working at O means learning how to knock down passes being thrown at you from all angles, often unexpectedly and without warning. No matter what, this woman is not going to score on me, so it's better to deflect swiftly and move on.

I pull myself up, legs off the bottom of the chair, and spring into a standing position, coffee lid much appreciated. "If you'll excuse me, I—"

"You're one of the strippers at O, aren't you?" Her eyes narrow, taking me in inch by inch, the look cold and calculating. "I've seen you before. But not in the daylight." She looks down at my running shorts. "And not with so many clothes on."

"Are you a member?" I keep my voice even. O Spa policy states that if you meet a member outside of the club, you act professionally. Master masseurs are "on" at all times.

Not on the clock, though. I ignore her stripper comment and put up my guard, knowing the best offense is to become a blank wall.

"Lifetime."

That means she shelled out six figures. She expects me to be impressed. But before I can come up with something to say, she reaches for both ends of my wet t-shirt around my neck, and pulls me close. Mocha and whisky blast my nose, her sour breath tinged with something elegantly sinister. That's not just coffee in that cup she's holding.

No surprise.

"I'm Eileen. What's your name?" One eyebrow goes up. "I know you're not Henry." She pretends to look a foot above me and laughs. "He'd stand out in a crowd of Vikings."

"Ryan." A split second too late, I realize I should have lied and given her Zeke's name. Then a warning bell starts to ding inside me.

Eileen. Eileen. I've heard that name before at work. But why?

"Ryan." It comes out like a purr and I'm her prey. Her eyes move slowly, like she has a right to check out the meat. *My* meat. Like she's bought me already. At work, I don't care. It goes with the job.

In public? With my heart barely in my ribcage after that moment with Carrie? Eileen's attention feels cheap.

I don't *do* cheap.

I twist away, gently taking her hand so I can untangle myself. But she's fast. Determined. The fine lines at the corners of her eyes, visible only when I'm this close, make me think she's well into her forties. Flat belly, though, and toned body.

A few years ago, I would have killed to have a woman like her want me.

Now all I want is Carrie.

Eileen's manicured fingers tickle my sweaty chest, a low, sexy rumble bubbling up her throat. Red, glistening lips part, her tongue peeking out as she gives me an uncompromising look.

"You have the body of an Olympian."

"And you have the lines of a pick-up artist," says a woman behind me, matching Eileen tone for tone.

I jump back, out of Eileen's grasp, my t-shirt dropping onto my foot.

"Hi Eileen," Chloe says, one arm firmly around Nick Grafton's waist, the other extended and ready to shake. "What a surprise and a delight."

Nick shoots me a look that says, *What's up?*

I give Chloe a look that says, *I owe you my firstborn son.*

As Nick and I shake hands and share masculine looks and death-grips designed to crush titanium, Chloe and Eileen do the fake air-kiss, murmuring comments about the resort and Grind It Fresh! Niceties that buy time while they size each other up.

"I'm here for a long-term spa stay," Eileen says, flashing Chloe a tight smile.

That's code for plastic surgery.

"You've worked so hard this year, Eileen. All that charity work. You deserve it," Chloe says smoothly. "Let me introduce you to my partner, Nick. Nick Grafton, this is Eileen van Donner."

They shake hands, Eileen's radar on high, scanning Nick for sex potential. We all feel it. Chloe starts to do a slow burn.

Hold on. Eileen van Donner. Now I remember. Cougar extraordinaire, something about trying to buy Zeke a while ago.

Literally *buy* him. People with money to burn will go to great lengths to get what they want.

"I see you've brought the help," Eileen jokes with Chloe, who looks genuinely perplexed.

"Help?" Chloe asks.

"I think she means me," I offer, jaw tight.

"Is Ryan available?" Eileen asks.

Nick starts coughing.

"Available? No. I have a girlfriend," I blurt out.

Chloe's eyes dart between me and Eileen like a metronome on high.

"I meant for spa services. I assume you're here to work?"

"No, I'm here for pleasure."

"Funny. So am I." She reaches for my arm and slips her hand in, fingertips brushing my bare nipple.

"Eileen, a former member of our O staff is getting married here at the Inn. You'll see many O staff members here as guests. They're not working," Chloe says pointedly.

"Not *officially*," Eileen asks, her intent clear.

"Not at all," I say firmly. "Remember my girlfriend?" At that, Chloe arches an eyebrow and smothers a smile. What the hell does that look mean?

Eileen pouts. It's hard to tell, but she manages it through chemical paralysis. "That's no fun."

"Everyone needs a break from work sometimes," I say, clearing my throat. Nick nods with sympathy. Or maybe he's just trying not to laugh.

"Don't think of what you do as work. It's more of a calling." Twisting my way out of her touch is easy as I break her grasp and suck down the rest of my coffee.

"A calling?" Chloe asks politely.

"All those women begging for God whenever Ryan touches them." I need divine intervention now.

Chloe's eyes narrow. "I'll ask you to treat Ryan and any other staff member like a regular person you'd meet at a resort."

"Who says I'm not?"

Chloe catches my eye. I give her a slight headshake that says, *I got this.*

Eileen puts her hand on my chest again and stands on tiptoe, coming in for a hug. Something pushes against the waistband of my shorts, right at the base of my spine. I don't have to look to see what it is.

"Room 422," she whispers, planting a waxy kiss on my jawline, the sour alcohol breath making me wince.

As she pulls away, I reach back for the plastic hotel cardkey.

And lock eyes with Carrie, who is walking toward us with an enormous flower arrangement and a dropped jaw.

Oh, no.

"There you are, Ryan!" Jessie calls out, hidden by the flowers. "We need your help moving the flowers for the brunch!" She's holding a similar batch of flowers and shoves them in my arms.

"You look like you need something fresher to hold, anyhow," Carrie says, her eyes narrowing as she blinks furiously, expression neutral.

My hands fumble to get a good grip on the basket as I process what she just said. Wait. Is she . . . *jealous?*

Casting a scathing look at Eileen's back, Carrie then turns to Chloe and says, "Was that Eileen van Donner? From O?"

"The one and only."

"She's the one who tried to hire Zeke to be her houseboy, right? Complete with a leash and everything." Carrie's eyes cut my way.

"Is she recruiting again?" She looks at the hotel cardkey in my hand. Then right into my eyes.

Red smudges on her cheeks indicate she's blushing, an angry, involuntary response to emotion. Carrie's chin juts up, her shoulders squared.

Jessie's chattering away a mile a minute about hydrangeas while Carrie stares me down, her chest rising and falling with emotion. She walks closer to me. The flowers in my hands suddenly become a welcome barrier between me and her anger.

Chloe reaches for my hand and plucks Eileen's hotel room cardkey out of it. "Poor Ryan," Chloe says in a loud voice. "Never off the clock. The clients love him so much. Even when he told her firmly he has a girlfriend, she kept trying. Unbelievable." Deftly, she takes the cardkey, walks over to a small stand with empty plastic bags for people who walk their dogs on the trails, and slips it in, tying a knot on the top.

"Trash goes in the trash can," she mutters, tossing it in a receptacle.

Jessie watches everything with hawklike eyes, clearly trying to catch up. I pivot, putting the giant garden in my hands on the table, then scoop Carrie toward me, caging her. Every muscle in her body is tense. She's trembling.

"You are the only fresh thing I want to hold, kitten," I say, just loud enough for Jessie to hear, just soft enough to let my real emotions come through in my voice.

Carrie's eyes dart all over the place, like marbles being dropped into a maze, as if she's scattered and unsure. Then she stands on tiptoes, her hands resting on my shoulders, and she comes in for a sweet kiss.

That turns hot in seconds.

"I don't like the idea of women turning you into a commodity," she murmurs against my mouth. "Only I'm allowed to do that," she adds.

Nick laughs. Out of the corner of my eye, I see Chloe tug him away, Nick nuzzling her neck and whispering something that makes Chloe chuckle in a low, knowing sound.

"Um, hate to break up your little makeout session, but we have more flowers to move because the planners relocated the rehearsal dinner across the resort, and my mom is breathing into random paper bags while—"

Carrie holds up a palm to Jessie as Angela walks up, grinning madly.

The gentle kiss against my lips, so chaste it makes me want the flip side of Carrie, the dirty, dirty sex kitten I am pretty sure she can be, nearly breaks me.

"C'mon! You two had all night together. How could you still want more?" Jessie whines.

"Look at him, Jess. How could Carrie pick flowers over *that*?" Angela's joking, but not really.

"Yeah," I murmur against her ear. "How could you?"

Carrie jolts, nervous laughter filling the sudden space between us, her hot breath tickling my collar bone.

"Um, we need to go. Something about a ribbon emergency," she says, patting my chest like a teddy bear wearing a vest she just buttoned.

"Okay. Just don't be gone for too long. Remember that nooner we scheduled?" Wink.

Angela starts to squirm.

Funny. As I walk away, I swear Carrie does, too.

The courtyard is full of people I don't know. As I dodge around guests in lounge chairs and tables full of folks drinking coffee, I hear a familiar voice.

As in, I just spoke to him a minute ago.

"I take it this goes with the territory," Nick says, surprising me from behind. It's not really a question, but I answer him anyhow.

"Nick! Thought you and Chloe were, uh . . ." I was about to say, *about to go off and have sex*, but that's probably not the best thing to say to Anterdec management.

He makes a sour face. "She just got a call from those idiot developers about the customer service phone tree. They want us to buy a European phone service that always hangs up on American cell phones and can only be programmed in French."

We share a laugh.

He shakes his head and runs his hand through his hair. "And they want her to add some crazy virtual reality feature with scent-o-rama."

I grimace. "I could see how that might get, um . . ."

"Messy?"

We share a sick kind of laugh. It's the chuckle you hear all the time from employees at O, a strange sound of *I can't believe this is what I do for a living* and *Damn, I have the best job ever.*

"You collect hotel cardkeys from clients like that wherever you go?"

"I can. Depends entirely on the client."

"All jobs have their downsides," Nick says with a boisterous chuckle. If I didn't know how comfortable he is in his own skin, I'd think he was envious.

"I didn't deal with any of this at my last job."

"Yeah? What did you do?"

"I was an electrical engineer."

Nick gives me a speculative look. "That's quite a career change."

I shrug. "Like you said, all jobs have their downsides. I make more money working at O and no one dies if I calibrate a sex toy circuit incorrectly."

Nick starts coughing again.

"Chloe started calling you the Renaissance Man. She wasn't kidding." Nick's broad grin makes his blue eyes stand out. He has a calmness, an alert confidence that makes the weirdness of this conversation disappear.

"I aim to please."

"Looks like you succeed."

With everyone but Carrie.

"How old are you, Ryan?"

"Twenty-seven."

Some weird look passes over his face, nostalgia and something contemplative as he gives me a crooked grin. "Enjoy it while you can."

"C'mon, man. I'm sure when you were my age, you had all the women you wanted."

"When I was your age, I was a single father to twin kindergarteners and a two-year-old. Women weren't slipping hotel cardkeys in my waistband. They were handing me carpool schedules for tiny tot soccer."

"That actually sounds like more fun."

A belly laugh comes out of him, booming and incredulous. "You've got every woman you could ever want at your fingertips."

"Yeah."

Nick's eyes narrow. He reminds me of a younger version of my dad, the one I played with when I was little, the dad who was still young enough to toss baseballs and teach me how to ski. I do some quick math and realize Nick's got to be my oldest sister's age.

"But you don't, do you?"

"I don't what?"

"Have the woman you want."

"What?"

He shrugs. Now he *really* reminds me of my dad.

Before he can answer, his phone buzzes. He looks at it and grins.

"I've got a woman of my own back at my hotel room," he says, waggling his plastic cardkey. "I've been summoned."

"Scent-o-rama crisis averted? Hey, man, don't let me delay you." I push the Up key on the elevator, legs too tired for the stairs.

By the time he's gone down the hall, the elevator doors open.

And I'm greeted with squeals.

"It *is* you! We saw you downstairs being interviewed and thought so. OMIGOD IT'S RYAN!" Twin blondes with hair down to their asses and eyes big as saucers gape at me. One of them grabs my arm and yanks me into the elevator. "You remember us from O? You did our eighteenth birthday party last year! Gia and Gina!"

SQUEEEEE!

I just smile. God has a sense of humor like Zeke's.

"And OMIGOD, Gia," one of them turns to the other, "Zeke is

here, too! We could get a foursome going." She winks at me. "Um, for golf or something." *Wink.*

As if summoned, I hear him shout, "HEY MATE! Hold the door!" Sweaty and holding a fresh beer, Zeke saunters on, literally dripping all over everyone as he turns in place and chugs half his brew.

"ZEEEEEEKKKKKKEEEE!" They scream as the doors close and I push the fourth floor, noting the only other button pressed was. . . . the fourth floor.

"What luck," Zeke says, burping. "I knew coming to this wedding was a great idea."

I'm too polite to point out he came because it was all free. As Anterdec subsidiary employees, we were able to get comped rooms.

"Whatcha doing tonight, Zeke?" Gia (or Gina) asks.

He puts his arms around both of them, looks at me and announces. "At least one of you."

"Why not both?" Gina (or Gia) giggles.

"Even better."

"What about poor Ryan? We can't leave him out." One of the twins speaks while the other applies lipstick.

Zeke gives me a fake sympathetic look. "Oh, girls. It's so sad. Ryan has a girlfriend now. He's taken. Off the market."

They pout.

"So you'll just have to share me."

"We like sharing," they say in unison.

"Nice shoes." Zeke's statement comes with a wolfish grin. I look down, wondering why the non sequitur about her footwear. Both women are wearing very ordinary high heels.

"Thanks!" More stereo responses.

"They'll look great against my shoulders."

Okay, then.

Ding!

Without another word, I get off the elevator, find the room, slip in, and press my back against the closed, locked door. Carrie's gone for the afternoon, attending wedding events like a good maid of honor.

The rehearsal is at 5 p.m. and she'll eat with the wedding party.

How do I know this? The color-coded Excel printout Jenny's sister gave us yesterday. Significant others have their own color (cerulean blue). My next optional appearance is at the wedding.

I'm here now, hiding and safe in my room. *Our* room.

Safe.

Whatever that means.

CHAPTER ELEVEN

Ryan

"WELL, I'M OFF to the bachelorette party," Carrie says as if she's headed off to renew her driver's license at the registry of motor vehicles.

"Don't sound so enthusiastic." I spent most of the day consuming calories, running on the beach, and trying to dodge the attentions of O clients. A bachelorette party is the last place I want to be.

"The rehearsal was bad enough. Jenny's family minister is about as interesting as listening to my father explain how to edge a window."

I laugh. She doesn't talk much about her parents. I know they own a paint store in Michigan, but other than the fact that her brother works there, Carrie's life before I met her is a vague mystery.

I should talk. She's met Tessa, Carlos, and the boys. That's it. I don't share much about myself at work.

"I'd imagine your father's home improvement lectures were a great foundation for your interest in design," I reply.

"Is that why you became an electrical engineer? Because of your father?" she responds, a hard-to-read tone in her voice. Either she's genuinely curious or a little pissed I credited her dad with her interest.

"No. I just like sex toys. A lot," I say with a grin. "I like them more when they're taken apart. It's like a 3-D picture in my mind, up against the skin, triggering nerve impulses in just the right calibrated motions to produce the desired outcome."

I get a pillow to the face in response.

"I'm sure Cal Tech had a lab for sex toys for undergrads to do research," she groans.

"No. Just Department of Defense-funded robotics labs. But someday, those wireless robots will do amazing things with a tickler."

She snorts. "Even when we're not working, we're thinking about sex, aren't we?" she says, giving me a saucy smile.

I hold her gaze.

"I mean," she adds quickly, "sex for work. Sex that sells. Uh—sex that gets women to open up."

I shove the pillow against my face, laughing too hard.

"Oh, stop! You're like Zeke."

"A horny asshole who fucks Uber drivers?"

Carrie gives me a squinty bitchface in return. I deserve it.

"What's so bad about the bachelorette party?" I ask, switching topics. "Seems like harmless fun."

She gives a one-shouldered shrug. "You know."

"No. I don't." I'm not part of the wedding party, so I'm not invited to whatever the groom's doing for a bachelor party, thank God. Zeke and I have plans to lift in the fitness center.

"I work at O," Carrie says with a knowing grin. "I'm surrounded by hot, mostly naked men all day. A male stripper is just run-of-the-mill. Boring. Like Wonderbread sandwiches."

I raise my eyebrows. "Really?" Folding my arms over my chest, I watch her as she realizes what she's saying.

And *who* she's saying it to.

"I—I—but—no, Ryan, I don't mean—I didn't—I'm not, oh, man." She's flustered and adorable. "I'm not saying you're run-of-the-mill or, you know—"

"Wonderbread?" I reply, enjoying her adorable awkwardness.

"No! No! You're not! You're like artisanal French countryside bread! Gourmet and handmade, fine organic sourdough! You're the opposite of what I'm talking about!" She's so damned earnest. Apologetic. Carrie actually thinks she's hurt my feelings, and that's what I love about her. The caring. The concern. Authentic and genuine, she's so real.

Every day, I work with women who can't get what they *need* elsewhere. Don't get me wrong—I love my job.

But there are enough clients who think that they deserve to get what they need from me no matter what—with no boundaries. Time after time, even here at the Inn, I've seen it. Off the clock, on vacation, but still viewed as 'the help.'

Carrie's the only woman in my life, aside from my mom and sisters, who doesn't think of me as a tool to be used.

It makes her gorgeous, inside and out.

"I'm sourdough bread? Crusty on the outside, chewy on the inside, made from white goo in a jar that's left out on a counter to go bad until it bubbles?" I smirk.

"Fine artisanal organic special—oh, stop!" She finally sees my shoulders moving from repressed laughter and hits me in the face with another pillow she tosses, hard.

I pounce. In seconds we're on the bed, Carrie squirming under me as I tickle her, the skirt of her dress riding up to show off creamy, bare thighs. My lifting shorts are tight lycra, designed for compression and sweat wicking.

Not meant for hiding anything.

"Stop! I give up! Oh, God, Ryan," she gasps, laughing until she snorts, then giggling with embarrassment. Her attempts to tickle me back are hilariously ineffective.

Until her hand brushes against my erection.

We both freeze.

Panting, I'm half on top of her, bare thigh to bare thigh, our chests rising and falling from exertion and playfulness. Her mouth is inches from mine, eyes asking me a question I can't quite answer with words.

I answer with my mouth anyhow, kissing her softly. Carrie's lips part and I'm on her, letting my weight press into her, blanketing her body with mine as she moves her hands up my back, inviting me closer.

The kiss is everything I want, more than I expected and less than I need. I rise up and deepen, her legs moving against mine, her hands on my waist, fingers touching a bare spot above my ass that makes my blood race.

Bzzz.

We both jump, Carrie rolling out from under me, jumping on both feet like a gymnast, grabbing her phone.

"That's Angela, wondering where I am!" she squeaks, running her hand through her mussed hair.

I can't breathe.

Don't leave, I want to say, sitting cross-legged on the bed, trying to make my mind line up with my mouth, my cock stand down from my heart.

Don't leave, I want to beg as the cool air between us sharpens my senses.

Don't leave, I want to demand as she grabs her purse and gives me a shaky smile.

"Now you look improper," I say. "Like someone who was making out with her boyfriend before rushing off to the bachelorette party."

"Boyfriend," she says, her eyes narrowing as she says the word. Carrie tilts her head, then takes one step toward me, hesitant. The air shifts, meaning filling the room, and I hold my breath.

I *really* can't breathe.

Then she dips her head and gives a sheepish smile. "Geez, Ryan." She laughs, shaking her head, as she retreats. "You're really good at this."

"Huh?" I choke out, confused again, body spinning faster than my mind—if that's even possible.

"You had me going there for a minute. Boyfriend. Right. Time to go out there and put on a show."

And with that, she leaves, closing the door softly with a click that is like a bullet being loaded into a chamber.

I shake it off, jumping to my feet, snatching up the hand towel I had on my nightstand, my phone and my cardkey. While Carrie parties with the bride and bridesmaids, I'm going to lift iron until my arms detach at the shoulder joint.

And then do still another set of reps.

Pure exhaustion would be a relief at this point. Danger is everywhere with Carrie now. I'm about to lose my fucking mind and tell her the game is up. None of this is fake.

It's all way too real.

I get to the fitness center, head for the racks, and load up barbells, curling until my biceps and triceps scream surrender. Zeke's running late, damn it. I need a spotter for squats.

Doing squats without a spotting partner is like having sex without using birth control. The chance that something will go wrong is slim, but the long-term consequences are forever.

I ignore the Olympic bar and decide it can wait. As I'm doing curls, I hear the door behind me open.

In walk Jamey and Kevin, dressed in full workout clothes, carrying matching stainless steel water bottles.

And wearing twin looks of discomfort as they spot me.

"Hi, Ryan," Jamey mutters, picking a bench as far away from me as possible.

"Hey." I rack more weight on my barbells, maximizing out, then lift. Kevin watches, eyes raised, counting my reps.

Jamey's mouth tightens.

"I thought you'd be at the bachelor party," I grunt out.

Kevin huffs. "They hired a stripper."

"Yeah? So?"

"A *female* stripper," Kevin adds in an acid tone. He and Jamey share an eyeroll.

"Gotcha. Maybe you should head over to your sister's party. Heard they have their own entertainment."

"Now there's an idea," Jamey says with a laugh. "Carrie and I could critique him while we drink w—"

I drop the weights, the gentle bounce of their heft on the lightly padded gym floor barely registering as I get right in his face.

"Leave Carrie the fuck alone," I warn him, breathing so hard, my exhale makes his hair lift off his brow.

Maybe it's all the testosterone unleashed in my blood by the lifting. Maybe it's my chewed-on tongue, sore from biting it. Maybe it's my frustration with all the kisses and caresses with Carrie that aren't real—but damn well feel like they are.

Or maybe I just fucking hate Jamey for what he did to my best friend. My fake girlfriend.

My—whatever Carrie is to me now.

"What?" he says, incredulous.

"You heard me. Don't go near her again—except for the bare minimum you have to do for the wedding."

"You can't tell me what to do. You don't control who Carrie spends time with."

"When it comes to Carrie being hurt, I damn well do."

"I can't believe she's dating a caveman."

"I can't believe she ever dated a piece of shit like you."

Air slides between his teeth as he sucks in an offended breath. "Fuck you, Ryan."

"Is that what this is about? Every time you dropped by the O Spa and watched all of us in our g-strings, you were just imagining fucking us? Not only did you use her for a beard, you . . ." I can't even complete the sentence.

Kevin inhales sharply.

"You don't understand," Jamey says, in my face with Kevin as backup. I almost laugh at the posturing, because I'm close to being the size of them—combined.

"Then explain it."

"You're straight. I'll bet you've always known you're straight. You have no idea how hard a struggle it's been for me. I started dating Carrie with the best of intentions. I like her. I even love her."

Kevin makes a sound in his throat.

I give Jamey a deadly, disbelieving stare.

"But she's nice and sweet and she just gives and gives and gives and after a while, it was impossible to leave. Impossible to really think! How do you *think* when someone's that nice to you?" Jamey practically shouts.

"You're blaming her niceness for the fact that you were a jerk to her?" I'd better not be hearing this. He's trying to make what he did Carrie's *fault*.

"It was agony, knowing I wasn't attracted to women, not even to Carrie. Denying it. Trying so hard to be the man she wanted. Trying even harder to turn her into the person I wanted. You don't understand. You can't understand."

"Here's what I do understand, you asshole. You had a choice."

"You're *blaming* me for being gay?"

"What? No! This has nothing to do with your being gay!"

He looks like I gut-punched him.

"What?" Jamey gasps. Kevin's eyebrow arches but he says nothing.

"Not one bit," I continue. "The fact that you're making it all about *you* is the problem. You didn't show even the slightest bit of respect for Carrie when you dumped her. You called her from the airport while you were running off with *him*," I point at Kevin, "broke up with her, and announced you were gay. And then you hung up." Kevin just blinks slowly, like an owl. Jamey's face drains of color. "You stripped her of her dignity. You don't get to do that to her. No one does. Ever again."

"I needed to make sure she knew," Jamey says in a small voice.

"Then you should have been a grown-up. A decent human being would meet her in person, say all the nice things she needed to hear about how good and smart and kind and attractive she is. Then you break it to her gently. Let her know it's not her fault. Let her know she's still valuable."

"Of course she's valuable!"

"You made her think she wasn't. *Isn't*. You broke her fucking heart, Jamey." I get in his face. "Own it. You were a prick to her. You made everything about you. You made your own selfishness *her* fault."

He staggers backward, nearly tipping Kevin over.

My hands reach down to the barbells, the metal grips digging into my palms, my heart speeding through my chest like a freight train. His eyes are wide with a scheming look that make it clear he's still desperately trying to make Carrie at fault for his own self-centeredness.

Bzzz.

My phone buzzes. I drop a barbell and look at it as it buzzes again, then I grab it. It's an actual call, from Zeke.

I answer.

"Hey! I need you. *Now.*" The last word out of Zeke's mouth is a bark, a growl, a primal sound that makes me want to pick up shield and sword and join my fellow man in battle.

"Where?" I snap.

"Courtyard by the chocolate buffet." Click.

That doesn't sound anything like a battlefield, but I am ready.

I walk quickly away from Jamey and Kevin, glad to be rid of them. The tension was getting thicker and thicker by the minute, and any break from sexual tension and alpha male preening bullshit is a relief. Whatever emergency Zeke's going through has to be better than that.

In the locker room, I throw on my clothes and then lightly jog to Zeke's location.

I turn the corner toward the chocolate buffet and find Zeke in the center of a group of women, down to his skivvies, while Jenny peels a red lace garter off his thick thigh.

With her teeth.

While wearing handcuffs.

If this is an "emergency" by Zeke's definition, the English have a very weird way of viewing the world.

But anything's possible.

"RYAN!" he bellows as Jenny nearly gives him a testicular exam with her bicuspids. He stands and starts clapping rhythmically, in tune to some music I didn't notice until just now. It's heavy Euro dance music with a little country thrown in, a fusion that includes a fiddle.

All the women in the semi-circle around him stand and look at me, clapping and cheering, hair mussed, eyes loose and happy, cheeks aglow.

The bachelorette party. I scan the group. No Carrie.

"The stripper no-showed for poor Jenny! No woman should be stiffed on the eve of her wedding, right? I'm helping her out."

"Stiffed," someone says, then giggles through hiccups.

I take a deep breath, body flushing with the creeping sensation of having forty eyeballs crawling up and down every inch of skin I possess. Even through my clothing, I feel them evaluating me. Smiling while they take me in. Appreciating what their looking does to their emotional cores, triggering fantasies that transport them.

It's what I do for a living.

But I'm not on the clock right now.

Planting my hands on my hips, I square my shoulders, taking a stand. "You're more than enough man for all of them, Zeke." I wink at one of the women, who is tonguing the cocktail stirrer in her fruity drink like it's some guy's mushroom cap. "No need for reinforcements."

Every woman groans in disappointment. "C'mon, Ryan! There's always room for more!" Angela calls out to laughter.

"That's what she said," Zeke shouts, triggering more groans and cheers.

Out of the corner of my eye, I see Carrie come from the building, brow furrowed with a puzzled look. She grins at me, then laughs at the sight of Jenny crouched at Zeke's feet.

"Carrie! Can we borrow your boyfriend?" Zeke shouts. "We want him to feed you sexy beasts!"

"What?"

"He means," says Angela, giving me a coy look, "we need another stripper. And Ryan's a professional, you know."

I hide my reaction. If I just stare at Carrie, no one will know I'm yelling inside.

Carrie is a people pleaser. She looks at Jenny, then Angela. Jenny's sister, Jessie, starts laughing, holding a glass of something alcoholic high in the air. Everyone in this batch of twenty women is drunk as hell.

"Well," Carrie says, uncertain, her face flushed, the hair along her brow a little damp with sweat. "Um . . ."

The way she looks at me makes it clear Carrie's loose and feeling no pain either.

I reach for her hand, her clasp tight and strong, fingers on her other hand roaming up my bare arm, tracing my tats. She pushes me into a chair and climbs into my lap, straddling me.

Her hair tickles my nose as she bends down and says loudly, "I don't want to share. Sorry."

Zeke lets out a loud wolf whistle. "Then don't! Ryan can do a special dance just for you."

The music stops, Zeke grabbing the iPhone from the speaker it's attached to, fumbling with the screen.

And then the opening notes to *Earned It* by The Weeknd starts, the slow, sultry tones from the *Fifty Shades* movie making women move their hips like they're already making love.

Carrie does a slow, sultry grind in my lap, whispering, "I don't know what to do," in my ear.

I don't know what to do, either.

"You are so luscious," I groan, my breath echoing against her jawline, my lips on her neck before I can think.

The women around us start moving in time with the intense, overpowering grind of the song and Carrie's hips move against my cock like she's fucking me.

Too much. Too little.

Too public.

I pick her up in one fluid movement, suspending her against me in midair as she whoops with surprise, her hair windswept as an ocean breeze blows through the crowd, whipping the flames from a fire pit and making Zeke call out with boisterous fun, moving from woman to woman to give each a little piece of himself.

I settle her in the chair I was just in and start to dance, locking eyes with Carrie, the music fading into my pulse, the women around us disappearing into a void.

All I see is Carrie.

All I feel is her skin.
All I know is her eyes.
And all I want is her.

Carrie

I'M SO HAPPY. Three mojitos happy. One mojito, two mojito, three mojito—four? Not sure, but they're all happy.

Ryan smells amazing, like salt and soap and sand, timeless and old, but young and fresh. When we kiss, it's like drinking the best latte you've ever had, the kind that makes you moan and want more.

Wait. Am I *actually* moaning?

I break the kiss and realize he's on me, hands in my hair, body gyrating, except I've never seen Ryan dance like this before. Two years of working together at O means I've seen him do pretty much everything with our clients.

Everything legal, that is.

But he's never been like this before. Our eyes meet and he's so serious. A woman could burn for a thousand years from one look like this, his smolder lighting me up.

Making me burn for him.

"Car-rie! Car-rie!" the wedding party starts to chant as Ryan grinds into me, his cock sliding between my legs, the friction of him against my clit too much. Embarrassment rips through me and I clamp my thighs shut, suddenly cold, suddenly self-conscious.

"Only you, Carrie," Ryan says in a deep, sexy voice. "I'll only do this for you."

Angela shoves her fingers in her mouth and does a wolf whistle. Diane's drinking wine straight out of a bottle. Jenny is still kneeling before Zeke, her face in his crotch, and Jenny's mom has a tiny, battery-powered fan aimed at her face.

Then under her dress.

The world swims, filled with Ryan's hot, muscled body on mine.

And then I remember.

It's all fake.

Every move he makes is a show. Every kiss he's given me has been staged. I put him up to this. I asked him to pretend. He's just being a good, dutiful friend.

This is what he does for a living. He's a pro.

I asked the best to do me a favor, and boy *is* he.

My mouth goes dry. My throat tightens. My nipples turn painful, and my skin just hurts. I'm sick to my stomach with the kind of grief that you swallow when you have no choice.

I haven't been acting, have I? At some point everything I've done with Ryan has shifted from pretend to real.

When did it become real?

I shove Ryan off me, so hard he crashes into Jessie, who is quick on her feet and wraps her arms around his chest, keeping them both upright.

She flattens her palms on his belly and shouts, "I count eight! Eight pack for the win!"

And then I run, shooting down hallways, running past people who are staring at our little party.

The party I can't escape fast enough.

"Carrie!" Ryan's calling for me, but I ignore him, yanking open the stairwell door and sprinting up the steps.

I can't.

I can't pretend any more.

A hot ball of emotion forms in my gut like a new star, roiling and twisting, hot and fevered.

What have I done?

I race to my room—*our* room—and throw myself on the bed, the cool sheets like my mother's hand against my cheek.

Within seconds, though, I realize I've made another mistake as I look up to see Ryan standing before me, hands at his sides, giving me that smoldering gaze.

And just like that, it's time to be real.

Ryan

"WHAT THE HELL was *that*?" she hisses as the hotel room door clicks shut. Carrie is on the bed. Whipping around, the hem of her skirt twirling slightly as she stands, she rears up on me like a frightened horse. "What did you think you were doing back there, Ryan?"

"Having fun. Putting on a show." My mouth fills with copper. The conflict between pretend and real is bitter, a sour taste I can't stomach any longer. My smirk makes her face go blank, but only for a few seconds.

The replacement emotion is unthrottled fury.

"I can't believe you danced like that for the bachelorette party! You're not here to work. You're here to pretend to be my boyfriend!" Fuming, she grabs a pillow and punches it. "Every woman in that room ogled you." Her words are incriminating, accusatory, weighted with unspoken expectation.

I broke a rule I didn't know we had.

I broke a rule I knew damn *well* I hated.

"You *do* know what I do for a living, right?" I can feel my eyebrows hit my hairline. I gesture at my body, undoing my belt buckle, sliding the belt out of the loops.

Snap! I crack the two ends and make her jump.

"What are you doing?"

I drop the belt, undo the button of my pants, then reach up and rip off my own damn shirt, buttons pinging against the ceiling, the lampshade, the ocean-view window. In seconds I'm standing there in my boxer briefs, hand on one hip, giving her a show.

A private one, this time.

"I'm giving you exactly what every other woman in that room got. Go ahead. Look."

Her pupils go wide, breath catching in her throat. A few strands of wavy hair have pulled out of her hairstyle, curling down the lobes of her ears, brushing against the tops of her breasts. Her cleavage is the pink tone of outrage.

"I've seen you in a g-string a thousand times, Ryan." She pauses, eyes going up and to the right. "Literally. Two years of work is more than five hundred days we've been at O together, and I've looked at you twice each day." She closes her eyes and swallows hard, then makes a breathy sound. "At least."

The dismissive huff makes my blood boil, pulse rolling like a boulder in an avalanche. The air between us is an electromagnetic pulse that shuts down my thinking mind until I am nothing but instinct.

Near-naked instinct.

"Then why do you suddenly care that Jenny's bridesmaids and mother saw me like this?" I cross the room, determined, my arms tense and akimbo. Every hair on my body starts to rise, standing at attention, the creep of awareness capturing my skin.

"Because . . . because . . ." She tosses the pillow at me. I catch it and fling it to the floor, moving slowly like a big game cat, prowling to her, unafraid.

I'm done with fear. Just *done*.

"Kissing you in public is part of what you wanted, Carrie." I've gone low and cold, my heart thudding in my throat like a bell tolling at midnight, warning the world of the thin layer between light and dark. She's about to tip everything—our friendship, this fake relationship, the last two years of working together—into dangerous territory.

And I'm ready.

But that doesn't mean what we're about to say to each other doesn't have consequences.

"You know, if we really were boyfriend and girlfriend, that's not how I would kiss you!" she shouts.

"Oh yeah? Then how *would* you kiss me? Because that kiss in front of all those people was damn hot."

"So was your dance!" Our faces are inches away, her breath sweet, the rum in the mojitos she drank earlier drawing me in. The skin under her eyes pulls up as she scrutinizes me. Carrie's trying not to look at my body.

I grab her hand and put it flat against my stomach, willing her to feel the pulse there, to touch my center, to feel my heat.

"What are you *doing*?" Her voice cracks midway through the sentence, body betraying whatever anger she has and making her take a step closer to me. One hip brushes against my erection. I close my throat so I don't react.

"You're angry all those women ate me up like I'm eye candy."

"I didn't—"

"Admit it."

A dawning look of something damn close to admiration and revelation ripples across her face. It's like she's seeing me through a new lens.

She tries to pull her hand away but I hold her to me with an iron grip, closing the inches between us, my other hand on her chin, making her look at me. Our eyes say a thousand words.

"I—"

Releasing her hand, I reach up and thread my fingers in the hair at the nape of her neck. "If we really were boyfriend and girlfriend, how would you kiss me, Carrie?"

"Look, I just said that because I was . . . ." My hand in her hair prevents her from looking down, looking away, looking inward instead of straight through the bullseye of my heart.

Where she can see so much more than my naked flesh.

"Carrie," I insist, pressing her, the stakes too high to step back into the shade of safety. "How would you kiss me?" I move so close but hold back that final half inch, tortured by the blow of warm breath from her lips, the hesitation I feel in her tendons and bone, my own need on display.

"Ryan." My name sounds like a promise. A plea. A cry for help. A koan. A question. A riddle.

An exaltation.

I close my eyes.

And realize that half an inch might as well be a mile.

Her hand moves from my abs up the center of my breastbone,

fingers tracing the lines of my collarbone. I look at her. To my surprise and agony, she steps back, her hand staying on me, eyes riveted. Without a word but with so much purpose, my C-Shel takes her time enjoying me. I'm rock hard as she uses her fingernail to brush the thick vein that pops from my forearm to biceps. My blood turns me into a furnace as she grazes her fingertips along my side, counting each rib. When she steps back, breaking our physical connection, it's the look on her face that keeps us in touch.

I can't do this.

I can't breathe without her touching me.

Blinking hard, she clears her voice, turning around and stepping backward. Her hands tap the base of her neck as if giving instructions.

And then she says, "Unzip me."

With stupid, clumsy fingers caught off guard I obey the request. As she steps out of her dress, I watch the exquisite frame-by-frame release of the cloth as it drops away, revealing a shapely bustier, black lace panties, and legs that go for miles in tall heels. She's damn close to my height, a fact I hadn't considered until now, the jut of her ass a dream come true as the height of the shoes changes how she carries herself.

She turns around.

"Now we're equal. How would you feel if I walked out into public looking like this?"

"No fucking way. I won't allow it."

"See? You'd be jealous, too, and besides, 'allow'? Seriously, Ryan, when did you—"

Whatever she was about to say is buried by my mouth, my tongue, my hands, my cock, all on her and touching, exploring and demanding, silencing and opening her. Anger makes her kiss back hard, teeth banging together, her mouth opening and sucking my lower lip, biting down as if pinning me in place, as if telling me I can't escape.

"I won't allow it," I inform her, slipping my knee between her legs, pressing up with a slow, grinding beat that makes her gasp, her hand moving over my ass, fingers biting into my hip, pulling me closer to her, "because you still haven't shown me how you'd kiss me if we were really together, Carrie. Show me. Show me now."

Carrie

I DON'T KNOW what he means. Panic splits my mind in two.

Desire weaves it back into one whole. The two forces fight in a dark corner of my mind while my body won't stop touching him. This can't be happening, right? This is Ryan. My buddy. My friend. My couch potato and Friday night television binge partner and holy hell, I'm kissing him like my tongue is a part of his body.

He tastes so good. How does a man taste like all my dreams in one hot, warm, wet tease? My arms are around his neck and his hands cup my ass, pulling me against him as he uses his leg to drive me crazy, my clit rubbing through my panties as he—wait, is he seriously doing this? *How* is he doing this? No man has ever moved my body with such expertise, kissed me like that with his tongue, moved his fingers like that along my nipple, made my own body work in concert with his to—

"Oh, God," I moan into his chest, gripping his arm for balance as I start to shake, something deep inside widening and narrowing at the same time, like a secret chime being called in my core. Electricity rushes to the surface of my skin and I whimper, legs tightening as Ryan reaches down with his hand to touch me and that's it.

I disappear.

In my place comes heat and sighs, groans and cries, my head tipped back and hair falling out of my updo, spilling down my back, Ryan's strong arms holding me to him, making it impossible to escape the sheer bliss he's giving me.

"I've never—I—what are you doing?" I gasp, trying to wiggle away, desperate to move closer, completely unable to calibrate my mind and body as chaos takes over and turns me into a warm, wet noodle.

"What I should have done long ago," he says firmly, bending

down to lift me, moving across the room with confident strides and dropping me on the bed. The room is a hazy spell, the air filled with my orgasm, a sexy scent that combines with his masculine musk. It hangs in the air with nothing but promises of more.

More.

We're—we're actually going to—I'm about to—

"Turn over," Ryan says, face serious in the moonlight. I don't question him. I do as he says. He swiftly removes my bodice. I start to pull my shoes off. His hand grips my ankle.

"No. Leave those on."

His voice is so different, yet familiar. Simultaneously, he's Ryan and someone else. This feels like having a one night stand.

With my best friend.

"You're beautiful," he says, on the bed above me as I turn over, almost naked before him, breasts pulled slightly by gravity, belly flat, high heels on the bed as my knees go up. Ryan takes his time to look at me, an appreciative, unhurried quality in his eyes that I've never seen before.

Ever.

In any man who has ever looked at me naked.

I curl my hands into fists to stop them from covering myself or ripping the bedspread off the bed and flinging it over me. Nothing about him says he's displeased. In fact, Ryan seems utterly captivated by, well . . .

Me. Practically naked, laid out before him.

My pulse quickens as I return the look, and now he's staring at me with eyes that pierce, his hands moving to my belly, one curved around my breast, a half smile forming.

"You're more beautiful than I ever imagined."

"You've imagined me naked?"

He just smiles.

"Because I never had to imagine you naked," I blurt out, awkwardness rushing in to replace everything good about this moment. "I mean, you know, you wear a g-string at work and those really show everything so I never need to really conjure up an image of—"

His smile widens.

He removes his boxer briefs and holy hell, am I wrong.

Way wrong.

Like, *hugely* wrong.

"Oh," is all I can say, struck dumb.

"Your turn."

"My turn?" I squeak.

His finger curls under the edge of my lace panties, a silent gesture that's pretty damn clear. But he doesn't peel them off, leaving me the choice. It's my move, his fingers say.

All mine.

I sit up and kiss him instead, needing the anchor of his embrace.

"You're such a good kisser," he says.

I bark out a really mood-shattering laugh. "I am no such thing."

"If I say you're a good kisser, then you are, Carrie. You're not the judge of your own kissing ability."

"But I—" I frown. "Okay. That's some strong logic. Fair enough. What makes me a good kisser?"

"You kiss like you mean it."

"Explain, please. Because I don't know what that means, but then again, half my brain exploded with that orgasm you gave me with your thigh." Did I really just say that? Oh, God. If I could smother myself with one of these twenty-seven decorative pillows, I would.

"I gave you an orgasm with *my thigh*." He looks at the body part in question the way some guys look at power tools.

"And a little help from your tongue and fingers."

"They played a supporting role?"

"You could say that."

"My tongue would like the opportunity to play the lead."

"That can be arranged," I respond, my voice suddenly a thousand miles away as he kisses his way from the spot between my breasts down my belly.

"Wait until you see the orgasms I can give you with other body parts of mine. But tongue first."

"Is it hot in here? I'm feeling dizzy. And hot."

"You're hot all right. Hot and sweet and I need to taste you. Now."

I've never been so aware of my own breath, of how my body and my mind work together. Reaching down, I cover Ryan's hand at my hip, taking in the feel of the back of his hand, the thick muscle of his palm, the simple majesty of the size of his masculine hands. He retreats, respectfully, and I jut one hip up, making it easier to slip out of my panties, sliding them down and over my thigh-highs.

Now I'm naked. Naked, in heels and stockings, with my best friend on top of me, eyes dark with desire, broad chest expanding with every hushed breath, the room thick with anticipation.

Somehow, the silence is comfortable. It shouldn't be. Two Carries are at war inside me, one fumbling and awkward, the other deliberate and yearning. No man has ever treated my body the way Ryan is right now, with an expression of worship, a gentle, slow absorption that makes me wonder how I've lived for so many years without knowing that a man can look at me like this.

A woman could bathe in this kind of attention forever, floating in bliss, enveloped by the high regard of a lover who is here, fully, to enjoy and be enjoyed.

All my internal weirdness drains out of me, fading into the shadows as if it's been told to step down, told to go back and rest. Heal. Recover from years of being on guard for a battle that never ends.

In Ryan's eyes I see a warrior, a peacekeeper, a general with reinforcements.

A benevolent king.

His eyes tell me I am a queen.

His queen.

As he bends toward me, one hand stroking my ribs, his mouth descends over my breast, tongue circling my nipple with tight, wet heat. It feels so good, my belly moving as I begin to breathe, excitement infusing everything. With hesitation, I reach down and run my fingers through his hair, enjoying his touch at the same time I keep thinking, *This is Ryan!*

He slides up my body, kissing all the way, until his hard heat presses over me like a protective forcefield, his mouth taking mine in a kiss that makes me think *Oh, yes.*

This *is* Ryan.

I run my hands across his shoulders, fingertips brushing along the big, built joints, covered with fine muscle that feels so smooth yet so calibrated, honed through effort. He is raw power in motion, a gentle giant with my body as he breaks the kiss and moves down, down between my breasts, over my navel, kissing his way to that line of no return where his hands smoothly part my thighs and his face, oh, his face is between my legs and he's about to—

"You don't have to do that!" I gasp, my hands on my breasts, frozen. I want to reach for his head but he's right there, breathing warm fire on my vulnerable, wet clit, which throbs so hard, pulling toward him, wanting what he's about to give but terrified of the unknown.

"I—what?" Ryan kisses the inside of each thigh, drawing out his moves, moving up to my torso and staring right into my eyes.

"You don't, you know. Have to do, um, that."

"Do what, Carrie?"

I wave in the vague direction of my screaming, throbbing sex parts. "You know."

"Say it."

A new wave of wet warmth rushes between my legs. His voice is commanding, soft and urgent, with a steel tone that makes me feel like I'm a student in the hands of the ultimate master.

"Erm?" I squeak.

"Tell me what you don't want me to do, Carrie. Tell me," he says between taking mouthfuls of my nipple, "what you don't want. Because I don't think you can."

"You don't think I can tell you what I don't want?"

"I think you want everything I'm about to do to you. With you. In you."

THIS IS *RYAN!*

"I just mean, um, I know guys don't really like to do, um, that."

"That?"

"You know. Oral sex."

"You think guys don't like to lick you. To taste you. To slip their tongue between your legs and bury themselves in your sweetness?" He reaches down and uses his thumb to perform magic between my legs. Pure magic.

All the heat in my body rushes to my face, breasts, and clit. All of it. My organs turn to ice and my blood has fled to Argentina.

"Um, well." Words escape me. They all went to South America, too, along with most of my brain.

Ryan pauses. My body sputters, hips moving up to catch his touch again. "Carrie, who told you that?" His words are so soft, so skeptical. A little angry.

"What?"

"Who told you men don't like to do this?" He crawls down my body, shoving my legs apart fast, putting my knees up and heels on the bed. A blast of chilled air hits my exposed vulva and he dips his head between my legs, giving me one beautiful, perfect lick that makes me arch up, body begging for more.

Self-consciousness wars with the desire to let go, to follow Ryan's lead, to actually believe what he's saying.

"Carrie? Answer me." He's looking at me from between my legs, confident and bare, intent on hearing my answer. I can't get out of this, his eyes say.

"Every guy I've ever been with." It comes out like a laugh, a choked sob, a confession, a charge. "Or sometimes I could just tell."

"Then you've been with the wrong men, Carrie. Let me show you how much I want to do this. Let me show you how much I've fantasized about tasting you for all these years. Let me show you how it feels to have a man who wants more than anything to give you what you need." He shakes his head, eyes stormy. "And when I'm done, let me do it again."

Every word he speaks is a permission slip submitted to the part of me that resists, each sultry, earnest pleasure vow a code that opens the door inside me.

I let go, closing my eyes, letting out a long sigh that I hope he understands.

His tongue tells me in no uncertain terms that he does.

It's not that no one has ever done this to me, but the way Ryan does it makes my whole body yield to his ministrations, interconnected and entwined. Sex is something I do to connect on a deeper emotional level with men I love. Intimacy forges bonds. It has a purpose. It's pleasurable and nice, the cuddling afterward is a welcome retreat into affection that feels settled. Safe.

Anchored.

As Ryan slips one, then two fingers inside me and I clench around him, his touch rippling through me as if he's pulling me in, daring me to show him all of me, every sound, every nuance, every *everything*, his tongue isn't just performing a task or a ritual.

He's enjoying this.

He's truly enjoying *me*.

I've never been so naked and vulnerable and alive and excited with someone who urged me to go further, to give way, to be wet and wild. Someone who takes his time, enjoying himself and in no hurry. I'm squirming as an orgasm of a new sort starts to take over, a soaring, swollen sense inside me that fills every muscle, making me hold my breath then gasp for air. It's too much. I move so his tongue stops touching the spot that makes me feel like every blood vessel in my face is about to explode into rosy fireworks.

"Is this good?" he murmurs. "Tell me what you want, Carrie."

"Is this good?" I moan, my clit lit up like a Fourth of July sparkler, all my nerves jangling. I sit up and he moves to me, like grey smoke in human form, so languid and graceful. Our kiss fills my mouth with my own juices and I giggle.

"So that's what I taste like," I blurt out.

Ryan's shoulders drop, his face a blend of anger and understanding. "Oh, Carrie." His grin is that of a predator as he backs away, finding his place between my legs again. "We're not even close to finished."

This time, I put both of my hands on his head, loving the lush softness of his hair, my hands guiding him to rhythms I didn't know I had in me. Some part of me detonates, sending shockwaves of heat to the far corners and curves of my body, my core tightening at the same time I hold my breath and climb, climb, climb to to the top of the world.

I try to draw back, curl in, because the feeling is too intense, too wet, too dry, too cold, too hot, too luscious, too bold, too—

"Oh, oh, oh," I cry out, grabbing his hair, grabbing the sheets, grabbing thin air as if I am about to drift into space. He flattens one palm against my hip, making me feel, making me endure, making me turn every part of me into every part of him and I can't move, can't freeze, can't stop panting, can't stop–

I become everything.

The world pulses with me as Ryan follows my moving body, my fingers digging into his neck, his mouth smiling against me, tongue working that mystical chaos that splits me open and swallows me whole. I scream, a sound in the back of my throat that is all my muscles from the inside out trying to cry out his name.

Blood rushes to my head, a pulse in line with his strokes, and I go limp, little shocks nipping at my clit, my walls, my nipples, my thighs. I release layers inside me I didn't know were tense, and just when I think I'm done, Ryan looks at me, moving halfway up my body, and whispers, "You're so real, C-Shel. So beautiful. "

"Come here," I whisper, reaching for his chest, running my hands all over his rugged body. He's thick and huge, breathing hard and so big. Big chest, big arms, big thighs, big erection.

I want him inside me. I want to give him the pleasure he just gave me.

"I can't believe we're doing this," I murmur, amazed by his body, touching it so intimately after two years of looking at it mostly naked five days a week. But we're alone now. What a difference. He's tanned and sculpted, skin going tight every time my hand sweeps across it.

His body responds to me as I sit up on my knees and just take him in.

While I touch him, Ryan looks at me until he comes in for a kiss, making it long and full. Vibrant and restrained, he's so present. The ocean beats against the shore outside, loud and then lulling, and all I hear is the water and our heartbeats. I lick his collarbone, leaving a small love bite, my hand moving down the corded terrain of his eight pack, finding thicker hair, then his shaft, ready for me.

The groan he makes when I wrap my hand around him is so gratifying. I'm in a place where the world still spins with frantic joy, so I bend down to taste him, finding warm silk. His sharp whistling inhale is punctuated by an exhale of my name. When Ryan says it that way, I feel emboldened. Brazen. Empowered.

Ready to give. *Wanting* to give.

He's big. So big. That's not some cliché, and while I can count on one hand the number of guys I've slept with and still have room to flash the OK sign, even *I* know that this is, well . . .

Special.

He's so open with his body that I relax and pull him in, deep, my tongue flattening, spare hand unsure. Abruptly, he stops me, and I'm on my back, Ryan over me, cock hard and wet.

"If you keep that up, I'll come."

I give him a sly smile. "Isn't that the point?"

The look on his face is so endearing, so brutally honest and stripped of facade that my heart expands, filling my chest until I feel it in the marrow of my bones. He cups my breasts, touching them with great care, then kisses me gently.

"The point is to do this right. I want to make love. Not just get off, Carrie. It's . . ." He frowns slightly, brows coming together, and I see a vein in his forehead pop out. He's restraining himself, fists tight, and I'm aware of more between us than we had even seconds ago.

I sit up and kiss him, widening my legs, and as he lowers me gently onto the bed he tears something in his right hand and reaches between us.

"Condom," he whispers.

"I'm on the pill."

"Good to know."

And with that, he's in me, his forehead pressed against mine, the slick sweat of our bellies gliding against each other as he fills me, more and more with each stroke, an impossible fullness that grows as he moves. Just when I think he's reached as far inside me as he can get, he finds a way to give me more.

This is Ryan, I think as we rock our way to orgasm, his hips rising and falling, moving at angles that render me mute, his powerful arms on either side of me, encasing me in a tiny world our bodies make with motion and flesh, friction and skin, kisses and strokes.

He moves faster, instinct making me widen my legs.

"Wrap your legs around me, Carrie," he urges, the sound of my name on his lips as we fight for what comes next so arousing I damn near come now. I do as he says, my heels digging into his ass, which moves like a wild animal, all dominance, no mercy.

Something in me breaks, a snap I feel in my heart, like a new ship's ribbon being cut, the cry of a newborn, the finish line victory of a marathon runner. Tears spring to my eyes, pinpricks that fill and fill and fill me like Ryan, who is gasping my name, face buried in my hair, our bodies saying two years of feelings.

This is Ryan, I think as my last coherent thought before ecstasy washes me out to sea.

This is *Ryan.*

CHAPTER TWELVE

Carrie

HAVE YOU EVER seen that viral video of otters swimming in a bucket of water? Then you know what I look like getting into my maid of honor dress by myself.

That's right. By *myself*.

I woke up to an empty bed the morning after we made love, the morning of Jenny's wedding.

No Ryan. Again.

I'm sure there's a perfectly reasonable explanation for why he disappeared after a night of wild passion with me. When I opened my eyes, the room smelled like warm sex and coffee. There was a hot latte next to the bed.

Latte, but no note.

I refuse to panic. As I finish putting on my stockings, an unsure smile makes me chew my lower lip. He'll be back.

Right? Of course he will. Don't be silly.

I admit this is a flattering dress, and it achieves that with structural engineering that probably requires a college degree like Ryan's. But how are you supposed to fasten a row of hooks in the back of your own dress? It's not like a garter belt, where you can fasten it in front and just spin it around. By the time I manage closure, there are dark circles of sweat under both arms.

But my breasts are higher, my waist is smaller, and my ass is perkier than they were when I started. Too bad Ryan isn't here to see me.

The bridesmaids have finished brunch, hair, and makeup, and now we're supposed to get dressed for photos, three hours before the actual wedding. You heard me—three hours. I've been able to get a driver's license faster. It would have been easier if I could have asked Ryan for help with these hooks. Judging by the way he unzipped me last night, he knows his way around women's garments.

At least, he knows how to remove them.

Is that from working at O? From past girlfriends? Or just from having four sisters? And why do I care, anyway? Last night was just . . .

I don't know what last night was. But one way or the other, it changed my life.

Forever.

I take a last peek in the mirror. Several wisps of hair have pulled free from my updo, and are hanging down in inconvenient places. There are mascara smudges under both eyes. I blot the black circles with a tissue. It looks like the morning after a long night and I haven't even left the room yet.

"Oh well," I sigh, "It's about how Jenny looks, not me. No one's going to be looking at me." I dust on a little powder and head out the door. Wherever Ryan is, he'll join me at the wedding.

Right? A date's a date.

The wedding party is gathered outside on the lawn overlooking the ocean below, and Jenny is indeed a gorgeous bride. She's always been tall and thin, but Bridal Boot Camp defined her arms and sculpted her back. Her gown is a perfectly simple column of white satin, and although it's a surprisingly warm day, the Atlantic breeze keeps the temperature perfect. There's something so romantic about a long white veil billowing in the air.

"Carrie!" She rustles over and hugs me, enveloping me in a cloud of Cristalle perfume. "Your flowers are over on the table."

"Jenny, you look so beautiful!"

"I should!" she laughs. "Six professionals have been working on me for two days! It's never going to get any better than this. If I weren't the one wearing a long white dress, Aiden wouldn't recognize me."

"Where is he?" I ask, looking around. "I don't think I recognize him, either."

"He's over there with the ushers. The hotel just sent over a tray of IPAs. And a Champagne cocktail for Jamey." She smiles, then looks at me sweetly. "I am so grateful you're still in my wedding, Carrie. And that everything's working out so well for you. Ryan seems like a really great guy. And it's obvious he really loves you." Her eyes fill. "I want you and Jamey both to be happy, as happy as I am."

Before I can reply, Jenny's mom appears at her elbow and points to the photographer, who has set up his tripod and is waiting. Another quick hug and she moves off to take care of bride business.

What was it she said? *It's obvious he really loves you . . . obvious he really loves you . . .*

"You look great, Carrie." Jamey is standing a step behind me, Champagne flute in hand. The ushers are all wearing navy blue blazers and tan trousers, with coral-colored neckties patterned with scallop shells. Jamey has his Ray-Ban Clubmasters on, so I can't see his eyes. "I love your hair in that relaxed style."

"It's not relaxed," I snap. "It's falling down. It's a mess."

"Well, whatever it is, it suits you." His voice is soft and sincere.

I open my mouth to say something bitter and sarcastic, to give him a piece of my mind, to make him sorry he ruined my life.

And I close it again. Is my life really ruined?

"Thank you," I say instead. "You're looking pretty snappy yourself."

I glance around, confused. Did I just say that? It sounded very much like normal polite conversation between friends. Couldn't have been me.

He leans forward, obviously relieved. "Frankly," he whispers, "the whole clamshell theme is a little bit overdone. Right?"

"They're in the centerpieces," I whisper back conspiratorially. I can't resist. "There are chocolate shells in the swag bags."

He holds up his paper cocktail napkin, printed with Jenny and Aiden's names and . . . yep. Clamshells.

"Etsy," we say at the same time.

An unexpected giggle bursts out of me. It feels familiar and good.

"I saw Ryan this morning, out for a run," Jamey says as we wipe our eyes. "You know, I always thought there was a spark between you two. Very hot . . . but isn't he kind of young for you? I mean, what do you talk about?"

I start to object, because Ryan's only six and a half years younger, actually six years and five months, and while that's a big difference it's not *that* big, but we're interrupted.

"We talk about politics," someone interjects. "Global warming. JD Vance's memoir, net neutrality, Amy Schumer's latest tweet. When we're not in bed, that is." Ryan is standing next to me, glowering, his shadow stretched out over the space between me and Jamey as if it seeks to intimidate. "When we're in bed, which is most of the time, we don't talk much."

"So," I squeak, "you've met, right? At O?" Of course they have. I'm just babbling again. Ryan is touching me for the first time since I fell asleep against him last night, naked and stunned, connected and overjoyed. My heart pitter-patters in my chest, pushing against the body-shaping structure of my dress, as Ryan becomes my world once again, consuming me.

"We've met," Ryan says, holding out his hand. "How've you been, Jamey?"

I do a little double take when I actually look at Ryan. He's wearing a lightweight tan suit, cut for his body, and a crisp white shirt with a light blue tie. His hair, still damp from the shower, is brushed back. He smells like limes and basil. He smells like masculinity. 10.5, headed for 11.

"Never been better, actually." Some weird tension crackles in the air, which is impossible, right? Because Jamey is gay, so it's not like there's any competition between the two men. What would they compete over, anyhow?

"Oh, I'm sure that's not true." Ryan looks at me with such un-abashed sensuality that even Jamey blushes. "Anyone who's ever dated Carrie knows that time spent with her can't be surpassed by anything."

Jamey's eyes narrow but he says nothing, looking at me as if this is my fault. As if I'm supposed to step in and fall all over myself to stop Ryan. As if I'm responsible for whatever comes out of my fake boyfriend's mouth.

As if everything is my fault.

"I really do wish you the best, Jamey," I whisper, trying not to die inside. Two voices scream inside the echoing cavern of my mind, one telling me to give Jamey my full blast of anger, the other prac-tically begging me to just give in and smooth it all out by sacrificing my dignity.

Or maybe by keeping my dignity. Smoothing it out wins.

Ryan squeezes me, just hard enough to make me gasp. He gives Jamey a dead-on, laser-focused stare.

"Too late, C-Shel. He already had the best." Then he kisses me on the cheek, pulling me even closer. My pushed-up breast smashes into his chest and the heady scent of his aftershave, soap, and the radiating, pure, righteous fury on my part that is fueling his words all fill my senses.

Unsure and reeling, I act on impulse, standing on tiptoe and turning my face toward his until we're kissing, his mouth angry, but not at me.

For me.

It's refreshing to have someone feel something *for* me.

The kiss is everything I've wanted from a partner, a soulmate, a live in-the-flesh man who desires me so much he'll slide his hand up my back, tangle it in my hair, kiss me breathless and ignore the uncomfortable sounds of people we're offending by this wild display of naked passion.

I break away, panting, my lips raw.

Because what's the point? This isn't real. Last night wasn't real.

Nothing is real.

Jamey's feelings for me weren't real. I mean, he thought they were, but they weren't. Ryan's anger might be, but the affection sure isn't. It's all an act.

And I'm tired of acting.

"You blew your chance, Jamey. Thank you for that." Ryan sticks his hand out again while his other arm grips me. Surprised, Jamey takes the handshake out of instinct. I watch Ryan grab hard, his forearm muscles flexing, part of his tattoo peeking out from under his shirt and bulging as his jacket and cuff ride up slightly.

"Uh, hey, man, my pleasure." Jamey looks confused, but he quickly covers it up, smile tightening to one of irritation, jaw grinding as he realizes what Ryan's doing.

"Actually," Ryan says loudly. "The pleasure will be all mine." He winks. "And Carrie's, of course." The look he gives me sucks all the air out of my body.

What is he doing? It's too much. He's pretending and I'm not, and the pain, oh the pain. My dress is too tight. The world is too heavy. Nothing allows me to breathe because I can't inhale in a world where what happened last night isn't real.

"Wedding party!" Jenny's mom shouts. "Wedding party to the terrace, please, for photos!"

Saved by formalities.

She deftly removes beer bottles from the hands of two ushers and shoos them toward the photographer. Coming to a halt in front of me, her navy blue chiffon sleeves fluttering in the breeze, she frowns.

"Carrie, what has *happened* to you? Your lipstick is all over your face and your hair is falling down, and we haven't even started yet! We need to fix you."

"Someone sure does," I say under my breath. "Good luck with that."

She glances at Ryan. "And her lipstick is all over *your* face, too." She hands him a tissue from her bag. "Jamey, they're waiting. Get over there," she continues, undeterred from her task of rounding everyone up. "You look very handsome, darling. Remember your left side is your best." She adjusts his boutonnière slightly and moves on toward the photographer's assistant. They bend their heads together, Jen's mom gesturing in my direction. The assistant nods, looking concerned.

With a small eye-roll, Jamey sets off toward the groomsmen, who are being pushed and pulled into alignment for the camera.

"I'd better go," I tell Ryan. "Are you okay just hanging out for a while?"

"Sure," he says, "I'm fine. I think I'll get one of those local IPAs from the bar."

"The wedding's supposed to start soon. After that, I'll be a lot more free."

"No worries. The reception'll be fun."

And then he meets my eyes.

For the first time all weekend, it's like we're really looking at each other. I mean, not in a fake-boyfriend, fake-girlfriend, performing-for-an-audience kind of way, but like we're completely alone. All the breath goes back into my body. All of it. Every bit of oxygen in the whole, wide world.

Ryan leans toward me and softly, gently, his lips meet mine. Not rough and hard, not muscular and groping, just . . . us. A kiss that connects us and holds us together in time, because that's what we both want. What we both choose. A kiss that lingers and breaks apart slowly.

Different. New.

I muster up my courage. "Ryan, we really need to talk—"

"Um, excuse me, you're Carrie, right?" The photographer's assistant, clearly embarrassed, looks like she's contemplating a career change. Taxidermy, maybe—something where the subjects stand perfectly still and exhibit no emotions whatsoever.

I can't answer her because I have forgotten my name. She soldiers on.

"The bride's mother asked me to, um, see if you, um, need any help with photo prep?"

I stare at her blankly.

"Um, makeup? Hair?" she tries. "They're shooting the brides-maids next."

Ryan's lips brush against my jaw light, light and feathery, enough to make me shiver and smile. "It's okay. We can talk later. I know you have wedding responsibilities." He eyes me appreciatively, his whole face smiling, eyes shining. "Go be the best maid of honor ever."

"That's not exactly a goal of mine," I admit, but laugh.

"You can't help it, C-Shel. Like I told Jamey, you're the best." He's standing so close to me, a few inches taller, the sun high in the sky. When he looks at me like this, his body shielding me from the wind, I feel so safe. Impossibly comfortable and filled with potential.

Maybe—just maybe—these feelings are real?

"Stop," I protest. "You don't need to flatter me." I can't let my-self dare crack open the vault of repressed emotion that allows me to function on a day like today. After opening myself up last night in every possible way—no matter how deliciously toe-curling—I need a little restraint.

His smile fades, replaced by an even hotter contemplative look. "Not flattering. Just telling the truth, Carrie."

The photographer's assistant clears her throat.

"I'll see you at the ceremony," he says. "I'll be in the back, on the bride's side. Ignore me until the reception."

Before I can say anything, he turns and leaves, long strides eating up the ground beneath his feet. My heart plays a tambourine in my chest as I reconcile the friends we were with the . . . whatever we are now. My belly tightens, tingling as I remember his hands on me last night, my legs around his hips, how he sighed against my neck, how his kisses went on and on and on until I floated away on the feeling of endless connection with Ryan.

Right or wrong, we crossed a line last night. Watching him dance in front of all those women, with his body over mine as he dipped and stroked, teased and moved in the moonlight until I couldn't stand it, couldn't keep pretending, made my flight instincts kick in. I fled.

And he followed.

Making love—can I call it that?—wasn't what I expected after I ran back to the room. But now it's all I can think about. Ryan's mouth. Ryan's hands. Ryan's naked body, so strong and powerful over mine, the interplay between our unclothed skin so new, so hot, yet holding so many questions.

It was real for me. Was it fake for him? How could it be so perfect if it was just pretend?

Funny how he looks like the perfect Instagram man, unposed, the light slightly off, and yet he *is* perfect.

In every way. I couldn't wish for better.

Ryan

FOR ONCE, I don't hate Jamey.

Just this one time.

He focused me, gave me an excuse to approach Carrie and touch her, feel her. Gauge her. This morning, I was up and out the door long before she woke up. Went for a run, but before that, I spent entirely too long watching her sleep, hair mussed, lips red from so much kissing.

Never enough kissing.

The reality of what I did last night—what *we* did—still hasn't seeped into the marrow of my bones where it should reside, permanent and lasting. Instead, it floats like tiny hairs on gooseflesh, rising to the occasion but unsure what to do next.

She's torn away from me by the photographer, ready to be paraded around and admired the way she should be, though today she's a backdrop. An extra. Part of the pretty scenery that showcases Jenny and Aiden.

At our wedding, Carrie will be in the spotlight, front and center.

Sweat breaks out on my forehead and palms.

Our wedding.

Where did *that* thought come from?

"Doing okay there?" Chloe asks, walking up to me as Nick holds her hand, fingers threaded intimately. He's using his other palm as a visor, watching the wedding party as they walk carefully up a sand dune, trudging to the top as the wind sweeps Jenny's lace veil like a kite tail, licking the heads of the groomsmen.

"I'm fine. Why?" I ask, struggling to keep my voice even.

"You look so serious."

I break out a sexy smile. You know, the kind I'm paid to flash. "This better?"

Chloe frowns. Nick drops his hand and gives me a neutral look. "Weddings make people re-evaluate their lives." He turns to look at Chloe, who meets his gaze. She's focused and ready, attentive yet contemplative. Even more than usual.

And very clearly trying to read Nick's layered statement.

"Weddings make women go crazy," I say, trying to lighten the mood.

Nick laughs, but he still looks at Chloe. "All the details take over, but underneath it all, you're promising forever to someone."

"Forever," she whispers.

They share a smile that makes my chest hurt. A deep breath just pushes the pain around, the buttoned business shirt under my suit jacket straining, my tie trying to kill me.

Everything feels tight. Close. Claustrophobic.

"Excuse me," I tell them, turning and walking away before Nick or Chloe can respond. I need air. Ignore the fact that I'm on the beach and a giant breeze is blowing.

I need space.

From my own emotions.

As I guzzle unsweetened ice tea from a big glass dispenser with lemon, lime, mint and cucumber slices—an entire produce section—floating in it, I look up just as the sun hides behind one of the rare clouds in the sky, making the line of men and women in the wedding party stand out against the clear, cerulean sky.

Carrie's on the very end, her skirt elegant, angled just so, laughing with such unrestrained joy I damn near can't stand it. She's captivating, a vision of pure abundance and love, her raucous, unremitting happiness the closest I'll ever come to seeing heaven.

Assuming I make it there.

A man could die in the middle of watching her laughing on the wind and be complete.

But I want more.

"Food's getting set up," Zeke says, suddenly appearing behind me, offering up a craft beer from some brewery in Maine.

"You're drinking already? The wedding is about to start!" As I judge him, I realize he's onto something.

He smirks. I take the beer and drink half. Why not? Liquid courage might come in handy later.

As I finish my guzzling, the back of my neck tingles. A drop of ice-cold water from the bottle's condensation drips on my wrist. I don't react.

Zeke's staring at me.

"What?"

"You did it, didn't you?"

"Did what?"

"Got laid."

I stare back.

He chuckles, a deeply annoying sound that makes me want to break the bottle and slice his vocal cords. The noise reminds me of being bullied, of the grunts of derision kids made on the playground, the mocking huff of someone judging you for being earnest.

Real.

Yourself.

"You did, didn't you? You're looser. Distracted, but all that tension you've carried in your shoulders is gone." Wink. "Drained right out of you." He lets out a low whistle. "Carrie any good in bed?"

The smell of beer and shock fills my nostrils as I grab Zeke's shirt collar, in his face, whispering in a deadly rasp, "You don't talk about her like that."

We're frozen, eye to eye, toe to toe. I'm a big guy. Zeke's a big guy.

Big guys can do a lot of damage to each other.

"I'm not your enemy, mate," he says in a controlled voice, the tone we reserve for the angry husbands who discover their wives are frequenting O.

"And I'm not some wuss you make fun of, dude. Lay *off*."

He holds his palms up, eyes round, the skin across his forehead folding with real emotion. "I'm sorry. I am. Crossed a line."

I let go of him.

"You did."

"You're really in love with her, aren't you?" He asks with a tone of what I swear is reverence. Impossible.

"Yes," I confess.

"Man."

"I know." As we stand down from nearly shredding each other, we go back to that easy friendship that comes from giving no fucks. I'm done. I just don't care anymore about pretending when it comes to my feelings.

"Must be nice."

"It's not. It's torture."

Suddenly, in the distance, the entire wedding party leaps in the air, squealing and shouting. Giggles and good-natured male laughter fill the air, carried to us by a thick breeze.

"I mean it, Ryan. Sorry. Good for you." He seems dejected.

"Why are you acting like we're at a funeral and not a wedding?" I'm calming down. Zeke's not my opponent. Jamey isn't either. No one is, really.

Aside from me. I'm my own biggest obstacle.

A quick head shake and he's back to grinning. "I'm not at a funeral *or* a wedding. I'm at a wake."

"A wake? For who?"

"For your poor cock. Paying my respects, because it's about to get tied down, and once you're tied down, might as well be dead." He salutes my crotch by touching the mouth of his beer to his forehead.

"You are so fucking weird."

"As long as I'm fucking at all, mate. Call me whatever you want."

Carrie makes her way toward us slowly, stopping to chat with the other wedding party members, then with Jenny's mom and dad.

"You gonna tell her? Or did you already?"

"Tell her what?"

"The truth about how you feel."

"I will. I just . . ."

"What?"

"Need to make sure she feels the same way."

"You *are* a wuss, Ryan. Have you seen the way Carrie looks at you? Of course she feels the same way. What more do you need? A billboard in Times Square?"

"I know. I guess. I—"

"She fucked you, right?"

I bristle. "We didn't fuck."

"I thought you said . . ."

"We made love."

I deserve his groan. I do. Even having this conversation with Zeke would have been impossible a few days ago. Who opens up to an asshole like him?

Me. I'm that desperate. Not desperate enough to talk it out with one of my sisters, but spilling my guts to Zeke is damn close.

"You're together, then?" Zeke asks, stuffing a giant bacon-wrapped shrimp in his mouth. The reception has been moved outdoors, with no need for a tent. He's filching food before it's officially set up, but Zeke clearly subscribes to the idea that it's better to ask forgiveness than permission.

"Together?" Even my own voice sounds idiotic.

"Real boyfriend and girlfriend? No more of this fake shit?" Smugness radiates from his pores. "I knew this would work."

"Knew *what* would work?"

"Convincing you to be her pretend date."

"You give yourself *way* too much credit. I was already thinking about offering. Besides, we're still not together."

"Oh, please. You're together. People like you don't just have a fun fuck and then walk away from each other. You're not pretending, and Carrie sure as hell isn't playing some game. I've seen how she is with you. This is real, Ryan. Better like the taste and feel of her, because that's all you're getting for the rest of your life." He drinks more beer, then shakes his head at me. "Sad bastard."

"You're wrong." But he's right.

"We'll see."

The string quartet plays a sprightly tune meant to get guests to herd themselves to the actual wedding ceremony. I put my empty glass on a tray and head over to the very last row of chairs, taking my place on Jenny's side.

Zeke follows me.

All I can say about the forty-minute wedding ceremony is this: good thing Jenny and Aiden aren't Catholic. Forty minutes of listening to them read vows to each other was more than enough.

Add in the fact that Aiden is a linguistics professor; the recitation of his vows in Gaelic, some clicking language from Africa, and Aramaic was overkill. Just rent a plane with a banner like the rest of us.

While the foreign languages went over my head, so did the rest of the words. I just watched Carrie, sweetly smiling, crying on cue, and supporting Jenny through the ceremony.

I just want Carrie back in my arms.

Weddings should be special, but they're not. Not to me. With four older sisters, I've been a junior usher, an usher, the guest book person, and worn a tux for too many fancy occasions. Caught two garters, too—both before I'd ever even kissed or been kissed.

The fast track to the reception is much appreciated by everyone but the parents, and soon people make a beeline for the food and alcohol.

More guests fill in the giant courtyard, holding glasses of Champagne and tea, milling about the food and beginning to sample. A small band, led by a jazz saxophone, plays smooth melodies, completing the Cape Cod wedding feel. Hours of fun and celebration extend before us, unstructured and unscheduled. Weddings are about love.

"Zeke!" Eileen van Donner says his name like she's having an orgasm. "I thought I saw you here. Can you spare a few minutes away from your friend to reconnect with me?"

"Reconnect?" Zeke makes it clear he understands that word is code for sex. "I would love to reconnect with you, Eileen." He winks at me. "Ryan's not able to reconnect. Ever. He's on perma-hold."

He leaves.

I drink beer.

I look for Carrie, finding her in a group congregated around the bridal party table. Jenny and Aiden are nowhere to be seen, but the rest of the bridesmaids and ushers are eating appetizers and drinking, looking a bit dazed from the wedding.

"Hey, beautiful," I say to Carrie, who gives me a bright-eyed look, then drops her eyes as she drinks from a Champagne flute.

Jessie is next to her, giving Carrie a jealous look. "You have a brother?" she asks me.

"Four sisters. I'm the baby."

"All the good ones are taken," she grumbles.

Bzzz.

I jump, my hand grazing Carrie's ass as the unexpected call comes in on my phone. "Excuse me," I say, just as Jamey takes the microphone and calls the guests to come for the best man's toast. I give Carrie an apologetic shrug and look at my phone.

Mom.

An uneasy feeling starts in my gut. Why would Mom call me so soon after our last conversation? As the guests find their places at tables, I find a quiet spot to talk, half-jogging out of the courtyard and into an empty hallway indoors.

"Hello?"

"Ryan? Sweetie? It's Mom." Something about her tone makes me go cold.

"I know, Mom. I have caller ID. Is everything okay?"

"It's your father."

"What's—what's wrong?"

"He's fine," she assures me. "He just . . . I think you need to come visit sooner rather than later. We were looking at old photo albums today and he didn't recognize you once you were out of childhood. Kept pointing at pictures of you when you were in high school and calling you Milt."

Milt is my uncle. Dad's brother. I look nothing like him.

"Oh." My hand shakes as I run it through my hair, shoulders hunching. Of all the times to field a call like this. Jamey's voice floats through the air, his toast about to start. I hear people moving chairs, instruments being tuned, the rush of the ocean and the beating of my own heart, steady but fast, over it all, under it all, merged in between.

"I know you're busy, Ryan, but—he recognizes Dina, Ellen, and Michelle. Tessa mostly, too. And this is the first time he couldn't place you in a picture as an adult."

"It's that bad? Really, Mom?"

"He's fine most of the time! And maybe I'm just being an alarmist. Next week he sees his doctor for a full evaluation. Sometimes these problems with memory turn out to be a side effect of medication. Maybe it isn't inevitable."

Inevitable.

A group of giggling women walk by, two of them familiar. One waves, fingers waggling, her look a come-on.

Gia. Gina. Twins. That's right—the ones with Zeke in the elevator the other night. Instead of flashing my professional smile, I turn away, ignoring them.

"I planned to visit in a month, Mom."

"Ellen told me about grad school. That would be perfect." I can feel the relief and expectation in Mom's voice.

I go silent.

"Don't be mad at her, Ryan. She's as worried about Dad as I am, and thought I should know what you're planning. I'm so proud of you."

"Don't be. Not yet. I haven't gotten in."

"You will. That's what you do, Ryan—you pick something you

want and you don't let anyone stop you. You've been like that since you were a little boy."

Mom's words make me blink.

You pick something you want and you don't let anyone stop you.

If I don't go to California, I won't be able to help with my dad. If I go, I lose Carrie.

If I ever had her in the first place.

"This is too much," I mutter. In the distance, Jamey's voice carries on the microphone system, his best man toast in full swing, people laughing at appropriate intervals. Music swells and someone announces the bride and groom as Mr. and Mrs., the air ripe with a song I recognize converted into a slow jazz tune for the first, symbolic wedding dance.

"I'm sorry. But I need to turn to you and tell you these things about Dad," Mom says.

"I didn't mean—it's okay, Mom." I sigh. "Tell me what you want me to do."

"Can you call Dad? Do that Timeface thing with him on the computer? Last time you were home you set it up for us, but then Dad fiddled with the computer and I think he broke it."

"Facetime, Mom. It's called Facetime. And yes, I can. I'll make more of an effort. Get Jane over to the house and she can fix it." Jane is my eleven-year-old niece, Ellen's daughter, and girl coder extraordinaire.

"Jane's here baking cookies. I'll ask her." Mom gasps. "Ryan! I completely forgot you're at that wedding. How is Carrie? Am I going to meet her someday?"

I happen to walk past a big picture window where I can see the entire wedding reception. Carrie's under a tall canopy with the rest of the wedding party, everyone's attention on the bride and groom as they dance. She's whispering something to Angela, both of them holding Champagne glasses, and then they laugh.

Carrie scans the room.

She's looking for me.

"Ryan? You there?" Mom asks.

Just as I open my mouth to reply to my mother, to tell her yes, she'll meet Carrie one day, that yes, I'm in love with her, that yes, Dad will be fine and yes—I can fix everything—I see Jamey approach Carrie and take her hand, kiss it, then lead her to the dance floor.

Something in me snaps.

"I'm here, Mom. And yes, you'll meet Carrie someday." *I hope.*

"Oh, that's great! I'm so happy for you, sweetie!"

"I have to go, Mom. Wedding stuff. Love you and Dad."

Click.

By the time I reach the reception, the band is playing a jazzed-up version of a Mumford & Sons song, Jamey holding Carrie close and talking to her softly, the other ushers and bridesmaids all paired off in couples that dance around Jenny and Aiden. The bride's parents and both sets of the groom's parents are dancing.

I don't care about decorum, so I cut in, interrupting Jamey mid-sentence with a look that says I assume he'll move.

He does. Smart man. And I think I see a little smile on his face as he moves off.

The second I'm touching Carrie, the world rights itself again. Her warmth, her scent, the soft press of her dress fabric against my palm, the brush of her loose curls against my nose all add up to a grounding I can't get from an anti-static wristband or a heel grounder. She's my emotional core, my heart's lightning rod, my true North.

And as I pull her into my arms, I realize it's time to tell her.

"Hi—Ow! Oof!" she says softly, moving her high-heeled feet to my left. "Ryan, can you lead a little more?"

I sway slowly to the music, my hands on her hips, one of her hands going up to my shoulder, the other on my waist. "Okay."

I crush her toes again.

"What are you doing? Quit joking around! I don't have enough toes for this."

"I'm not—what do you mean, joking around?"

"Ryan, you're a master masseur. You dance at work. There's

no way you're really this clumsy. You must be pretending." Carrie winks at me.

Pretending.

"Uh, no. I really am this bad at slow dancing." It's like I'm in eighth grade again, terrified to touch a girl, mind racing a million miles a second, my body not quite mine. None of that is true, of course. I'm twenty-seven, sexually experienced, the size of a tight end and a piece of eye candy manmeat for O Spa clients, but it doesn't erase the old Ryan buried deep inside me who is standing here in disbelief that a girl is letting me touch her *at all*.

Carrie laughs. "You faker."

I lean down, barely dodging her foot, and whisper, "I'm not faking, Carrie. Not in any way."

Her whole body quivers, a violent shake that lasts for less than a second. Is that because *she's* really faking? Last night was too real. No way.

No fucking way was that pretend.

Before I can spill my guts and tell her how I really feel about her, the music ends, an abrupt transition that leads to applause for the bride and groom, wine glasses chiming in the night as people tap forks on them, chanting "kiss kiss kiss."

We're not the bride and groom, but who am I to disappoint a crowd?

Carrie

I'VE HAD TWO glasses of Champagne. Or three. Obviously that explains this bubbly feeling as Ryan kisses me. I think I might be a little tipsy. Why else would I be having this much fun?

As his lips press against mine and his hands touch me like he means it, I find myself letting go in his arms, just wanting this to be real. Ryan and I need to talk. We need to do more than talk. A *lot* more.

Right now, all I want more of is his mouth.

It's just a normal wedding reception, with a normal band. The usual steak dinner, the usual cake. I probably go to four of these a year. But this one is so much *better*. For some reason, I feel wonderful. I feel . . . like the world is full of goodness and possibility.

Strange.

I am dancing. With Ryan. With his arms around me, and stepping on my toes, and laughing. I want to do that again and again. I need to do that. I break away, regretfully ending the kiss, and smile at him.

"I need a minute," I say, patting his chest, reaching up to run my finger along his jaw.

That look. The way he's staring at me, like he worships me. It can't be pretend, can it?

Can it?

We really need to talk.

But first I need to use the ladies' room. And there are *a lot* of women in here.

Because I go to so many weddings, I can tell you that there is always a traffic jam in the ladies' room at the reception, and it's not the peeing that's the problem. It's the mirror. There are at least eight women ahead of me, waiting for mirror space.

There's no one in here I know, so I pull out my phone to pass the time until it's my turn. And find a text from Ryan: *They're playing Cotton Eyed Joe, where are you?*

Smiling, I type: *Be right back*

This is definitely a great wedding.

"This is ridiculous," Chloe says at my elbow. You should see her dress, oh my God. Ice blue with lime green flowers embroidered on the skirt. Lime sandals. *So* cool. And she always looks like she just threw it on, no effort involved. "I have a purse mirror. I'll hold it for you if you'll hold it for me. We can use hand sanitizer for our hands."

"Deal," I tell her.

Three minutes later, we emerge from the ladies' room with powdered noses and fresh lipstick. We stand for a moment, scanning the crowd.

"Having a good time?" she asks me. "How's it going with Ryan?"

"I'm having an amazing time," I confide. Just hearing his name gives me a happy little shiver.

"I know you told me in the coffee line that you were both acting, but I have to say, it doesn't look pretend," Chloe says.

I laugh. "He's seven years younger. A masseur at O. We're not exactly, you know, compatible."

A waiter squeezes between us with a huge tray of wedding cake slices and strawberries, interrupting my words for a moment or two. A noisy group of guests shifts to make room for him, and he passes through without an accident.

"Not compatible on the surface, I mean. Most people would never guess we have as much in common as we do. We've been friends since the day we started work, and we hang out, but—I don't know—something feels different now. Remember what you told me that day in your office, when I was so upset?"

"Remind me," she smiles.

"I think you said that I would never find the right person if I was totally focused on Jamey. Actually, I think you said 'the wrong guy,' but that was Jamey." I take a deep breath. "There's just one problem."

"What's that?"

"Ryan really *is* pretending. He's doing it for me, as a favor, so I don't have to look pathetic in front of everyone. I'm pretending, too."

"No, you're not." Chloe's reply is so fast, so matter-of-fact that I gape at her.

"*What?*"

Chloe spots Nick across the room and waves, then turns to me and puts her hand on my arm. "There is one thing I know for sure," she says seriously. "One of the most dangerous things you can do in a relationship is assume you know what the other person is feeling. Never, never assume. Talk to him. I see the way he looks at you. It's really obvious you have deeper feelings for him, too."

"I know. I need to talk to him."

"Sooner rather than later, Carrie. I think he'll surprise you." She gives me a quick hug before chasing down Nick, the two of them laughing as they begin to dance.

Nick doesn't step on Chloe's feet even once.

Ryan

I HEARD THAT.

Loud and clear.

" . . . not exactly, you know, compatible." Straight from Carrie's mouth to Chloe's ear. No ambiguity. No what-ifs. No does she or doesn't she?

She doesn't.

For someone who was pretending, last night was so real. Maybe I made it more real than it really was.

No *maybe*.

I did.

Shit. My heart speeds up in my chest like a motorcycle at full throttle, gaining asphalt, eating gravel. It's trying to climb out of my chest and run away.

Flee.

Escape.

She doesn't feel what I feel. This really has been fake for her. All those kisses, the touches and the caresses, the making love—

Stop it.

Not making love.

Fucking.

Zeke's right.

We fucked. That's it. That's all it was. Carrie's been pretending and the sex was what—an afterthought? A rebound from Jamey? I was just a convenient tool for her.

I was a tool, all right.

A fine, slippery sweat breaks out all over me, down my back, rippling across my shoulders, coating me in a wet armor that chills me as much as it heats my shaking skin.

I need to get the hell out of here.

I was so wrong.

The only way out, though, is past Carrie and Chloe. Might as well walk on hot coals while balancing all my body weight on the tip of my cock.

That would be preferable to this.

Deep breath, Donovan, I tell myself, remembering every point of failure in my life. The time I lost the spelling bee in third grade. Who thought it would be a good idea to add a silent W to *wreckage*? Dangling from Mr. Aglioti's fence. Asking Rachel McMasters to junior prom and having her laugh in my face.

Being tossed in the pool at high school after-prom by the football quarterback. Didn't even need a linebacker to manage that with my scrawny self back then.

None of that compares.

Not one fucking bit.

I was wrong about Carrie, but I was right, too.

Right to be afraid.

For the last two years, she's been dating Jamey. I'm a nice guy. Carrie's fun to be around. But I've been friend-zoned the entire time.

A sick laugh comes out of me, turning into a cough, making me curl into myself from the searing pain in my gut as the emotional punch kicks in.

The taste of her. Open-mouthed kisses that made me open my heart. The feeling of sliding into her, how she grasped my hips, her sighs and moans of pleasure making me feel whole. The prism of life turning slightly, allowing me to see Carrie differently, to be seen by her as more than a friend, as an intimate, as someone *more*.

"It doesn't look pretend," I hear Chloe say, the words loud enough to cut through my pain, earnest enough to turn me stupid again, filling me with hope.

The crowd of wedding guests jostles and shifts, laughing and calling out. For a minute I can't hear a thing, but then Carrie laughs.

"Ryan really is pretending. He's doing it for me, as a favor, so I don't have to look pathetic in front of everyone. I'm pretending, too."

That's *it*.

I take a few fast, shallow breaths, hands curled into fists, and look sharply to my left.

Jamey's standing there, watching me. He's heard every word. He's looking at Carrie with a perplexed expression.

Then he catches my eye and shrugs unhappily.

My ears fill with the sound of jet engines starting, the *whoosh* of my own blood beating against my ears and skull too exquisite, too full. I walk past them. Carrie gives me a startled look, then waves.

I wave back, Chloe a blur of big eyes and a wine glass that glitters in the sun. Carrie's face is flushed and she looks a little guilty, like I caught her doing something wrong.

The walk to the hotel room is a blur. Packing takes two minutes when you don't care, all my shit thrown into my suit bag and zipped up, shaving cream and deodorant rolling around in the bottom. I storm downstairs to valet parking and wait impatiently, crawling out of my own skin, my body trying to shed it like poison.

The second the Miata appears I bolt, flinging open the driver's side and tossing the first bill in my pocket at the guy.

"Thank you!" he shouts as I peel out, half-blind and turning the wrong way, ignoring road signs. I need wind. I need air.

I need space.

But most of all, I need to get away from the one person I invested so much of myself in, the one who turned out to be such a disappointment because I was too clueless to face reality.

Not Carrie.

Me.

Carrie

IT FEELS LIKE about a week since I woke up this morning.

My weekend started with coffee on the beach and ended with cocktails in a ballroom, went from blue jeans to near-black tie. In between, I have appeared on local television and smiled through approximately two thousand wedding photos (both professional and Instagram). I've laughed at the punchlines of everyone's toasts and been a really good sport about the stupid bouquet-tossing ritual (dodged that bullet when Jessie caught it). I have pretended to remember all of Jenny's cousins, to tolerate cougars, to like Kevin, to love Ryan and not to love Ryan. Most of it while wearing four-inch heels and being pulled into videography sessions more choreographed than the Oscars.

I am completely exhausted.

"Have you seen Ryan?" I ask Angela. She's got her now-wilting flowers in one hand and a bottle of water in the other and appears to be headed for the door. With Aiden's brother, Nolan. Who is carrying her purse.

Huh. Weddings.

"Not since you were dancing," she says, glancing around the still-crowded ballroom. It's after ten p.m. "He must be here somewhere. See you tomorrow." She kisses my cheek, unconcerned, and puts her arm through Nolan's as they move on.

Very true. He must be here somewhere. I make one more circuit of the room, but no luck. Not by the bar, not at our table, not on the dance floor. The only place I can't look is the men's room. I retrieve my bag from under my chair and pull out my phone.

Hey where can you be? I type and send, then squint at the screen, which says: *Hey when can you bed?*

Damn autocorrect.

where I add. **be**

Nothing.

"Carrie!" Jessie comes over to me, breathless. "We forgot to get a picture of you with your fabulous centerpieces. It'll make a hole in the scrapbook. We need you to hold this empty wine bottle and we'll photoshop in a centerpiece later."

An hour later, the photographer has 244 versions of me holding an empty wine bottle.

I check my phone. No text from Ryan. No actual Ryan. What on earth is going on?

I hydrate. I eat yet another piece of white wedding cake with a fondant rose. I make small talk with Aiden's grandmother's cousin's plumber (who had to be invited as an exchange for someone in Aiden's family being invited to his daughter's wedding). I find blisters on my feet and change into the flipflops Jenny gave us.

Still no Ryan.

I force myself to do the Funky Chicken Dance. Without Ryan.

Ryan, I text again. *I'm worried. Please reply. Where are you?*

Three bouncing dots appear, and then:

nowhere

Well, that's odd. What does he mean? A little stab of worry pierces my stomach.

I'm so tired all of a sudden, want to leave? I send back.

No response. The worry stabs again. It's a familiar feeling.

Maybe he's already gone up to the room. I should say polite good-nights to everyone, but Jenny and Aiden are surrounded by a group of people I don't know, chatting and laughing. Guiltily, I take my bag and my bouquet and slip out the door. I'll see them in the morning.

On my way, I check the wing chairs in the lobby and poke my head around the corner to see if Grind It Fresh! is still open. Ryan might have felt the need for caffeine after all the partying? I could use a latte myself. But it's closed up tight.

When I let myself in, our room is dark and blessedly silent after the noisy reception. I snap on a light and drop my things on the bed.

"Ry?"

Still silent. I check the bathroom. Just my pink-striped makeup bag on the counter. His shaving kit isn't there. I spin around and scan the bedroom. A few quarters on the desk, and a half empty water bottle, but nothing else of his. I run to the closet and pull it open.

One suitcase: mine. His hangers are empty.

I grab my phone again and type out: *Ryan where are you?* My fingers are shaking. I switch to the recent calls list and press his number.

I know there's not going to be an answer, but I try three times anyway. The little stab of worry is now a giant sword of hot fear.

"What could have happened? Why won't he pick up?" I am talking out loud, anything to fill up the silence, to hear a voice. I can't understand this, we were having so much fun! I mean, weren't we?

Eventually I get undressed and pull on a t-shirt. It's a lot easier getting out of the dress by myself than it was getting into it. I strip off my stockings and jewelry and stuff it all in my bag. I feel pain and numbness, physically in my feet from dancing in heels.

Dancing. With Ryan.

I lay down on top of the bed with my phone in one hand and wait for morning. Which eventually comes. It always does.

Hours later, when the sky begins to grow light, I turn off the bedside lamp and pick up the phone:

Ryan, please, where are you? Are you okay? I'm so worried

Nothing for a moment, then my heart leaps as the three dots appear.

Then disappear.

And reappear.

Then, nothing. No dots. No answer.

There's a farewell breakfast on the terrace at 9:30 a.m. That's three hours from now, which is so long, it might as well be Tuesday. What on earth am I supposed to do for three hours? I pace around the room, considering my options. They're not good.

1. Call Angela and pour my heart out? I'm guessing Nolan would not appreciate that right now. Or Angela either, for that matter.

2. Go for a run on the beach? Right. The only time I run is when the subway doors are closing.

3. I can't think of anything else.

Suddenly I stop pacing, so fast that I almost lose my balance. I am getting out of here, now. They do not need me at the farewell breakfast, and in fact probably no one will even notice my absence.

I brush my teeth, pull a pair of grey yoga pants and a pink top out of my bag, and gather up the few last items in the room. I drop my bouquet in the wastebasket, where it lands with a thump.

Something is sticking out from under the bedskirt, and I bend down to see what it is. My black lace thong is lying on the carpet. It must have gotten kicked under the bed the other night. I pick it up and stare at it for a long moment, remembering how Ryan slid it down and off, then ran his hands back up the inside of my thighs . . . I throw it in my bag.

Two texts must be sent:

Jen, I'm not feeling very well, heading home early. Sorry to miss break-fast. Call me the minute you get back from Bermuda! Happy honeymoon, love you!

And

Angela, I'm so sorry, not feeling well and heading home. I know you can grab a ride with Diane or maybe Nolan? See you next week, really sorry xo

"I'm definitely not feeling well," I mutter. "Truth."

That's it, done. I've piled my belongings by the entry. I pull open the heavy door and start dragging the bags out, when a clicking noise makes me look up.

Jamey's standing in the hallway outside their door, wearing the t-shirt he bought when we went to an Adele concert last year. His hair is wet.

"Hey," he says, obviously surprised to see me. "Where are you going? What's going on?"

He looks so familiar and yet different, like somebody who used to be your best friend but now you've grown apart.

Which, come to think of it, is exactly what he is.

And that is when I finally break down. The uncertainty and frustration of the weekend—hell, the past month—overwhelm all my control mechanisms, and the tears spill down my face.

"Ryan's gone," I say, trying not to sob. "I'm going home."

"Gone?" he repeats. "Gone where? That doesn't sound like Ryan."

"I don't know! When the reception was ending, I couldn't find him, and he won't answer my texts or calls. Well, he answered one text, but that was all, and I don't even know what he meant!"

"What did he say?"

"I asked him where he was, and he said, 'nowhere.' What could that mean?"

"I have no idea. But at least you know he's all right. And he did answer you." Jamey steps closer. "You two haven't really been together very long, and this was a pretty stressful weekend for everybody. Under the, you know, circumstances."

I nod and sniff.

"Kevin and I have been getting on each other's nerves, too," he confides in a lower voice. "You and Ryan will work it out. You just need to talk. He really does love you, Carrie."

"No, he really doesn't," I say sadly, shaking my head. "You don't understand."

"I understand more than you think," he says, and opens his arms, wrapping me in a hug. He kisses the side of my head. "And I do still love you, too. Not like I think Ryan does, but I hope you know that. And I'm so sorry. I never really gave you the apology you deserve."

He smells so good, so sweet, so friendly. "Thank you," I say, sniffing again, emotions a jumble of really tangled wires inside my chest. "I love you, too. Just, you know . . ."

"Not like you love Ryan. Or like I feel about Kevin."

"I don't love Ryan," I protest.

Jamey pulls me away and looks at me at arm's length. "You are the worst liar, Carrie. Always were."

My tears make it impossible to tell him he's right. I hate that he's right.

"You can't drive home all upset like this, you'll have an accident. I'll drive you. Just give me a minute to get my stuff."

"No, no," I protest, taking a long series of sniffs, clearing my head and wiping my eyes with the hem of my shirt as Jamey scrambles to hand me a linen handkerchief, one I used as a stocking stuffer for him last Christmas, bought at Ten Thousand Villages and made by

Nepalese Buddhist nuns. "I'm fine. Don't be silly. Jenny's your sister and I'll be perfectly all right."

He peers at me closely. "Are you sure? I don't mind at all." Then he grins. "One more meal with my entire family will probably make Kevin disappear, too. Gram keeps asking him why such a handsome young man doesn't have a girlfriend."

I smile in spite of my misery. "She knows, doesn't she?"

"Of course she knows! She just likes watching him squirm," Jamey chuckles. "Gram's a piece of work." Jamey's eyebrows drop in confusion. "Everyone's been so accepting. It's almost like my family didn't have a closet for me to be in. I'm really lucky."

"You'd better stay and protect Kevin from Gram," I tell him, on emotional overload and unsure how much more I can handle. Even positive emotions can be overwhelming in bulk. "But thank you for offering. It means a lot."

I throw my purse over my shoulder and pick up the bags, then hesitate. "Call me next week," I offer. "Maybe we can meet for a drink."

He brightens. "I'd love that! I'll definitely call. You can fill me in on Ryan. It's going to be fine, Carrie." I had him back his wet handkerchief, which he stuffs in his pocket. "And don't forget the Straight No Chaser concert in November. We have to go together."

"You're not taking Kevin?"

"Turns out he doesn't like *a cappella*." Jamey makes a sour face.

My jaw drops. "Who doesn't like *a cappella*? How is that possible?"

"I know, right?" We share a warm smile, a few beats passing, and then it's time.

I wave my fingers and start off, then drop my bags and turn back. I give him a big kiss on the cheek. He smells good, just like always. "Love you, Jamey."

"Love you back, sweetie. Always will."

CHAPTER THIRTEEN

Carrie

T'S JUST ANOTHER day at work.

A regular Tuesday.

Nothing special.

Unless you count avoiding the kitchen, hallways, lobby, and the area outside the bathrooms as special. Unless you mean bringing my own thermos of coffee and a lunch that doesn't need refrigeration. Unless you mean reapplying lipstick every twenty minutes just in case I am forced to leave the safety of my cubicle and might accidentally run into . . . someone from the spa side.

And in addition to these complicated logistics, I am expected to *think*.

Ridiculous.

I did get to come in late today. There's a divorce party tonight and it's my turn to be on duty, representing the corporate side in case anything unforeseen comes up.

Which it so often does at O.

I used to like the late nights in the office. It's a good time to catch up on work with no one around to interrupt, and sometimes these funny things happen: once, a new divorcée and a new fiancée—of the *same guy*—were having celebrations in adjoining rooms. Which probably would have been fine, they never would have known, but the cakes got switched. It wasn't pretty—there was cake *everywhere*, and some people got scratched. But the video did get the most hits on YouTube for three weeks straight. Like, over a million. You saw it, right? Membership applications went up over 200 percent.

We're asking for more information now when an event is booked . . . part of the phone tree script, as a matter of fact. The PR was great during Cake Switch (that's what the YouTube title was), but Anterdec legal was nervous.

Anyway, whoever's around after a scheduled party—Ryan and me, sometimes Zeke, sometimes a few of the other dancers—usually goes out for pizza and beer. They've burned off a lot of calories during the evening, and they always have stories to tell. It's really fun.

I'm guessing that's not going to happen tonight. Or ever again.

But with my extra time this morning, I did manage to shower and put on an actual outfit. Because, you know, I might have to appear in front of the clients tonight. I should look put together. Professional. Pale grey skirt and sweater with a grey jacquard leopard pattern, grey heels.

Someone around here should be fully dressed, in clothing that does not sparkle or light up, and is not edible.

A message from Hayley pops up on my computer screen:

Carrie, are you there? Snacks for the performers just arrived.

Okay, I type back. *Can you just take them over to the break room?*

I can't leave the phones. Can you take them?

I sigh. Normally I wouldn't mind, and in fact I'd enjoy the change of scene. But not today.

The idea of seeing Ryan makes my stomach turn over with either desire or dread. Not sure which.

Both.

Sure, np. I answer.

I pull out my makeup bag and start touching up. There is no way I'm going over there looking less than my best—or my work-best, anyway. I haven't seen him since the reception. I'm not going to repeat the Jamey break-up show, dragging around here looking like a dead cat. *Poorcarrie.* I mean, Jamey wasn't here to see me destroyed. Ryan is.

A girl has to have some pride.

I start down the hall to get the food from Hayley at the reception desk. Whatever the snack *du jour* is, I hope I can carry it in one trip. I'm really not dressed to juggle deli trays.

"Carrie?" Chloe calls out as I pass her door.

I back up.

"Can you come in for a minute?"

I step into her office, which is pristine, as usual. Her raincoat and tote bag are on a chair by the door, ready to go. Since she became a mom, she tries hard to leave on time every night.

"You look great," she observes. "You're on duty tonight?"

"Thanks, and yes. The food just got here."

"I'll only keep you for a minute. I have a proposition for you."

"You do?"

"You've been doing a fantastic job, Carrie. Your design is first-rate—it's like you know what I'm thinking before I even know. And you have all the details under control, budgets, installation schedules, everything. Suppliers love working with you. It's very impressive."

"Wow," I stammer. "Thanks." This is unexpected.

"You know O San Francisco is slated to open next year."

"Yes." I start to get excited. She's going to send me out there to check on construction! California is a dream business trip—and if the timing works, I can stay over a weekend and go to Napa. Mini-vacation!

"I can't believe I'm even saying this." She shakes her head, swinging her hair. "But what would you think about moving out there as Associate Director of Design? I need someone I trust on the West Coast. O LA is in the works, and they're talking about Seattle in 2019. It's a lot of work—a huge amount, actually—but it would mean a promotion and a raise. You'll be responsible for all the West Coast design, plus have a hand in staffing and operations. It's a lot like my job here, but you'll have me to back you up."

I drop down onto one of the chairs in front of her desk. I just look at her.

"I mean, take a couple of days to think about it," she says. "It's a big decision. I don't know how I'll do without you here, but we'll still be working together, just not in the same city."

"Chloe, I . . . thank you," is all I can manage. It's too much to absorb.

"You have totally earned it," she smiles. "You made it happen. Now go get the food before the guys come looking for it."

As I reach the door, she says, "How did the weekend end up? I haven't seen Ryan hanging around your desk lately."

"It's fine. It's all working out for the best," I say weakly. "Thank you again."

Three thousand miles. He definitely won't be hanging around my desk.

Ryan

IT'S JUST ANOTHER day at work.

A regular Tuesday.

Nothing special.

Unless you count groaning when I realized I had a divorce party today as special. Unless you mean leaving my car at home and taking the T to avoid being in the parking lot at all. Unless you mean taking the stairs to prevent any elevator awkwardness in case I got trapped with . . . someone from the administrative side.

Like I said—nothing special.

I put on my cop uniform, adjusting the g-string with the flashing blue and red lights on the pouch, moving the battery pack and wires. Over the weekend, I perfected the device, swapping out the ridiculous 9-volt battery for a slim lithium system that makes more sense.

And doesn't give me an unwelcome prostate exam.

"Ingenious!" Henry says in a low voice filled with admiration. "You really have a way with electronics and design."

I just grunt my thanks.

We're in the O Spa locker room, getting ready for our shift.

Divorce party at 6pm. Big affair, all hands on deck (so to speak). Which means Carrie's working late and will be on call in her office to manage any blips.

"Ryan? What's up?"

I look at my crotch. "Nothing."

Henry rolls his eyes. "That's a Zeke answer." His hand goes on my shoulder, the gesture respectful but filled with concern. "You seem distracted."

"I'm waiting to hear about a grad school application," I say, mind scrambling to find something to say other than *I love Carrie and she doesn't love me back.*

"Really? Where are you applying? What field?"

"Electrical engineering."

"Nice. Which schools? MIT? WPI?"

I appreciate the fact that he immediately goes to top schools. Henry's working on his master's degree at Harvard. He doesn't judge me by what we do for a living.

"Stanford. Berkeley. Cal Tech," I admit.

His eyebrows go high. "You're leaving us?"

"*Shhh.* Only if I get accepted. There's a professor at Stanford with a huge grant and he's considering me as a research assistant for a January start. Maybe next August. Not sure."

"I'm impressed."

I shrug and center the police light right over my balls.

"The Bay Area is home." This is weird. Awkward. I've spent two years working here and this is the most I've revealed about myself to anyone other than Carrie. Guys don't stand around in g-strings and sex-play costumes talking about their *feelings.*

"Good luck."

"Yeah, thanks. Hey, don't say anything to anyone, okay? It's not official. I don't want to lose my job because Chloe thinks I'm not serious here."

"You've more than proven yourself. We'd miss you if you left, but no one wants to hold you back from moving forward with your real career."

Real career.

"Right."

"Besides, you don't have anything keeping you here." Henry smiles. "No girlfriend. No wife. No mortgage. You're still free to be."

Free to be.

"Uh huh." My fake gun belt cuts into my hip. I move it, unholstering the plastic pistol and checking to make sure the candies it shoots are properly loaded.

"Change is good. Grad school is great. Good for you."

And with that, he leaves.

I can stall for only so long, other masseurs and staff streaming in. Finally, the time comes.

I walk into the hallway, starting the swagger I have to allow to inhabit my hips, my thighs, my shoulders, the cocky walk we create as part of the fantasy.

Fantasy.

That's what my entire life is now.

Nothing but fantasy.

"Ryan," Chloe says as I finish pinning on my fake badge. "Can you come to work on Thursday morning for a phone tree meeting?" Nick Grafton is behind her, holding a black leather portfolio and talking on his phone.

"Sure." Shit. Carrie's running that meeting.

Nick gets off the phone and looks me up and down, clearly suppressing a grin. "I like how you helped with the software issue. We need someone with more knowledge to take a look at their proposal."

"You mean you want me to tell you whether you're getting shafted by an overbid," I reply.

He grins. "Have you thought about a different job here at O?"

"You mean one where I don't wear cop lights on my dick?"

Chloe's big, mink brown eyes turn into headlights. "Ryan!"

I ignore her.

"I suppose the software developers can wear whatever they want if you're so attached to that feature," Nick muses. The dry wit goes over my head for a second.

Then I laugh.

"Most of them just wear stupid sarcastic slogan t-shirts and jeans, though," he adds.

"I'm good in the job arena," I tell him, not wanting to share my future plans. "But thanks."

He nods as Chloe's phone buzzes. She turns away, murmuring something about her daughter into the phone, just as Carrie comes down the hall carrying a giant flat white box of City Donuts.

Like something out of a comedy, she catches my eye and stops short, tripping just enough that the entire box crumples up, the top flying open, the donuts bouncing up and pelting her chest and face like a little sugar missile test being conducted by the pastry version of North Korea.

I move to catch the box before it falls to the ground, everyone in slow motion, glazed sugar coating Carrie's face and top while Nick catches a powdered jelly donut in each hand.

As I pivot and manage to get the half-filled box before the contents all hit the industrial-strength hallway carpet, something in my crotch pulls hard, a yanking feeling that brings tears to my eyes.

The unmistakeable sound of police sirens fills the air.

"Is your crotch on a 911 call?" someone behind me asks.

Snickers fill the air. I look down. Blue and red lights make my package look like Rudolph the Red-Nosed Reindeer is fighting a Smurf in my pants.

"OH.MY.GOD!" Carrie finally gasps, hands splayed at her sides.

"You look like Carrie," Zeke says with a snort. "You know. From the horror movie? Only instead of covered with blood, you're covered with blueberry compote and cream filling."

Carrie peels a maple donut off her right breast and wings it at him, so hard it whacks him in the eye and he screams like a little girl.

I can't help it. I start laughing. But something in my crotch warms up.

JULIA KENT and ELISA REED

Zeke, ego wounded, grabs the box of donuts from me and turns them into sugar bombs with Carrie as the target. She ducks into a conference room.

Nick stands in the middle of everything, his expression alternating between the need to assert control and the desire to join the food fight.

My crotch starts to smoke. The siren makes a dying sound, and I grab my belt, ripping the pants off at the Velcro seam down both sides.

My dick is on fire.

Literally.

"Ryan!" Carrie screams. "Your penis is on fire!" She grabs a Boston Cream donut from the floor and drops to her knees at my feet. Taking aim, she shoves the donut over my smoking genitals and squeezes.

Hard.

Goo covers my balls, my penis, the g-string pouch, the little plastic red and blue light chambers, and most of my groin area. Carrie starts patting my cock with the now-empty donut hull.

Someone starts humming the melody to Donna Summer's song *Hot Stuff.*

"Stop it," I hiss to Zeke.

He points to Nick.

Who just shrugs. "I've never seen a crotch do an imitation of a Samsung Galaxy 7 before," he says.

"You giving Ryan a moisturizing treatment there, Carrie? A sugar scrub?" Zeke jokes, everyone around us laughing as Carrie realizes she's basically giving me a hand job with a donut.

My perverted teenage self came up with lots of really inventive ways to whack off, including a Playtex glove/Crisco combo that I'll take to the grave, but it never occurred to me to use a hollow cream-filled donut as a vessel for emptying my nuts.

"Oh!" Carrie falls backward, then rolls over, flashing me a nice view of her ass. As she stands, I smile at her and she smiles back, unguarded and embarrassed, the absurdity of the situation cutting through our mutual discomfort.

For about three seconds.

I take off for the locker room, turning my back on the giant mess behind me. Just as I open the men's room door I hear Chloe chewing someone out, calling for staff to clean up the mess.

Zeke's on my ass as I strip naked and check out my junk. No injuries.

"Short circuit? Nice."

"Shut up."

"Carrie made your cock ignite."

"Shut UP!" I roar, naked from the waist down, wearing a fake cop's uniform on top, hat and all. The associate professor at Stanford in charge of the wireless robotics project I would love to work on would, I'm sure, be impressed with my credentials right about now.

"Geez, Ryan, it's just a joke."

I tear the rest of the uniform off (easy to do with Velcro) and take a very fast shower, washing off the sticky cream filling and other bits of sugar all over my legs and midsection. Two minutes later I'm re-assembling myself.

My outside self, that is.

My insides are a whole different issue. I feel like someone squeezed me, hard, and made *my* gooey center fall out.

I shove on a non-electric g-string and glare at Zeke, who is leaning against a locker, arms crossed, making it clear he's going to torture me with conversation. "What?" I bark at him.

"What the hell happened to you at that wedding?"

"Nothing." *Everything*, I want to scream, but I don't.

"You and Carrie . . . ?"

"I told you. I did her a favor. It was all pretend."

"You know damn well it wasn't."

"We're not *compatible*." The last word tastes like contempt.

"You are!"

"Turns out I was wrong."

"At the wedding, you were grabbing my shirt and threatening me when I talked about you and Carrie fucking. Now it turns out I'm right?"

"Yeah." I slam my locker door and adjust the cop uniform. My basket will have to be enough. No flashing lights. The air smells like singed hair.

My singed hair.

"Bullshit."

I shrug. "Believe what you want to believe."

"Ryan, you know damn well nothing you did at that wedding was pretend."

"It was pretend for her. All of it. That's what she said."

"She said that?"

"Yes." I don't mention she said it to Chloe. I'm sick of this conversation. Parts of my body are zooming from Carrie's touch and the pyrotechnics display.

My heart's zooming, too.

Zeke lets out a low whistle. "She's more of a player than I thought, then." He washes his face with his palm, rubbing his upper lip with his index finger. "She's hard core."

"Yeah."

"You okay?"

"I will be."

"You need to get laid."

"If that's an offer, my answer is no. You're not my type."

"Gia and Gina want to see me next weekend. How about—"

"Sure." I wave him off. "We're late for the divorce party." The last thing I want to do is dance for a bunch of bitter women, but it's better than what just happened with Carrie.

Zeke follows me, hand clapping my shoulder. "We'll get you out there and over this, Ryan. I guarantee it."

"Right."

As we walk into the hallway, Carrie suddenly exits the women's locker room. We're inches from each other, face to face. She smells like coconut body wash and is wearing a new outfit, a simple but tight dark red sweater and a long, pencil skirt made of deep blue. Her makeup is fresh, a smudge of powder on her collar.

I don't touch her.

"Um, thanks for catching the donuts," she says.

"Thanks for putting out my dick."

Zeke starts wailing with laughter.

Carrie gives him such a glare he begins coughing, hard, and disappears like a rabbit. She looks at me, uncertainty making her painted face softer.

"Ryan, we should talk about—"

"Using a donut as a fire extinguisher?"

"Ryan," she pleads. "This is hard enough."

"What's there to talk about?" I imitate Zeke, minus the accent. It's the only way I can get through this moment, this pain, this anger. "We had a fun weekend. I did my job. You knocked 'em dead, Kitten." I give her a grin that I can't feel in my eyes and pat her shoulder twice. Exactly twice. "It was good fun. Now we're back to reality."

I can't look her in the eye. I'm a coward. I admit it. If I looked in those beautiful honeyed pools, what would I see?

Pity.

A man can handle many, many insults, but being pitied by a woman he slept with, one who doesn't reciprocate his feelings, isn't one of them.

I turn away and give her a little wave, headed for my roomful of horny divorcees who know I'm pretending, and who pretend right back.

We're even. Equitable. On par.

It's simple—I just made my feelings balance with Carrie's.

She was pretending last weekend.

And I just pretended back there.

CHAPTER FOURTEEN

Carrie

"**O**H, MY GOD, how much sex are you having, Jenny? Every single wrinkle on your face is gone. You look nineteen again!" I squeal as we hug in the Grind It Fresh! flagship coffee shop in the Seaport District. Jenny's finally back from her nearly month-long honeymoon and has time for coffee with me.

I'm pretty sure she knows about the mess with Ryan, because Jamey is constitutionally incapable of keeping a secret from his sister.

Well, other than his own big one.

"You didn't know me when I was nineteen, Carrie," she says sensibly.

"If I had, you'd have looked like this. A long honeymoon suits you."

"I credit Aiden entirely. He picked Bermuda, he picked the resort, but best of all—he picked me." She beams. "And who would have guessed there are cruise ships to Bermuda directly out of Boston?" Her eyes wrinkle at the corners just like Jamey's. When she smiles, she looks like him, warm and smart, playful and attentive.

"I'm so happy for you," I say, sitting down across from her at a table made of broken shards of ceramics and some lightweight metal shaped like a *Game of Thrones* sculpture.

"What about you and Ryan?" She winks. "You seemed really cozy at the wedding." Leaning in, it's clear she expects me to dish.

And by *dish*, I mean describe every second of fabulous sex.

Jamey must have kept his mouth shut about what happened with Ryan after all. There's a first time for everything.

"About that," I jump in, deflecting. "I'm sorry again for missing the brunch. I drank too much."

"So did everyone. You didn't miss out. We basically spent a small fortune for people to drink water and munch on plain bagels while begging for ginger ale. Everyone was shitfaced."

"Oh." Guilt returns when I remember that morning. As maid of honor, I really dropped the ball.

Then again, when your heart breaks, you don't exactly worry about whether your hair looks good. I wasn't in any frame of mind to be at a brunch and do my duties. I just couldn't.

She gives me a one-eyed squint. "Something's off."

I touch my hair. "What?"

"You. Ryan. What happened?" She peers at me, hard. "What *really* happened?"

Best friends can read you so well.

Too well.

"Nothing. That's kind of, well—nothing. It was just—"

"Just?"

"Okay. Ryan was pretending to be my date. I was so embarrassed with everything involving Jamey. He was a gentleman and stepped up to the plate, acting like my date. It was all fake," I confess, throwing my hands over my face and peeking between my fingers.

"Then he's a damn fine actor, Carrie. That didn't look like he was pretending. And everyone knows you're incapable of lying. One look at you and your feelings for him were obvious. In two years of dating my brother, I never saw you look at Jamey like *that*."

"It was all in good fun." The words taste like pity, a bitter, acrid flavor I never want to taste again.

"Carrie." She touches my knee, her rings glittering. "You don't have to pretend with me."

Commence waterworks. As Jenny watches me with eyes so close

to Jamey's, so kind and understanding as I turn my latte salty with my own tears, she can't help but look like my polar opposite. Jenny's tan and happy and well-fucked.

I'm pasty white and pathetic and, well—

fucked.

"It's just that I, I *was* pretending! I really was! Ryan offered to be my pretend date so I wouldn't look like the pathetic unwitting beard that Jamey turned me into and so I went along with it."

"Mmm, hmmm?" Jenny hands me a handkerchief. Perfectly pressed, monogrammed with her married initials, smelling like baby powder and lilac.

"And, and it was great! Ryan was the perfect fake boyfriend."

"But it wasn't fake, was it? You really care about Ryan."

"It wasn't fake for me!" I wail.

"Good grief, Carrie. I've known you had a thing for Ryan for a while. Jamey wondered, too."

My sobs turn to a single sound like Godzilla gagging on a Xanax. "What?"

"You two are perfect for each other. Ryan's casual and smart. So are you. You both love those stupid reality television shows. You even like the same kind of pizza!"

"But he's my friend."

"So? Aiden was my friend before he became my husband."

"Yes, but you and Aiden are well matched."

"What does that mean?"

"Look at me! Ryan and I have a 6.5 point difference!"

Her head snaps back. "You do not!"

I am so grateful I can speak in code and not have to explain the attractiveness math scale to her.

"He's a 10.5! I'm a 4!"

"This again?" she groans. "You're not a 4!"

"Then why did he ghost on me? And after we slept together at your wedding?"

"You did?" she squeals. "Was it good?"

"What do you think, Jenny? I finally sleep with a guy who thinks a woman's body is a buffet after only being with guys who treat me like I'm gruel. Of course it was good."

She snorts.

"It was great," I admit. "It was everything I never knew I was missing."

"Then why aren't you with him?"

"Because he disappeared right in the middle of your reception. Came to work a couple of days later and commented on how it had been 'fun' pretending."

"Ouch!"

"I know. Trust me, *I know*."

"Carrie, I know how he looked at you at the wedding. He wasn't faking."

"Jenny, no offense, but you were too busy complaining about the squeaky corks in the Chardonnay to notice how Ryan looked at me."

She doesn't deny it, regret clouding her face. "I'm sorry. I really was too self-absorbed. Jamey's breakup with you and coming out was an emotional rollercoaster on top of the wedding. But Jamey told me. Commented on it. I think Ryan managed to make my gay brother a little bit jealous." I could do without her waggling eyebrows.

"I am not even going to attempt to parse that out. I need three psychologists, a sex therapist, Dan Savage, and a Freud puppet to even try."

"Bottom line: your gay ex could tell Ryan feels more for you than some pretend feelings."

"Then Ryan has an awful way of showing it," I sob, sniffling and dabbing my eyes with logo-covered napkins. Coffee shops should be stocked with tissues. Preferably the kind with lotion built in, so criers like me don't look like coke fiends after having a good cry in our lattes.

"Sounds like a big misunderstanding to me."

"No. It was clear. He disappeared right after that one dance we had, and then all I got was a stupid text. I asked him where he went and he just said, 'nowhere.'"

"Huh. I don't know him that well, but it doesn't add up."

"Right. It doesn't. And when things don't add up, you know what that means?"

"It means you need to talk to him to clear the air."

I was about to say you avoid, avoid, *avoid*, but okay. I'll let Jenny think she's right.

"I guess so."

Too bad Ryan's been gone from work for over a week. I have no idea where he is, or why he hasn't been at work, and aside from Chloe's offhand mention of a health problem his dad is having, I know nothing.

And why should I know anything? It's not like I'm his girlfriend.

Bzzzz.

I look at my phone. Chloe.

"Oh, man." I stand and sniff, then blow my nose. "I need to get back to work. Customer service phone problems."

Jenny stares at me, hard. Then her eyes get huge. "No way. O really went for the phone sex line? Last year they were thinking about it, but I never imagined they'd actually do it."

I shrug. "Never underestimate the power of a determined woman."

"You mean desperate and sex starved."

"Same thing."

We say our goodbyes, and by the time I'm back at the office, Chloe's at my desk, beaming.

"Carrie! You've been crying!" she says, dismayed, as I hurry into my cubicle, head down, wondering if Ryan's back yet and praying he's not. Her smile has turned to a concerned frown.

"Allergies. You know."

"In November?" Can't fool Chloe.

"Climate change," I say, as if that explains everything. "Why are you in my cube?" I ask, trying to change the subject. "Not that you're not welcome, but . . ."

"We got a new bid on the phone system for the master masseurs.

Forty percent cheaper than the other guys."

"And will the new vendor be forty percent less sexist?"

We share a knowing look. "You can't have everything," she says. "But Nick was impressed with Ryan's coding knowledge and took his advice on a few things. Between you and Ryan, this project is going to fly."

"That's great."

She hesitates. "What's actually going on between you and Ryan, though?"

Do I seriously have a face that shows every single feeling I experience?

"Um, nothing."

"Carrie."

"That's just it, Chloe. Nothing is going on between Ryan and me! NOTHING!"

Here I go again. Dehydration via crying is a real thing. Someone get me coconut water and alpha hydroxy night serum.

"Well," she says, frowning. "I guess that's good, then."

"Good?"

"It'll make it easier for you to take the promotion and transfer."

The promotion.

"I really, really think you should take it, Carrie."

I do, too. But not for the same reasons Chloe thinks. Mom and Dad will be sad I'm moving even further away from Michigan, but I gave up a long time ago on the idea that they'd ever visit me in my own life. I shouldn't make them a factor in deciding.

This is mostly about Ryan. And Ryan's made it very clear I'm not a part of his life anymore. So . . .

"Okay. I know. And I will."

A big smile spreads across her face. "Make it official. Send an email to corporate and cc me."

Bzzzz. That's my phone. I do a quick check.

Then a double take. Tessa. Ryan's sister? Why is she texting me?

Carrie I'm so sorry. Ryan's out of town and I have a babysitting emergency. Carlos got hurt at work. Is there any way you can you help me?

My expression makes Chloe give me a sharp look. "What's wrong?"

"Ryan's sister. She's having an emergency. Her husband's hurt. Needs a babysitter." A helpless feeling fills me.

"For God's sake, go!" Chloe makes a shooing gesture. "Don't worry about work. Any mom in that situation is more important. *Go!*"

I run out of the office, pause at my desk, and text Tessa.

I'm coming right now, I say.

The drive to Tessa's is miraculously only twenty-three minutes. Amazing how clear Route 3 can be in the middle of the day. I have to actually concentrate on driving faster than a turtle, which is unusual. My life experiences are set by external factors—rush hour with everyone else, grocery shopping on evenings and weekends like everyone else, vacation when everyone else goes.

You get the picture.

I pull up to Tessa and Carlos' house, a small raised ranch in a Boston suburb. It looks exactly like the houses in my hometown, but actually costs six times as much, with a fourth of the land.

Why do I live where everything is so expensive? And why am I about to move to a housing market that is even *worse*?

Pushing all that aside, I race to their front door and knock hard, wondering how bad Carlos's injury could be. What kind of occupational hazards do accountants face? Finger sprain on the calculator?

The front door flies open. No one's there until I look down to see Elias, wearing a Batman hat and Spongebob underwear. Nothing else. Just that.

"Carrie!" he squeals.

"THANK GOD!" Tessa shouts. As I scoop Elias into my arms, he gives me a big hug, then wiggles down, doing a running leap onto the big L-shaped sectional by the television. "Carrie, thank you so, so much! I'm waiting to hear which hospital Carlos is at."

"What happened?"

Tessa rolls her eyes. My fear and worry instantly goes down a notch. "They have this corporate wellness competition at work. Never get a group of desk jockey accountants together and throw a fitness challenge with financial incentives at them. It's a recipe for injury."

"Huh?"

"They went to a giant fitness center and had to do an obstacle course. Part of it involved a rope climb. You know, the knotted rope hanging from the top of the roof?"

"Yeah. I hated that as a kid."

"Everyone hated it! So, of course, they made that part of the challenge." Tessa keeps nervously looking at her phone. "Apparently, Carlos made it up, but his ankle got caught. He lost his grip and was suspended at the top for about ten minutes, upside down."

"Oh my," I gasp, covering my mouth with my hand. I'm actually trying not to laugh. The image is pretty bad.

"Go ahead. Laugh." Tessa snorts. "I would laugh, too, except he may have broken his wrists trying to untangle himself."

"Couldn't anyone get him down?"

"None of them could climb that high. Took a while to find gym staff capable of getting up there. Meanwhile, Mr. CPA insisted on trying it himself. Got halfway down and then *bam!* He fell. Broke his fall with his hands."

"Ouch!" I shudder. "Did you say wrists? As in, plural?"

"Yeah."

"Oh, my God!"

"They should heal before tax season, but still." Her eyes are unfocused, the words robotic. Shock makes people say strange things.

She checks her phone again. "I really appreciate this, Carrie. I'm pretty sure they're taking him into Boston, so as soon as I know, I'll leave. My mother-in-law will be here in about four hours, so it's not forever."

"Even if you need longer than that, it's fine. Don't worry about the boys. I've got them." I give her a big hug. She grabs me back, hard. I can feel her worry through the facade of emotional control she wears.

You can tell she's Ryan's sister.

Tessa pulls back and looks at me, eyes a little watery, but she's not letting herself cry. "You're so nice. I see why Ryan fell for you."

"Why Ryan . . . what?"

Tessa does this twist with her mouth that makes her look so much like Ryan for a second. Must be a family trait. "Oh, screw him. He's so stupid. Why are men so stupid about love?" She sighs. "Ryan's liked you since the day you two met at work."

"What? He said that?"

"He never had to. I know my brother."

"But he never said a word!"

"You were taken. You met Jamey the same day, Ryan said. Something about Jamey visiting his sister and you started dating right away?"

I *did* meet Jamey the same day I met Ryan. Jenny was training me for my new job, and we had lunch together at a little Asian-fusion place on Congress Street. Jamey popped in, saw his sister, and an hour later he asked for my number.

A simple twist—being trained by Jenny—changed everything between Ryan and me?

"Carrie?" Tessa hands me a half-full pint of my favorite ice cream. I take it and open it, eating directly from the pint. I don't care.

"Ryan's right. I met Jamey at lunch that first day at O. But it's not like I was engaged to him. I mean, Ryan could have—"

She squints at me. "You expected my brother to snipe you from another guy? *My* brother, who didn't have his first date until he was nineteen? Little Ryan Donovan, who never went to a single dance in high school?"

"WHAT?" I practically scream, the chocolate brownie mixture in my mouth muffling my surprise. "Ryan *what*?"

She gives me a rueful look and walks past me, bending down before a big bookcase with cabinet doors on the bottom. Rifling around, she comes back with a big photo album, flipping through pages. Tessa settles on one and thrusts it at me.

Class of 2008, the picture says. A very thin guy who looks like he's twelve is in the picture, all glasses and braces, wearing a t-shirt with a joke from the television show *Big Bang Theory*.

"Who's the twelve-year-old?" I ask, my voice trailing off as I recognize the muted brown eyes behind those coke-bottle lenses. The melted ice cream in my mouth turns to cement. "No way!"

Tessa laughs. "Yes way."

"That's *Ryan*?"

"He was a late bloomer."

I stare at the picture. "That's like saying sloths can be a little slow. He was, um . . ."

"Not at all like he is now."

I swallow my mouthful and stare, dumbfounded. "No. Not a bit. He looks so much like the guys I dated in high school."

"Really?" Her voice floats so high with skepticism.

"Other than my gay high school boyfriend, yeah."

"Oh, honey. We all had that one gay boyfriend back then. Hell, I grew up in the Bay area. It was basically a rite of passage."

"But what does this have to do with Ryan never telling me he, that he—"

"Loves you?"

The room spins, and not just because Elias and Darien somersault into me, making my ankles weak. They giggle in stereo, then look up at me. Elias looks so much like a little version of Ryan that I just stare, time stopping. All I can do is breathe.

Love.

Bzzz. Tessa grabs her phone, looks at a message, and rushes out the door, shouting.

"Speaking of love—Carlos! Got to go. Only one hand has broken bones. The other one just aches. He says they transferred him and now I need to go to Beth Israel Deaconess. He says the best hand surgeons are there." Freezing, her eyes go unfocused, staring over my shoulder. "Hand surgeons. Oh, geez."

Tears spill over her lower lids and her hand grasping the phone starts to shake. I reach for her, holding her shoulders.

"Do you need me to drive you? We can all pile into a car and I can drop you off."

She sniffs and wipes her tears, squaring her shoulders, stretching her neck. "No. I'm fine. It's just—'hand surgeon' makes this more real." She looks over at the twins, who are deeply engrossed in a Peppa Pig episode. "I guess I should be grateful it's just his hands." She sniffs again. "When it rains, it pours. You heard about my dad?"

"Your dad?"

"The stroke? Ryan didn't tell you?"

"Um, sure," I lie. "I heard about it. Is he okay?"

"Better than okay. They think he had a slow brain bleed that led to what we thought was dementia. He's got more clarity now than he's had in a while. Still not out of the woods. Ryan's been there for over a week."

"Oh. Right. The last thing you need is Carlos getting hurt."

She shrugs. "That's the risk."

"Risk?"

"Of life. Of love. Getting hurt. Watching them get hurt. It's all part of being alive. The alternative isn't all that great." She gives me a quick hug. "Thanks. I'll keep you posted."

And with that, she dashes off, leaving me reeling.

Ryan

"I'M SO GLAD you made the time to come home, sweetie. It's been wonderful having you here for so long." Mom pours coffee out of the same machine she bought when I was in high school. Having an old-school engineer father means that every product in the house is meticulously maintained, fixed instead of thrown away, on strict maintenance schedules. I'm sure Mom cleaned the coffee machine with a vinegar cycle at some point this month.

And if she didn't, Dad did.

The four-bedroom house where we grew up is outdated but

clean, a well-oiled machine that's a throwback to the 1970s, when Mom and Dad bought it. As the Bay Area gentrifies and billionaires consider our modest two-story a "teardown," we call it home.

For now.

I'm in my pajamas, sucking down a second cup of coffee, about to go for a run. My oldest sister, Ellen, bursts through the front door, her arms filled with bags of yarn.

Taryn, her oldest daughter, tags along behind with a little yappie dog on a leash. The dog, Cupcake, is a new addition to Ellen's growing menagerie of animals.

"Thanks for the help, Ry," Ellen says dryly as I watch her stagger into the house and dump the yarn on the couch.

"It's yarn. And I'm the annoying little brother, remember?"

Taryn smirks and gives me a thumbs-up.

"Peacock hair this time?" I ask her. She's a high school sophomore and what we would have called Emo ten years ago.

A mouth full of metal greets me as she grins. "Close. I was aiming for puke green and got this instead." Sections of shiny green and blue peek out from her auburn hair.

"Looks good."

Taryn eyes my forearms. I still can't get over seeing my sisters' faces on their kids. It's disorienting.

"I want a tat like yours."

"Over my dead body," Ellen calls out from the kitchen, where she's chattering with Mom about knitting sweaters for dogs for some charity project.

"If I wait until you're dead, Mom, tats won't be cool. And I turn 18 in two and a half years! You can't tell me no then!"

Taryn reaches for my right arm and follows the design with her fingertip. "Fractals, right?"

I give her an admiring look. "Yes. Most people don't realize that."

She shrugs. "You got me coding when I was in third grade. I'm, you know, pretty good at science and math."

"Nice."

"Those tats are dank," she says.

"'Dank' is good?"

Taryn gives me an eye roll. "Sometimes you're like Mom, and sometimes you're like, you know, cool. Could you pick one, Uncle Ryan? I'd like to know who I'm talking to."

Cupcake jumps in my lap and starts licking my arm.

"I'll do better next time," I say. Then I extend one arm and pretend to touch my nose to my other arm's inner elbow, a gesture I've been told is called "dabbing."

A long, aggrieved sigh is my answer.

I guess I'm not cool anymore.

"How's Dad today?" Ellen asks, eyebrows together, as Taryn raids the fridge. When she makes that expression, she looks ten years older. More like Mom.

"The doctors say he's on the upswing. The stroke took so much out of him, but his memory is really improving," I tell Ellen.

She and Mom just look at me. Uncomfortable silence fills the air, interrupted by Taryn pouring herself a Coke.

"What?" I finally ask, scowling as I stand and make another cup of coffee.

"I'm just not used to you being here. Being part of Dad's issues." Ellen touches my shoulder. "Sorry. It's nice. It's . . . different, but good."

"I love it," Mom declares unequivocally. "And if you move back home, you can have your old room."

Taryn shoots me a sympathetic look. Hey, I'll take it.

"If I move back, Mom, I'll have my own place."

"No one can afford apartments around here, Ryan!" Mom scoffs.

"I have some money. I've been saving. And if I get the grant-funded position at Stanford in the electrical engineering lab—"

Mom's eyes light up. "When will you know?"

"Any day now."

"And you'll start in January? That's just two months away," Mom says, excited.

Ellen's eyes narrow. She looks like Mom, but with brown hair, although a few strands of grey are peeking through, just over her ears. Worry lines cross the corners of her mouth, etched there. That's new since I last visited.

We're getting older.

"Dad's birthday is in January. It would be so nice if you could be here," Mom adds.

"It would," Ellen concurs. "So you're serious? You plan to move back here if you get the grad school spot?"

Taryn snorts. "No pressure, Uncle Ry. You know."

"Tessa will miss you, of course." Mom's words make me frown. "She and Carlos love having you nearby in Boston. Did you know that nice friend of yours helped her yesterday?" Mom's eyes sparkle. It's a relief to see her cheer up a bit. But what's she talking about?

"What friend?"

"Carrie."

I sit up straight, like someone ran a finger down my spine. "Carrie?" My damn voice cracks in the middle of her name. "Why would she help Tessa?"

"Oh! I didn't tell you. You were out and then I was at the hospital and when I came home, you were asleep. Carlos got hurt at work. Tessa needed you to babysit, but you're here. So she called Carrie." Mom watches me carefully, evaluating my reaction.

Which is considerable beneath my skin. Inside my chest, there's a big bass drum banging away. Might as well fire off a few cannons and a fireworks display, too. Carrie. I haven't heard her name in over a week.

That's not technically true, if you include my own inner voice, which says her name a thousand times an hour. Let's not count that.

"Is Carlos okay?"

"He will be. Tessa said he fell at work and broke a wrist. Who knew accounting could be so hazardous?" Mom's eyebrows go up. "Tessa said Carrie was a lifesaver. She really likes her." Propping her elbow on the kitchen counter, Mom scrutinizes me further. "So?"

"So . . . what?" The thought of Carrie being nice, helping my sister, makes my gut ache. That's what friends do, right? They help each other out. I helped Carrie with her wedding date problem, and she helped my sister in a moment of crisis.

We're even. But it feels weird that I didn't know about it.

"Maybe Carlos could get transferred here. I'd love to have all my kids nearby," Mom continues.

"You have five kids, Mom. Good luck with that."

Mom rubs my head. I feel like I'm eight again. "Ryan will get that lab spot. I know he will. And Paul will make a full recovery and I'll have you all—" Her voice chokes with emotion and she turns away. Mom's really good at expressing positive emotions.

But the negative ones? No. This is freaking me out. Ellen, Taryn, and I all look at each other, frozen in place as Mom grips the kitchen counter's edge, her shoulders tight but shaking in small movements.

Oh, shit.

She's crying.

Ellen looks at me like, *You're the man—go do something*, and it occurs to me that I *am* the man. The only son.

The one who becomes the patriarch when Dad is gone.

Responsibility fills me like lead weights in my blood as I stand and go to Mom, putting my hands on her shoulders, pulling her in for a hug. She's solid but still somehow frail. I tower over her. Nothing's changed in nearly ten years, after I shot past her my first year of college.

And yet everything has changed.

"I know you have a life in Boston," Mom says to my chest, sniffling. She pulls away and looks at me, eyes red, the skin underneath loose and wrinkled. For the first time, I see her as a woman, as my dad's wife, as a person.

Not just Mom.

She's scared and worried, and I'm reminded, bizarrely, of the moment Carrie kissed me for the first time, forever changing how I viewed her.

"I'm not tied down there, Mom. I'm glad to move back home."

"What about Carrie? I know you started dating. You went to that wedding together right before your father's stroke."

"No, we're not—that was just me doing her a favor."

Taryn raises one eyebrow. Pierced.

Busted by the zirconium-wearing teenager.

"If that's the case, then there's no reason for you to stay in Boston, is there? And if you get an offer for grad school . . ." Mom's voice drops and she smiles up at me as she wipes her eyes.

I'm breathing. Deep and full, the breaths making me bigger, older, wiser. My life is about more than me. Ellen catches my eye and doesn't react, watching me. Evaluating.

She's looking at me the way I just watched Mom. Like she's realizing I'm more than a little brother. Like I'm a man. A man with a wonderful, interwoven family, and with aging parents who need me.

A few years ago, leaving home felt like a kind of freedom. Pushing aside my electrical engineering work, finding meaning in using my hands and body as a tool, working at the O Spa filled something in me that had been hollow.

But now?

Coming home makes the most sense.

With my eyes locked on Ellen's, I answer my mother's question.

"Then there's no reason for me to stay in Boston, Mom. Not a single one."

♥ ♥ ♥

THE LETTER FEELS heavy as I slide it into my breast pocket of my coat, pressing over my heart like a stone.

I'm resigning.

The day before I got on the plane to come home, I got two calls. One from Stanford, one from my alma mater, Cal Tech.

No matter what, in January I have a job. Turns out all that sex toy circuitry has medical research value, and my skills are, shall we say, valuable in more ways than one. Ellen doesn't like the idea of Cal Tech because it's too far away, but a short plane ride from LAX or Burbank to SFO is way better than the long haul BOS to SFO. And no time change.

Besides, she has no say in my choice.

I'll give O two months' notice. My apartment is already sublet from someone else, so I can leave easily. Cleanly.

Quickly.

And with no attachments. Free to be.

Unraveling a life shouldn't be so simple, but there you go. Maybe it's my own fault. Maybe I came here and never put down roots for a reason.

Maybe I was right all along not to tell Carrie how I really feel, because some part of me knew that putting down roots means intertwining yourself with people and places. Once those vines weave their way in between the cracks, seeking light, you have to cause pain when you rip them out to uproot.

This is all for the best.

As I walk into Chloe's office, my heart pounds against the resignation letter like a hammer tapping on a nail. She looks up and smiles, then dips her head back down, ticking things off a list with a pen in her hand.

"Ryan! You're back." *Tick. Tick. Tick.*

"Sort of."

Now I have her full attention. Chloe drops the pen, pushes her paperwork aside, and gestures to the chair in front of her desk. "Have a seat."

I do, then reach in my breast pocket, pulling out the slim envelope.

Her face falls. "Is that what I think it is?"

The envelope seems so final as it passes from my hand to hers across the wide expanse of clear glass desktop. "Yes."

The fewer words, the better.

I shift in my seat, uncomfortable, unaccustomed to wearing a jacket so often. The wedding last month, the visits to professors and deans, and now here. Being this formal feels right, though. It's what grownups do when they're being serious.

Dress the part.

"I'm resigning, Chloe."

"No!" she gasps, her lips compressed, her face twisted with a kind of pain that surprises me. "Is this about money?" She's hopeful, immediately trying to find a way to fix this. To make me stay. "Because we can renegotiate your rates."

"It's not about money."

"Your father? Oh, how rude of me. I should have asked first. Is he—how is he?"

"Making a good, solid recovery."

She leans back in her chair, body relaxing with relief. "Thank goodness. It sounds like you're close with your parents."

I shrug. "I guess. About the same as everyone else I know."

A really funny look crosses her face. "My mother is still alive and well, living in Florida with Howard, my guardian angel."

My turn to give her a funny look.

"It's complicated," she says with a sigh. "Charlotte can be . . . imperial."

"Charlotte's your mother?"

"Yes."

"Why do you call her by her first name?"

"It's a very long story." It's clear she doesn't want to tell it to me. "Ryan, really? You're really leaving us? You're so good with clients. They absolutely adore you. And frankly, you're one of the best employees on the spa side."

"I am?"

"You don't have an ego, you're fundamentally kind, and you don't create drama."

"I've never seen any of that on my performance review, Chloe."

We share a smile. "It's a softer skill set, Ryan. The kind employers love to find in workers. The kind that makes your life better, too."

I drop the smile. I don't know what to say.

"What are your plans?" she asks, biting her lip, looking at the envelope with such sadness.

"I'm moving back to California. To be closer to my family."

Her slow nod makes it clear she gets it as she opens the letter, scanning it. "January?"

"Yeah. I know how crazy it gets here with the holidays. I'll stay through New Year's."

"Oh, bless you!" She lets out a whoosh of held breath. "Finding a replacement for you is going to be damn near impossible."

I don't know what to say so I just grin.

"And . . . Carrie? Does she know?"

Grin disappears. "What?"

"Carrie. I know you two are really close."

"No."

"Excuse me?"

"No. We're not close."

"Ryan." She sounds so much like Ellen when she says my name like that. "You two . . . what happened? You've been friends since you came here. Then there was Jenny's wedding. And now you're avoiding each other like the plague."

"I'm not avoiding her. She just—we just—it was all, you know."

"None of that was a complete sentence. Or even a complete thought."

"She put out my burning penis with a cream donut the last time I saw her, Chloe."

"Is that a positive or a negative observation, Ryan?"

I can't help but laugh. It's a sad sound. "Why are you digging into my personal life?" My fingers grip the edge of the chair to the point of pain.

"I shouldn't." She sets the letter down on her desk and leans forward, threading her fingers together in a clasp. "But I am. You and Carrie both look like someone shot your dog."

"Maybe we both have sad things going on in our lives."

"Or maybe you *are* the sad thing in each other's lives."

"I didn't come in here expecting to have you interrogate me about my personal life, Chloe. You're my boss."

"You're right. But I'm also not going to watch people I care about make stupid mistakes and not say a word. Tell me, Ryan—were you pretending at the wedding?"

"Sure." Shrug.

"Were you really? Because Carrie wasn't."

Anger surges through me. "Bullshit, Chloe. What's your game here? Are you and Carrie fucking with me? I heard you two at the reception. Heard you both laughing about how it was all pretend." I stand up, flexing my fingers. My shoulders feel like marble. Hot marble with lead poured on top.

"You heard *what*?"

"You were coming out of the bathroom and Carrie told you we weren't compatible. Loud and clear. That it was all pretend."

"That's what made you leave? Carrie said you disappeared during the reception." Her eyes narrow, calculating. "Instead of asking Carrie what she meant, you just ghosted on her?"

"What? No! I didn't—that's not how it went. She asked for a fake boyfriend. She told you it was all pretend. Told you we weren't compatible, that I'm too young for her. So once she was done needing me to be the hot, young piece of meat she could parade around to save her ego, I left. Mission accomplished. Job done."

"You don't believe a word of that, Ryan." She's on her feet, walking smoothly around the giant glass desk. Her eyes are so earnest, I almost fall for it. "That's not the conversation I actually had with Carrie."

"Don't gaslight me. Jesus. I *heard* it." Rage makes my vision swim. I turn around to leave. I need to get the hell out of here. Working for the next two months was going to be hard enough.

Now it'll be a living hell. Maybe I should just quit on the spot.

"You heard part of it. *Part*. After she said you weren't compatible, she also added that it just looked that way. That you really did have something deeper beneath the surface. That she assumed you were just pretending. I told her not to assume."

I'm in the hallway, about to pivot right, when what Chloe says sinks in. "Carrie said that?"

"Yes."

My palm goes flat against the wall. I need it for support. "Say all of that again, Chloe."

"Carrie wasn't pretending. She assumed you were. But she said everything had gotten deeper than she expected, and needed to talk about it with you. Needed to see if you felt the same way. I told her no man looks at a woman the way you look at her without being very, very real."

All I can do is blink. Blink and let this wall hold me up.

"I don't normally meddle in employee affairs, Ryan, but Carrie is more than an employee to me. She's a friend. And she's hurting. She'd be very upset if she knew I was telling you all of this, but too late. Cat's out of the bag. You two need to talk."

"She wasn't pretending." I'm muttering to myself more than anything now.

"No. She wasn't."

"Oh, God. I just . . . oh, shit."

"You need to fix this, Ryan. Are you quitting because of Carrie?"

"What? No. I would quit no matter what. But it was easier when I thought she didn't—when I thought she was pretending."

"And now that you know she's not?"

"I need to go see her. Now. Is she in her office?" I look at my phone. It's just after six p.m. Maybe she's still here.

"No. She's gone for the day."

I start jogging for the elevator banks.

"Wait! Ryan! You need to know about Carrie's promotion! She's getting—"

I see the door for the stairs and shove it open, pounding my way downstairs, Chloe's words fading as I run.

This time, *toward* her.

Not away.

CHAPTER FIFTEEN

Carrie

"**Y**OU'RE MY BEAUTIFUL best friend, the person I want to wake up with, get stuck in airports with, make love on the beach with, laugh and cry and sing karaoke and have kids and get old until we forget everything and only remember each other."

"I'm older than you are—I'll forget everything first."

"I'll be there to remind you. I'll remember every single day of our lives and I'll whisper it in your ear until you can see it all again."

My breath catches in my throat and a little sob escapes. These are the exact words I have wanted to hear from Ryan for so long, longer than I even knew, and I can't believe I am hearing them now.

From Dermot Mulroney. In "Starcrossed." Thanks, Hulu.

I reach for the remote and click the volume down a notch.

With my chopsticks, I dig around in my container of lo mein, looking for any stray shrimp that escaped my notice. When you're alone, you can do that. You can forget table manners and pick out the best bits for yourself. Yet another benefit to being single.

BZZZZZZZZZZ

Door buzzer. Probably someone in the building forgot their keys.

"Yes?"

"Pizza," a deep male voice announces.

I glance over at the table. Yep, there's my lo mein. Pretty sure I didn't order pizza?

"Not mine," I say into the intercom.

"Shelton, apartment 3B. Sausage and mushroom, extra cheese. Paid for."

That's what Ryan and I always ordered. Must have come up in their system by mistake.

Great. It's like the entire world is trying to remind me of what I almost had, and lost. WTF?

"Okay, come on up." Might as well. I buzz him in, then crack the door open and start rifling through my wallet for tip money. I can hear the delivery guy's steady footfalls as he climbs the stairs. Nothing in my wallet but a twenty-dollar bill, and that's too much even if it *is* a third floor walkup. I pull open a kitchen drawer and I'm searching for my spare cash envelope when the door swings in.

"Just one sec," I tell him, still digging through the drawer. "I didn't order that, but I guess I can wrap it up and have it tomorrow."

"You can," he replies. "You can have it tomorrow or the day after. Or now if you want."

NoNoNo.

I look up, very very slowly. There's no pizza box on the counter.

"*NoNoNo*," I whisper.

"Yes," Ryan says firmly. "Repeat after me: Yes. Yes, please. I will have that today, tomorrow, and forever. Thank you."

My tiny apartment suddenly seems so vast, like the ceiling has been ripped off and I'm blanketed by the night sky, stars shining, clouds covering the moon as if it's being modest. I inhale, then exhale. I know I'm alive, because every bit of my skin prickles, excitement rocketing through my blood. Ryan wouldn't be here if he wasn't—if he didn't—*right?*

"Ryan, what are you doing here?"

"I . . . was in the neighborhood and thought I'd drop in," he says with a tone of finality, as if there's nothing to question, no reason to wonder.

I close my mouth and breathe carefully through my nose, his cologne just strong enough to make my knees weak. Finally, I slowly turn. His back is to me as he closes my door. The same strong, powerful shoulders that faced me at the Chatham Beach Inn our first night together. My eyes comb over his body, taking in the snug business-casual slacks, the business shirt and tie, the dark suit jacket. He looks like any businessman in the Financial District, coming off the Commuter Rail for his day at work on State Street.

Only hot as hell, poised and sophisticated. Why is Ryan wearing a business outfit?

And why is he *here*?

"This neighborhood isn't on the way to anyplace," I argue. Trust me. I know.

"I haven't been able to find my, um, cuff links?" He's such a liar. Those golden eyes are wide and seeking, his hair longer now, brushing against the tops of his eyebrows. The look he gives me is a dare. "I haven't seen them since the wedding, and I thought maybe you have them," he continues.

"For Pete's sake, Ryan. Every girl in the world uses that excuse: 'I think I left my earrings at your place, can I come over and look for them?'"

He looks sheepish—or pretends to. "Where do you think I got it?" The grin that makes his face light up is like watching the sun rise over the ocean. You know it's coming and you know it will be a spectacular sight, but when you actually experience it you're changed forever.

I glance around for something to throw at him, but there's nothing that I wouldn't mind if it broke. There's another apple pie I made yesterday, but that would make a huge mess. I need to touch something, hold it in my hand, cradle it to remind myself I'm still part of this world, because there's no way Ryan is doing this. And then I need to throw it at him, because *"Where do you think I got it"*?

No way. This can't be real.

He notices me scanning the counter. "Don't hurt me," he says with a little grin, mouth pulled to the side, dimples on display. I forgot how irresistible that grin is. But then it fades, and he's looking at me seriously.

"I hurt enough, Carrie. I hurt so much I can't breathe. And you know what the worst part is? I think you hurt, too." One step closer, he moves with that liquid grace he possessed in bed. My belly tightens and my heart starts to move faster and faster, as if chasing time.

"Me?" I draw myself up with what dignity I can muster, juggling my body's response to him with my rational mind's defense of my hurting heart. "Hurt? Why would you think that? I'm fine," I lie. "Everything is great. I've been offered a promotion. I am moving to San Francisco, probably."

His jaw drops a little in surprise, chin pulling back, hands going to his hips. "Did you say *San Francisco?*"

"Yes. Chloe offered me Associate Director of Design. I accepted." I glance away. I can't look at his face. That conversation with Chloe feels like another lifetime. One where my former pretend boyfriend wasn't delivering pretend pizza to me.

"When?" He leans against the counter, his ass shifting those long, thick legs and the end of his suit jacket hitches up, pulling out his shirt, showing a band of skin at the waist, with muscle that goes into that tight V at his hip I see when he's in a g-string at work.

And—blank. My mind goes blank. My salivary glands and clitoris, however, take up the slack. I focus on that spot of his skin. It's easier than answering his question.

He waves slightly. "Hello? Carrie? San Francisco?"

"I don't know exactly," I confess. "When OSF opens, I guess. Maybe sooner."

"That's great. Congratulations." Why is he blinking like that, staring at me like I told him I won the lottery?

"Thanks."

"I got accepted to grad school," he blurts. "Stanford and Cal Tech."

I stare back at him. "Stanford has a massage program?"

"Engineering," he says patiently, inhaling sharply, suddenly, like a gasp he's trying to control. "It's time to get serious. Nobody can dance forever. And I have to make a change—even Zeke says so. Not that I'm taking advice from Zeke now. Or maybe I am." He looks a little alarmed at that thought, but takes another breath and soldiers on. "I can't just spend my life waiting for you to love me back."

"Love you *back* . . . ?" I echo.

Snappy comeback, right? Hey, less than three minutes ago, I was trying to find four one-dollar bills for a pizza delivery guy I wasn't expecting, who is now standing in my kitchen doing a pretty fair imitation of Dermot Mulroney. You try being witty under those circumstances.

With a tiny voice in your brain screaming *Why didn't you wash your hair today when you showered?*

"Yes, love me back. Pretending was my idea, I guess, so I only have myself to blame, but I wasn't pretending. I love you, Carrie. I've loved you since that night you came over and we made tacos but we used tuna fish and they were awful and we had to order pizza."

That was a year and a half ago. I stare at him, in awe.

"Sausage and mushroom, extra cheese," I whisper.

"Don't interrupt," he says. "I might lose my courage."

I press one hand over my mouth and remember to breathe through my nose, my own hot breath all I can feel.

"And we laughed so hard and then we watched a movie and you fell asleep on my sofa," he continues, starting to pace. Except my kitchen is about eight feet by ten feet, so he can only take three steps in each direction.

"'Gone Girl.' You made a joke, you said I was gone before she was . . ."

He glares at me, looking fierce and sophisticated, like one of the billionaires in a drama about power and dominance. I clap both hands over my mouth and shut up as the rest of my body screams for him.

Yes Yes Yes.

"I looked at you curled up and sleeping, with the light shining on your hair, and I just knew." Soft love fills his eyes, the corners turning up, memory capturing his heart. I want to cry, his words like little thorns, so beautiful on a rose yet so painful.

"But I was dating Jamey," I finish for him.

Ryan nods, eyes sad. "Yes. I wasn't going to say anything when you were with someone else." He looks away.

"And then last month," I whisper, trying to understand how this all connects, trying to figure out what to say next. "He broke up with me. And I texted you and you let me come over and oh, God," I groan. "My broken vagina kiss!"

He walks around the counter till he's standing right in front of me, and pulls my fingers from my lips. He holds them tight, his thumbs slowly caressing my palms.

"That was the best kiss, C-Shel." His mouth warms my fingertips, eyes looking up at me with expectation. Grounded and centered, this Ryan is my friend, my television buddy, my—well, he's everything.

More than ever before.

"And now you know my vagina's not broken."

He laughs. "We'll get to that later. Let me—I thought all the way over here about what I was going to say to you, after Chloe explained."

"Chloe?" My voice squeaks. "What does—"

This time, it's *his* hand that covers my mouth.

"But here's the thing you need to know," he goes on. I stare down at his fingertips, eyes crossing. "That night on the Cape when we made love? That wasn't pretending. Not for me, anyway. When I was inside you for the first time—look at me," he says urgently.

Slowly I meet his eyes again, his words making blood pound from the inside out, my body drawn to him.

"When I was inside you for the first time, everything in the world was in that moment. Every question I ever had was answered. I don't know how to say it better than that. I just *knew*. That was as real as it gets. Carrie, I was never pretending. Not then, not before, and certainly not now."

I cannot believe my ears. That's an expression, but I mean it literally. I am questioning my own sanity.

"Wait just a minute—*never* pretending?" An indignant feeling starts to bloom in my chest as his words sink in. "When this all started, you said we were going to pretend. And then I thought maybe I wasn't pretending but you said you were, and then I thought maybe you weren't but I heard you tell someone you were, and then we had sex and I definitely wasn't pretending but who *knows* what a guy is thinking?"

He makes a sound of protest, but momentum propels me onward.

"You're not just any guy, of course, because you're Ryan. You know—my friend. My stupid reality television friend. My work husband. My—"

"Soulmate," he interrupts, the word so quiet that it can't be right.

I'm inventing this, aren't I? Reaching down, I pinch my inner thigh and yelp from pain, then look back up.

No. He's still here, though his eyebrows are now knitting in confusion, eyes on my pinching hand. I'm going to have a nasty bruise on my leg, but I've confirmed this is actually happening. Worth it.

"And then maybe I sort of said I was pretending because I heard you say you were, and I didn't want to be the only one who wasn't . . . and then we were both pretending again at work because a few people knew although most of them didn't, and *now you are telling me you never were?*" I press my palms flat against his chest, ready to give him a huge shove or a passionate kiss, unsure which will happen first.

Fury has driven every tender feeling out of my body. I pull my hands away and take a step back, panting.

He just stares at me, saying nothing.

"*Ryan? You were never pretending?*"

"Nope." His voice is calm and steady. "I'm sorry, C-Shel. I loved you the whole time."

"No."

We look at each other, all pretense gone.

"Yes."

"No! Impossible! You're a 10.5 and I'm a 4."

"Stop it. Stop that *now*," he says, all gravel and fire, his voice so serious. "You're my 10.5 Carrie. I can't give you a number. You just *are*. Tell me you feel the same way. Please."

"I loved you, too, Ryan. I'm sorry I didn't know it when I was pretending. But I know it now. I love you, I do . . . love you."

He just stands there for a minute, taking it all in, our eyes locked as he searches my face, our breathing fast. My chest rises and falls, seconds ticking by, our breath in sync, all that I am vulnerable and raw.

I can't stand it, blurting out, "What do we do now?"

Before I can finish, his mouth is on mine, the fine fabric of his suit jacket tickling my forearm, his hot mouth eager and demanding. In seconds, this moves out of reunion territory into something magnetic, all-consuming and torrid. I can't touch him enough, pulling his shirt out from his pants, running my hands up his bare back, his hand cupping my breast, in my hair, cradling my jaw, all of him pressed against me, every part of us needing more.

"I've missed you," he says, voice thick with emotion, hands on my ass, my back, my shoulders, his desperate need to stay in contact with my body matching how I feel about him.

"I can't believe any of this is happening," I admit, the thought overwhelming, stronger even than the physical need for Ryan's heat, his scent, the way his nose nuzzles my neck, how my hands slide up under his open jacket and it falls to the ground. We're in my kitchen, the counter's edge digging into my hip, but we might as well be worlds away, alone and in need of nothing more than each other.

"I can't believe you ever thought I was pretending, Carrie." He speaks between kisses, my heart soaring.

"What was I supposed to think, Ryan? I took you at your word." Shaky and shaking, I correct myself. "And I was too afraid to say anything to you. Afraid I was imagining it all."

"I'll never lie to you again. Never," he says fiercely, dipping his head down to kiss me, pulling me up to him with hands that hold my hips, thumbs anchored at my waist.

"Two years," I marvel, about to let myself get caught up in all the time we've wasted, all the misunderstandings—but then I gasp and pull back in horror.

"Oh, God!" I choke out, my hands and feet going numb with the aching reality of what I've just done. "I told Chloe I'd take the promotion! I'm about to *move*, Ryan! Three thousand miles away!" Hyperventilation has never been a character trait of mine, but it's quickly taking over. The thought of losing Ryan after finding him makes my chest physically hurt.

"C-Shel. Hey, Carrie," he soothes. "It's okay."

"No, it's not okay! I finally—we finally—"

"Stanford," he says slowly, his penetrating gaze so calming. "I'm going to Stanford."

"Stanford?" I'm having trouble keeping up.

"Stanford," he repeats firmly. "You made my decision for me. And my family is in the Bay Area, so this is an easy choice. I choose *you*."

Laughter, unexpected and completely hysterical, pours out of me like a bottle of prosecco being uncorked. "You choose me? You *choose* me? I was fleeing you! I took the promotion to get away from working with you because it hurt too much to be around you but not with you. And now you're telling me you're moving to San Francisco, too?"

"No."

"No, you're not moving?"

"Yes, I'm moving. But no. I'm not telling you anything. We'll talk later. Let's," he says, kissing me gently, "stop talking."

Ryan moves suddenly, sweeping one arm around my back and the other under my knees, his thighs brushing against my ass, his movement so easy, like he's lifting a feather, a ball of yarn, a pint of ice cream. We're kissing, Ryan carrying me without breaking his stride. I melt into him and let the swirling thoughts that tornado through me settle down, absorbing myself in the feel of his skin against mine, the brush of cotton caressing my throat, how his arm stretches under my knees.

It's a very small apartment. He knows where my bedroom is. I don't care where he is carrying me, I only want to go with him. A part of the world closes, separated by a giant door constructed of pieces of our souls, giving us privacy and time.

Time to get real.

He lays me down on my bed and I shimmy out of my yoga pants, kicking them away as he strips off his pants, his movements hurried, impatient. Normally, I'd savor this, but the air between us feels so charged with emotion, so much to unravel between us, the only easy form of communication one that happens when we're naked. Words matter, but they can wait.

My body can't, though, because my heart is in it, craving him, beating a rhythm that calls for more of Ryan. My bedroom's in order, the room of a self-possessed woman, wholly on her own. No more, though. As I move the covers and beckon to Ryan, he turns on my bedside lamp, a salt crystal that glows, casting his sublime body in shadow and dim light, all hard lines and deep presence.

"Come here," I say, direct and clear, unambiguous.

I hold out my arms, urging him, needing him with me, in me, part of me. I've been with him before. I know what is possible, and this time we don't need to tease. Pretense is a distant memory, one we'll talk through in our own time, at our own pace. Wounds don't have to bleed to hurt. Pain doesn't have to create scars to leave a mark.

Healing comes in so many precious ways, and right now, I need to stretch against Ryan's bare body, to feel him over me, to press up and kiss him with the fullness of my soul.

Bedsheets made of high thread counts move against my bare flesh like silk, the in-between space as Ryan sinks in beside me a warm cocoon. Hungry hands cover me, roaming and free, moving with the abandon of a man given blanket permission to do as he pleases.

And to please me.

"Ryan," I whisper, tears welling in my eyes as emotion overcomes me. He's stroking my face, compassion softening his features, and if we had more light in the room the shadow over his face would reveal worlds unseen, love unfelt, time unlived.

"I do love you, Carrie. Have for a long time. It's killed me to wait, but now here we are." His palm goes flat against my cheek, gliding slowly, achingly meandering down my shoulder, over my collarbone, leaving a trail of tingling anticipation. Ryan's gaze goes dark as he looks at me, following his hand, the smooth, confident touch growing bolder.

As his fingertips close over my nipple I gasp, a tight pain zinging through me, followed by a wellspring of desire that courses through my body, making me ache to have him in me. So soon, I know, and yet I can't wait any longer.

We've waited too long already.

"Kitten," he says, making me smile, the nickname a shared secret, an inside joke that makes me want him inside *me*. Forcing myself to slow down, I press my fingertips into his shoulder, the layers of definition mine to explore. Mine.

"This is Ryan," I say, reveling in the words this time, unafraid and with a finality to my tone, shoulders lowering, body relaxing.

"Yes," he says, his hand moving down, finding me wet and very, very ready. "You were expecting someone else?" He's playful but serious.

"When we were at the Inn, I kept thinking to myself, 'This is Ryan,' because I couldn't believe we were naked and in bed and that you were touching me and we—" The sheer beauty of it all makes me stop, my throat tightening. He moves his hand to my hip, forehead touching mine, his eyes closed as he honors what I'm saying. Grief has no place between us now, and yet a sliver of regret has to be let in for this to remain honest.

To remain real.

"This is Ryan, Carrie. I'm here, all the way." His kiss makes sure I know it. "I'm not sure I can hold back," he adds as I stroke him, enjoying the feel of him, his body rising up as I touch him, hips drawing toward me.

"Then don't. Don't hold back. Don't ever hold back," I implore him, my fingers traveling down the wide plane of muscled torso, reaching for him with a greedy hand and a needy soul.

And then he's between my legs and I open to him, fully and freely, whispering his name as if it's become my heartbeat. As he enters me he groans, the sound resonant and I am so wet, he slides straight in, making me gasp with joy, enjoying the power of having someone so close to me.

This is Ryan, indeed.

"I'm here. Not going anywhere, Carrie," he says as he thrusts, so slowly, the movement reverent. All the ways that I feel disconnected from the world fade away as he moves inside me, my hands on his ribs, fingers divining the way to his heart. I feel it beat beneath my flattened palm, my appreciation for his very existence mingling with the soulful, steady gallop.

He finds my hands and moves them beside my head and weaves our fingers together as he begins to thrust and I meet him, bracing myself with one arched foot. I can see my other foot above his shoulder, stretching to the ceiling and the universe beyond, the feel of him exquisite, the feelings inside me more ecstatic.

This is all I want in the universe. Ryan.

"I never, ever want you to doubt me," he says tenderly, kissing me as he makes love to me, my hands now finding all the corners and curves of him, yearning to show him all my corners and curves, too. We're just planes of existence folded and twisted by life and love, and it's the unraveling, the blossoming of a tight bud that allows us to let the love in.

"I don't. I doubt myself, but not you. I wish I'd seen you as you are, like this. I never thought I had a chance with you," I murmur in his ear as he dips down to take one nipple in his mouth, teeth doing something that makes me tighten, makes me spiral to a place without form, without anchor, where pure pleasure fills in the gaps of who I am.

"You're all I want, Carrie. Let me love you."

"Let me love you back," I beg, unable to talk, moving against him as I match his quickening pace.

I can't hold back any longer, the lovely buildup reaching its intense peak and cascading over, going on and on as my sounds tell him it's time and he lets himself go, exploding into me with such force. I can feel every pulse, all shyness long gone, our openness more erotic than any stroke. He is still for a moment, then he moves again, his breathing ragged, his cheek against mine, all his weight on me.

I love it. I can't move, can't escape, can't avoid.

Can't help but love him.

My body is like thousands of ribbons blowing on the wind, carefree and unmoored, following nature's plan. We are still feeling the last waves of our lovemaking, Ryan's hands pressing into the mattress as he lifts himself up, kissing the tip of my nose as I smile.

"Sorry," he whispers. "That was fast."

"What? No. That was perfectly normal."

"Normal isn't good enough, kitten. You deserve far more than normal." He rolls off me, resting by my side, every bit of his thigh, hip, and torso touching me. My side boob rests against his arm like an obedient, well . . .

Kitten.

I frown. "If that was just 'normal' sex in your world, Ryan, what the hell is 'great sex'?"

He grins, a shock of brown hair matted to his sweaty forehead. "Give me ten minutes and I'll show you."

"Ten minutes?" I lift the sheet, look down at his endlessly delicious body, and raise one eyebrow. "Besides, twice in one night? No one does that."

"What's your sample size of experience?" he asks, reaching for my breast, stroking until I can't quite answer him. He shakes his head. "No one does that?" he mimics, face hard to read. "We'll see."

"Why didn't you ever say anything sooner?" I gasp, rolling against him, lifting my knee against his thigh, my curves against his muscles a beautiful paradox.

"Because I was stupid. Cowardly. Afraid you'd reject me." He rolls slightly toward me until we're face to face, breathing each other's breath.

"Reject you? You?" I wave at his body like my hands have become hummingbirds. "Who in their right mind would reject *you?*"

Like a wounded animal, his shoulders hunch, just for a second before he squares them and answers me forthrightly. "Lots of women."

His heart speeds up under my hand, like someone pressed the gas pedal of a car. I trace the thick, colorful outlines of the tattoos on his left arm. Mandelbrot Set. It was one of the most compelling details about Ryan when I first met him. Anyone who tattoos fractals on himself has a commitment to nonconformity.

"Carrie, I wasn't always like this."

"Good in bed? Bad at blurting out feelings? Wasn't always like—ohhhhhh," I say, grasping his meaning. "You mean your high school graduation picture."

"My *huh?*"

"Tessa showed me. Class of 2008." I do the math. 2008—2001 (my graduating class) = 7 years age difference. When I'm old and wrinkly, he'll be seven years less old. Less wrinkly. Then again, I have longer life expectancy, so the balance favors me.

Ryan sits up sharply, the covers falling off our bodies. I look down, soft moonlight giving us a stippled glow, our legs tangled. "Tessa *showed* you? I'll kill her."

"No—Ryan, it's actually good. It helped me to understand. And you look like a lot of the guys I liked back in high school."

The shy look he gives me makes my heart say *Awwwwwwww.* "I've changed a lot since then."

"Haven't we all?"

"More on the outside than the inside," he says, clearing his throat. "I didn't realize it until you were available and I could take a chance. Tell you how I felt. Suddenly, though, it was all too—"

"Real?" I interrupt, snuggling against his chest, listening to his heart. Who knew pillow talk could be so revealing? When Jamey and I talked after sex, it was mostly about the new deCordova museum art exhibit or whether Blue Ginger was still worth the hike out to Wellesley.

Ryan talks about *feelings.* Naked. Feelings and nakedness combined are lovelier than any new trend.

His hand strokes my shoulder. "Yes. And I'm sorry I ran away from the wedding. That really was cowardly of me. I heard you and

Chloe at the reception. You told her we weren't compatible."

"No, I didn't!"

"Yes, you did. But that's all in the past."

"Ryan! I told her we weren't compatible on the surface, but deep down we were."

"I know. Chloe told me."

"You talked about me with my boss?" My self-respect starts Irish dancing in my throat.

"I went to O to resign, and Chloe—"

"You *resigned*?"

"Yes. I really am moving back to California." He squeezes my hand. "With you."

"California." My words sound breathy, like an ocean breeze. A Pacific Ocean breeze.

"Stanford it is. My mother is going to love you." He kisses my temple.

"Your mother?"

"My dad's sick. She wants me to move back home anyhow. So I'll go for Stanford instead of Cal Tech."

"We're both moving to San Francisco." I sit up and stare at him, heedless of my bare breasts, suddenly comfortable being on display. Enjoying it, even. "Less than an hour ago I was eating takeout and hating on Dermot Mulroney. Now I'm naked, in your arms, and you're talking about moving to San Francisco with me to start a new life."

He smiles. It's electrifying. "Sounds about right." His arms tighten, pulling me closer.

"Don't you think it's all kind of . . . fast?"

"No. We wasted two years, C-Shel. I can't be with you fast enough." Tension fills his body, all of the parts of me touching him shifting as he turns into one giant, gorgeous rock. "Unless you're having second thoughts."

"What? No! Hell, no." I crawl up him, my bare belly against his, straddling him as we kiss, a deep wet affair that leaves me with no doubt that Ryan's ready for round two, should one of us call for it.

"Fast isn't fast enough for me, either."

"You look incredibly beautiful," he says softly, as our heart rates slowly return to normal, our kiss a seal on a deal we've been waiting to make.

A self-conscious laugh escapes me. "Yeah, no . . ."

I know for sure—I've heard from Jamey and his predecessors— that this is *not* my best look. Messy hair that I should have washed today, flushed face, lipstick long gone (was I even wearing any?), maybe a little sweaty . . .

What is he doing now? Ryan flips on top of me, pinning me in place, but he has twisted sideways and he's rummaging on the floor next to the bed. He comes up with his phone in one hand and swipes at the screen with his thumb.

"What are you *doing*?" I crane my neck, trying to see what's on the other side of the phone.

He slides over next to me and holds the phone at full arm's length. His face is pressed right next to mine and he is smiling at the screen, which reflects us.

I know what this is, and I screech "WHAT ARE YOU *DOING*?" as I yank the bedsheet up over my face, trying unsuccessfully to stop the selfie from being taken.

"I am saving this moment forever. For all time. So someday I can show you how gorgeous you are and how much we love each other. In case you ever forget." A heated kiss follows his words, tongues dancing, mouths saying more than we can in any other way.

"But it's my mission," he adds as he pulls away, leaving me open-mouthed and panting, "to make sure you never, ever forget."

I close my mouth. I narrow my eyes. I drop the sheet. This is me, trusting him. After all, making things look better *is* in my blood.

A huge smile spreads across my face as he pulls me in the frame, as is, perfect just as we are, rumpled and disheveled, wild and free.

Click

THE END

♥ ♥ ♥

Dear Readers: a huge thank you to all of you. Elisa and I deeply appreciate your taking the time out of your busy lives to read Ryan and Carrie's story. If you haven't read *Our Options Have Changed*, which is Nick and Chloe's book, we encourage you to grab your copy now and sink into their unconventional tale.

ABOUT THE AUTHORS

JULIA KENT

Text JKentBooks to 77948 and get a text message on release dates!
New York Times and *USA Today* bestselling author Julia Kent turned to writing contemporary romance after deciding that life is too short not to have fun. She writes romantic comedy with an edge, and new adult books that push contemporary boundaries. From billionaires to BBWs to rock stars, Julia finds a sensual, goofy joy in every book she writes, but unlike Trevor from *Random Acts of Crazy*, she has never kissed a chicken.

She loves to hear from her readers by email at jkentauthor@gmail.com, on Instagram and Twitter @jkentauthor, and on Facebook at *facebook.com/jkentauthor*

Visit her website at www.jkentauthor.com

ELISA REED

Elisa Reed is a journalist-turned-fiction-writer whose snappy, irreverent prose combines with an irrepressible zest for the simpler, and often intimate, pleasures of life to produce fun(ny) contemporary romance with a focus on second chances.

New England born and bred, Elisa Reed now lives, writes, and plays in New Orleans and along the sugar sands of the Gulf Coast.

You can find her on Facebook at: *www.facebook.com/elisareedauthor*